PINK
SLIPS

Dear Wendy-

Thanks for
your ♡

Beth
Aldrich
-2017

ALSO BY BETH ALDRICH

Real Moms Love to Eat

BETH ALDRICH

Restoring Essence, LLC
Winnetka, Illinois

restoring
essence

Printed in the United States of America

Cover design by Sarah Hansen, Okay Creations, LLC

Formatting and design by Jovana Shirley, Unforeseen Editing, www.unforeseenediting.com

ISBN (paperback): 978-0-692-86600-9

To my family, for giving me countless reasons to smile.

I lied. As the weeks pass the truth will come out. But Steven will get over it. He always does. Sometimes a lie is better than having to argue your point. At least that's what I tell myself.

A recorded message blares over the loudspeaker, announcing the incoming train's arrival. The Metra clanks down the rails and makes a scraping halt inches from where I'm waiting on the gusty platform. In my peripheral vision, I catch a glimpse of a tall man wearing a dark bomber jacket and knit hat, staring right at me—giving me a chill. His random screams, directed up at an indefinite spot above us, cause me to jolt in place. The other people on the platform are ignoring him, too, knowing that when you engage with a crazy person, it only incites a conflict.

Don't look at him, Betsy.

My heart is hammering as I avoid eye contact. I turn to face the train and pause, waiting for the doors to open— keeping my senses vigilant.

Sheets of heavy rain whip past the wall of the station house and the tracks, flecking my pant legs like bullets. I scan the platform, trying to locate anyone of authority just in case this person decides to attack. Not sure I can count on my fellow passengers.

I clutch a folded slip of paper containing a phone number, protecting it from the stray droplets. My call to the dog breeder earlier today went to voicemail, so I need to keep her information handy to call her from the train. I don't want to lose this puppy to another family who calls her first. Despite the chill in the air and my concern about the screaming man watching me, the warmth inside my heart gives way to giddy butterflies, anticipating our new arrivals. Soon I can share the truth with Steven. Two newborns will be joining our family—a puppy to surprise him and in seven months, our new baby. Once he gets used to the idea of the pregnancy, he'll come around. He always does. He's been on the fence about starting a family, but now is as good a time as any.

The moonbeam reflects off my kitchen ID badge hanging from the handle of my bag as I step into the train car and over the gap exposing a strip of trash and soot-laden gravel below. Joining a handful of other late-night riders, I settle far from spying eyes, in a back-row seat, before the jagged jerks of the ride begins.

The sliding door behind me swoops open, allowing a gush of damp air to spill in from the vestibule between train cars. The man in the dark hat thumps his heavy boots down the aisle, his shadowy gaze fixed downward, mumbling. When he reaches the other end of the train car, he turns back to stare at me. I shift my attention to the bag sitting on my lap before he catches my glance. The whoosh as he exits sends a chilly rush of air whirling up the bottom of my chef pants. I rub my arms to erase the goose bumps forming under my shirt and push the thought of him out of my mind. After dialing the number again, I slide the phone number in my coat pocket... only to hear a recording, asking me to leave a message.

As the train comes to a halt at my stop, I race out of the station and down the escalator to avoid being followed by the man who freaked me out on the train. I'd prefer to avoid any contact with him this late at night, with so few people around.

The dimly lit parking lot on Canal Street, not far from the Ogilvie station, is eerily quiet this time of night. I concentrate on putting one foot in front of the other.

The forceful blow comes out of nowhere as he grabs me from behind, the same way a great white shark barrels into an unsuspecting seal floating on the surface of the ocean. The incensed, loathsome constriction around me tightens.

"Help, someone! Please, I'm being attacked!" I wail.

I can tell the veins in my neck are bulging underneath my turtleneck. I think of my wallet containing the large cash withdrawal from my bonus check, tucked under my chef's coat and apron, deep inside my bag—sheltered from the sheeting rain and prying hands. I knew I should've waited to cash that check until tomorrow. What was I thinking? I was so proud to earn that money after working hard all year long. I'll be damned if I'm going to let some vagrant steal it, unless it means my life.

My screams for help may fall on deaf ears, given the lack of foot traffic, but I continue. It's worth a try.

"Gimme your money or I'll cut you." His voice is raspy, his breath overbearing. As he yanks me, I tighten the long muscles of my legs to maintain balance. *I wish I remembered to bring my pepper spray today. I could really use it right now!*

I avoid looking at him as I see his distinct image in the reflection of a car window. I take note that he's wearing a black ski mask and a bomber jacket, is at least a foot taller than me, and is solid. His grip confirms his muscular strength. He looks like the guy from the train, but I can't see his face through the mask.

Unrelenting, he shouts, "Give it to me now! I got a knife." He's poking me with a pointy edge through my raincoat.

He continues his fury, determined to get what he wants as I try to distract him from what's deep inside my bag. "I don't have cash," I whisper, my voice lost in my throat. "Take my watch" is all I spit out as he pulls me closer to his chest. I can replace the treasured gift from my husband five times over with the cash in my bag.

I lift my arm and show him the shiny gold face and burgundy leather strap. The pressure from his twisting grip hurls pulses of pain up my arm with numbing force. *It's not worth keeping if the alternative is a knife piercing my back.*

He's not buying it. The heat from him intensifies, forcing his energy to cave in harder.

He yells, "Bull! You paid for the train. I tracked you... rich urban scum."

"I used my pass and ID, not cash."

Thank God, I leave my wedding ring at home on work days.

As he pulls on my shoulder bag, a muted voice in the distance calls out, "Hey! Hey you! Is everything okay?"

I shake my head as I hear the faint steps of the Good Samaritan picking up his pace and heading in our direction.

The attacker seems to sense a losing battle against whoever may be coming our way. He throws me down, my hip and cheek slamming to the cement, and hurls the steel toe of his boot into my midsection. The kick lands inches from my pregnant stomach. A wail escapes my throat as the searing pain shoots through me like a bolt of lightning. I retighten my grip on the bag with one hand, preventing him from whisking it away; the other clutches my belly, attempting to shield my unborn baby. The cherished watch is still on my wrist, but the warm blood coming from in between my legs indicates he's stolen something much more precious.

My screams echo throughout the parking lot while I roll onto my back, begging my baby to "stay, hold on." Quiet sobs follow my rage as I lie in a puddle, whimpering. The attacker disappears in between cars through a heavy veil of rain, and my baby finds a way out of me. The distant sounds of sirens merge with my moans as the kind stranger holds my head in his lap.

———

In the ambulance, a paramedic peels open the crunchy paper covering a panty liner to catch the clots. Another medic wraps a stretchy, beige bandage around my waist to secure my ribs.

The ice pack I'm holding against my cheek is causing my fingers to tingle. The frost around my heart is numbing. The ambulance drives through jarring potholes on the gloomy downtown streets headed toward Michigan Avenue on our way to Northwestern Memorial Hospital. The seasoned officer, who wasted no time taking my statement in the drenched parking lot, averted his gaze from my bloody chef pants—respectfully, for my loss.

The throbbing beats in my head, my wrenched neck, and the searing pain in my abdomen dominate my consciousness as I offer a silent prayer to my baby. My white turtleneck has stains of mud and blood like my pants, proof that the horrible evening took place. The bumpy driveway leading to the ER entrance jiggles me in place on the cold stretcher, magnifying the gravity of my injuries. The loading zone is surprisingly deserted at 1:30 a.m. on a Thursday, so I'm wheeled directly to triage. My bag sits on top of the itchy blanket partially covering my body, hiding the growing bloodstain by my groin.

The nurse – who's a spitting image of my younger sister Brenda, with emerald eyes, radiant skin, and long legs – takes my ID and insurance card and processes my forms while I wait for the doctor on call. My work badge, which is usually connected to the outside of my bag, is missing. I pray to God that jerk didn't take it.

I continue to cradle my empty stomach, soothing the phantom baby, fixating on a blurry spot of blood on the floor. The nurse's pale blue scrubs and scuffed white clogs appear worn and washed too many times. Blood has a way of staining things. I'm going to rip up and burn these pants when I get home—these horrible, bloody pants.

The nurse pulls the pen from the base of her curly blonde ponytail and notes my details. Because of the attacker's swift kick, I'm confident I broke a rib and have a shot uterus—hopefully it will repair before I try to get pregnant again. *That man… he stole my baby.*

"Name."

"Huh? Oh…um, R-Y-A-N, Betsy Ryan."

"Age?"

"Twenty-eight."

"Height and weight?"

"Five-four and about one pound lighter."

She shoots me a curious smirk, glances, and sees an area of my pants not covered by the blanket, then nods, agreeing to skip that question. Her sorrowful response reminds me that I miss my sister, who's traveling the world. I need to hug my sister, my baby sister.

With a much-needed prescription for pain medicine, ample bandages, maxi pads, and an instruction sheet in hand, I am finally wheeled to the waiting room where Steven is sitting. I can't look at him. I stare at the ground as he leaps to his feet and rushes to my side.

"Oh, my God, honey! I am so sorry this happened to you… to us. I didn't know." He slides a single curl from my forehead and kisses it as he floats his hand on mine—already on my belly.

The nurse turns and leaves me sitting in the wheelchair so we can talk in private. I glance back at her and say, "Thank you for all of your help."

"You will be okay, just take it easy this week," she calls out as the doors to the ER close behind her.

My attention drops to my red, scraped hands clasped over the vacancy as I inhale with bitter confidence, determined now more than ever to focus on the future. "We need to revisit our conversation about moving to the suburbs."

His silence tells me he's open to listening to my point of view this time, so I continue. "Steven, we have to try again to have a baby. This time I will tell you when I get pregnant. I won't keep it a secret." The rush of air escaping me is a silent exclamation mark. One he can't ignore any longer. He always listens to my point of view, but we end up doing what is best for him every time.

I won't give in. I want a baby to love. I know if we get a puppy, it would add to the happiness around the house while we try to have another baby.

A year after we were married, Steven's old cocker spaniel, Benny, peacefully passed away in his sleep, so when a good friend referred me to a cocker spaniel breeder south of the city—who will soon have a puppy available in her sought-after champion litter—I jumped at the chance to get in touch with her. The hole left in Steven's heart from Benny's passing is still raw, and I know getting another puppy would be good for him and for our marriage. The hole in my heart from losing this baby will be raw for a long time to come. I hope we can try again soon.

Through sobs, I tell my husband, "Steven, it's time to settle down and try again, to grow a family—in the suburban bubble. I need leave this city and the crime that comes with it. I want to see more trees. Trees to hold a swing for our child and a treehouse and a place where our new puppy sits to chew bones."

"You're right, Betsy. I'm ready to grow our family."

Ten Years Later

Someone is watching me, I know. Dr. Deller is lecturing me about my high blood pressure during pregnancy while his fingers sit on my wrist to check my pulse, but all I can think about is the note I found on the side door of my home last night: *I watch you, woman. Almost touch you.* I should tell the doctor, or even the receptionist, about the vile note, but I don't want to get other people involved. Plus, what could they do to help me? I'm not sure who left it, but it's sick, reminding me of the horrible man who killed my baby years ago—no physical description. This time all I have is a flimsy piece of pink paper with scribbled black words on it. I plan on sharing this note with Steven when he calls, but I'm just not sure it's something he can deal with while he's out of town on business. It's creepy, but it could also just be some teenage prank. Either way, it's weirding me out.

While getting dressed to leave, I linger in the mirror for a quick second studying my eight-months-pregnant belly. I really hope the note was just a prank. But maybe it's related to what my seven-year-old son Kyle told me about the man outside last night? I shouldn't have dismissed it as his childhood imagination so quickly. It's too coincidental. I must get home and call the police.

At the reception desk, Donna takes a pen from the ceramic cup on her desk to meticulously process my insurance information and schedule my next appointment. Urging her to hurry along is like rushing molasses out of a jar—there's no use in trying. I exhale as I purse my lips into a phony smile, then check my phone for messages.

Finally, she reaches over the counter, smiles, and says, "Here's your reminder card and receipt. Stay dry out there."

I grab the invoice and my credit card and shove them into my handbag. "Thank you!" I reply, hoping she doesn't hear the feigned cheerfulness in my voice as I turn for the door. My attention shifts again to last night's menacing note, but then a little wiggle in my belly brings me right back and I smile.

"Oh, Betsy," the receptionist says. I turn back to see her holding out an envelope, a silver bracelet dangling from her wrist. "I almost forgot. Did you leave this on my desk earlier when you checked in?"

"What? No—maybe, let me see it." I squeeze my eyes shut, and as they open, she's still holding it—much like the envelope containing the threat from last night. I take the note from her as a bead of sweat forms on my upper lip. I try to hide it as I rub my lips together, thank her again, and slip out the door. My fair complexion pales even further. I sense the baby's movement, and my blood pressure starting to increase. *I need to leave.*

Pregnant at thirty-eight makes it hard to get away as fast as I could have if I were in my twenties—but something inside pushes my feet to a sprint in my size-seven loafers. I glance both ways as I dodge puddles and a whirl of brown-and-orange leaves, and almost trip over a parking block on the way to my car at the back of the lot. I steady myself and continue to wobble-run.

The droplets in my hair slide down to my collar then onto my chest as I shake off an uncontrollable shiver. With one hand, I fumble to locate the key remote. With the other, I clutch the note and the hood of my fluttering raincoat tighter, leaving open only a small peephole. I'm exposed outside in the rain, just like I was ten years ago. The familiar *chirp-beep* of my car lock is music to my ears as I jump in and exhale, causing a lone blonde wisp to jump up and down in front of my face. Looking behind, I confirm the back seat is empty. Thank God. Years of practicing the power of proper breathing in yoga and meditation classes are paying off, as my breathing tempers and the throbbing in the long muscles of my legs starts to fade.

No bad guys carrying notes are chasing me through the hospital campus parking lot—at least from what I see—but those few minutes outside my car gave me the creeps. I wish I knew who was following me. I crinkle the envelope in my hands and fight off the urge to cry. Pressing my palms against my full chest, unable to breathe again, I gulp for air as I look up and realize my mascara is covering my face with uneven, swirling black lines. *No time for vanity or to sit and commiserate with myself and give in to fear. It's time to go.* I toss the envelope on the seat next to me and start the car.

A *tap-tap-tap* on my window causes me to jump in my seat. It's only Donna standing patiently outside my window in the pouring rain, her oversized raincoat hiding her full figure. She's all smiles, holding a red-and-blue-striped umbrella and *my* cell phone.

I try to wipe my face with my wrinkled blue sleeve and fake a small grin as I put the car in park and roll down the window.

Donna leans and says, "Betsy, you ran out and left your phone on the counter."

"Oh," I reply as the damp, musty air swooshes inside my car, causing the front windshield to fog. "Sorry. I'm late picking up my sons from school."

As I make up an excuse for my rushing, my nostrils flare in and out, ever so slightly—a tell my husband pointed out once when he caught me fibbing about spending way too much money on cookbooks. I consider fibs less offensive lies. Cheating on your spouse? Now that's a lie.

"Well, here you go," she says.

"Thank you, Donna. I'll see you soon." I smile, take the phone, and slide it into my purse. I roll up the window and let out the breath stuck in my lungs.

This time the shiver stuck in between my vertebrae isn't as easy to shake. I rack my brain trying to figure out who's placing these notes. I've been to this doctor's office so many times over the past few years; anyone could've seen me coming and going. Until I know for sure, I'll pay extra attention to people lurking around, especially near my home.

I'm not thrilled about getting home to an empty house and possibly facing a crazy stranger before I've had a chance to calm down and figure out what to do. I need to regroup. I wish Steven were here.

I still have time before I get the kids from school, so I drive a far and safe enough distance away from the doctor's parking lot and pull over onto a street with busy foot traffic— there's safety in numbers. My heart is dancing in my chest as I swallow and pray this note isn't like the other one.

With numb fingers, I examine my scribbled name on the outside of the envelope. The multiple people walking up and down the street with their umbrellas in hand give me a moment of relief before I rip open the note and expose the end of a rose-colored piece of paper—identical to the other. My stomach twists when I imagine what this sicko intends to do. Is it a man? Or maybe a woman? Without thinking, my hand reaches for my growing belly.

That side door where the first note was placed, camouflaged with hearty boxwood bushes, is behind a locked gate—so much for privacy. I thought our fence was secure and safe? I guess not. While I'm thinking of it, I grab my to-do list out of my purse and add another item to the ever-growing collection of chores: *Install a stronger deadbolt on side gate— maybe a higher fence. Move hidden key from under rock.* I'll scratch that one off the list right when I get home.

I take a breath and read the second note.

I want your baby.

My face heats as my hands stay icy. I shake my head. *Well, if the goal was to scare the tar out of me, the stalker is succeeding. Let's hope it's all words and no actions. Let's hope he or she is* unaware that my husband is out of town.

The intense beat in my temples escalates as I fight off a sensation more crippling than falling from a cliff. Ever since the attack in Chicago, I scrutinize everyone I meet; the tangle of anxiety ignites my nervous system whenever I'm away from home or work. These notes justify my fright as I relive being pushed to the wet pavement and kicked in the gut. The attacker didn't steal my bag or my beloved watch, but he did rob me of my first baby... and gave me cuts and bruises as a reminder. That rib still gives me trouble.

The notes prove there's someone wanting to hurt me again, someone who hopefully hasn't broken into my house and injured my dog. *Oh God! I need to get home and protect Barney!* I check the door locks, then stuff the new note into my purse and race home.

I try to calm down as I turn onto my street. The lush, warm-hued rainbow of leaves on the trees and sculptured bushes along this strip of road reminds me that I live in a picturesque suburban bubble. Still, as I pull into the driveway, I realize I've turned my home into a fortress—for good reason.

I pull into the detached garage and shut the door. Sitting inside my car, I finally let it all out like a breaking dam—it can't be stopped. I clench the steering wheel, shoulders shuddering, propelling uncontrollable sobs—tears of fear *and* regret for fighting with Steven before he got on that plane to San Francisco. He swears he doesn't cheat on me, but I fear the distance and days away might tempt him just like it did a few years ago with his secretary. At this point, with two kids and another on the way, I have no other choice but to believe him.

After several minutes, my fit subsides as I sniffle and catch another glance of myself in the rearview mirror. Forget the rain—these tears certainly do a number on mascara. I rummage through my purse and grab a tissue to get rid of the smeared makeup on my face. After texting my parents to ask them to pick up my sons at school and come over right away, I muster the courage to work my way through the rain and get ready to confront this threat, head on, as I quickly dial 911.

Thankfully, Barney is fine. I hurry to double check the locks on every door and window on the first floor as Barney follows close behind, his collar jingling with each step. I know they're locked, but being paranoid is part of who I am these days. It never hurts to double check. The boys' beds are a rumpled mess with clumps of dirty shirts and underwear on the floor. The master bath still has a little puddle on the marble in front of the shower door. My wet loafers squeak on the polished surface as I grab a towel and dab the spot, then toss the towel in the hamper in the corner. I hurry down the stairs and onto the dark hardwood floors. I wobble-jog past the hall table and through the kitchen to double-check the latch on the door to the back patio, then pivot and proceed to greet the police officers as the doorbell rings.

The officers in front of me are wearing their official uniforms with shiny badges, telling me they're Officers Flaggler and Wilson. The guns holstered on their hips, not to mention the lack of wrinkles and gray hair, distract me.

After a brief greeting, Office Flaggler, the young male officer, asks, "Ma'am, when did you notice the first note?"

"Last night."

"What time?"

"It was after I walked my dog. I don't know. Why does the exact time matter?"

"Ma'am, I'm just doing my job."

My cheeks fill with pink as I reply, "I'm sorry. It was after dinner, so I'm guessing between seven and eight last night."

He doesn't look up as he writes down each and every word.

"... and you say you received a second note today at your doctor's office?"

"Yes. It was left on the counter, so they didn't see who left it."

"Do you know anyone who would want to threaten you like this?" he asks.

"No, not really, except—"

"Not really, or no?"

I shoot him a sideways glance and answer, "No." *Who's on trial here?* "My son told me he saw a man across the street, the other night. He just told me about it this morning. I didn't think the person he saw was related to the first note because it was delivered last night. Honestly, I thought my son may have just seen our neighbor, Mr. Swanson. However, after receiving a second note today, it appears they may be related. I know I should've called you about it first thing this morning, but I didn't take it as seriously as I should have."

Office Flaggler nods. "I've added it to your file, so don't worry about that right now. We've searched the perimeter of your yard, around the patio and grill area, and along the doors and windows and didn't see any signs of forced entry." He reads from his notepad, then looks down, raising his eyebrows, "Did your son get a good look at the man?"

"He only said the man was big. He said the man was across the street—he couldn't get a good look at him."

"Have you noticed anything disrupted around your home or property?"

"Like I told you, I found the note taped to my side door, that's it. We always keep our gates locked. There hasn't been any damage that I can see."

"Perhaps the person has a key, or they hopped your fence to put the note there?"

Good point! Inhaling through my nose and forcefully pushing it out again, I squish my eyebrows and respond, "What else can I do?" I didn't want him to think I was rude, but this whole ordeal was really frustrating for me.

"We'll file a report and keep it open just in case something else comes up."

"What would come up?"

The female officer chimes in. "What he's saying is, until we establish more clues or catch the person, we will continue to work on it from our end. If you figure out the identity of the stalker, then you must come in to the station and fill out a formal stalker no contact order. This is an official form filed to identify who is stalking you. That way we'll have it on record. If we don't have an identity, we can't proceed with legal action."

My clenched fists release. "Will you offer me security guards around my home?"

Officer Wilson shakes her head. "Mrs. Ryan, we don't have the manpower in this district to offer that type of exclusive protection, but rest assured, we will have more squad cars roaming the area. That should deter any future notes from being placed on your property." She puts her hand on my shoulder and gives it a little squeeze.

The warmth in her hand and the use of my name dispel any unsure thoughts I had about her age earlier, reinforcing my love for this small town. "Thanks. I'll contact you if anything else happens."

Officer Flaggler hands me a business card and says, "Here's our contact information. Call anytime." He flashes the first grin I've seen on him since he arrived, signaling to me that he's satisfied with the report. I hope they make some headway and catch this stalker.

Swinging the door shut, I ask Barney, "Well, buddy, what do you think? They did exactly what I expected they'd do. Not much."

My dog stands next to me, looking up, and lets out a half-groan, half-bark as if he's yelling at me. My running about and anxiety he's witnessed today must be quite a lot to handle for a sensitive dog like him.

Now that I've reported this crime, I'm hoping my nerves will calm down a bit so I can sit and relax for five minutes. I find relief in the form of my safe and comfy leather chair in the corner of our family room. Leaning back on the soft throw pillows, I wait for the microwave to complete its task of warming the water for my tea. I grab my leg above the ankle and place it on the opposite knee, giving my hip a good stretch. It's amazing where stress hides in the human body.

When my parents come in with the boys, Barney sits at attention by my feet while the baby is jolting my rib. I fiddle with the fringe on a pillow, making a tiny braid as I glance over at my mom, who's watching my sons place their backpacks on the hooks in the mudroom. My dad is close behind, ushering them into the other room to "do homework," while telling Morgan how awesome he is since learning to write his ABCs in kindergarten. I imagine another little blue or pink backpack hanging on a third hook soon.

A warm sensation comes over me as I realize Barney is trying to get my attention. A thought comes to mind: *He'll always protect me.* I lower my eyes to meet his as he intently stares back. He wags his stub of a tail, rhythmically knocking it on the floor, as he pulls his mouth into a dog smile. I return the smile and reach down to scratch behind his ears.

The microwave's *beeeep* rouses me from my warm seat in the living room to retrieve my mug and add my favorite medicinal brew. Herbal tea has always soothed and centered me, and I'm hoping today it does the trick to steady my shaking hands.

I consider my next words to Mom as I wait for the tea to steep. I flick my eyes to her. She's sitting on the overstuffed couch, thumbing through a magazine. Her soft, gray hair almost blends in with the painting hanging on the wall behind her of a calm lake, reflecting smoky clouds and a deep teal mountain ridge. We're waiting for the kids to leave the room so I can tell her what's going on.

I swallow before speaking. "Here's the deal. Last night, I received a threatening note from someone I may or may not know, something about how I'm being watched." I see her eyes widen as the weight of this incident rests on her heart. "And then another arrived this afternoon—at my doctor's office. Before you and Dad brought the boys home, the police arrived to check on the house and take my statement."

"Good heavens, Betsy." My mother gasps, causing the weathered skin on her forehead to crease. "Are you okay? I knew something was up when you texted us. What did the authorities say?"

"After they took my statement, they also snapped pictures of the notes, looked inside and around the house, and even through the bushes in the yard. They told me to call if I spot the stalker or receive another threat. That's about it. Since I saw no one, the notes were the only evidence—not much else to go on. They told me that once I have the identity of the stalker I should go in and file a stalker no contact order. Then they can zero in on my case."

After throwing the saturated tea bag into the sink, I join Mom on the couch, next to where Barney is sitting on the floor, to continue our conversation. This is one of many private discussions he's been privy to over the years—without regard, aside from his chuffing and woofing.

Mom's taut shoulders give her frame an uneven look as she smiles and says in her most comforting voice, "Well, at least they came and have it on record that the incident happened. I guess they're doing the best they can. We should spend more time together and keep our eyes open until Steven gets back in town. Have you spoken to him since your most recent disagreement?"

"Yeah, I agree. I expected more from the authorities." I sigh. "As far as Steven goes, when he left the other day, we agreed to discuss the possible move and his late-night meetings when he returns. He's been traveling back and forth from the West Coast for work a lot this month while his company finalizes the corporate merger, and it's beginning to bother the boys."

"How is it bothering them? Did they say something?"

Repositioning myself on the couch, I reply, "This morning, Kyle told me about a man he saw across the street the other night, but I assumed it was just the neighbor. I know he witnessed the disagreement me and Steven had, so I'm sure the two things combined are concerning him."

My mother's eyebrows raise, and her eyes widen again as she shoots me a look, one I haven't seen since the attack years ago. "What man, Betsy? This is serious. We can talk about your marital bumps later."

I push my tongue to the roof of my mouth to refrain from snapping at her. "Kyle told me that the other night he got up to go to the bathroom and he heard a strange noise outside. At the window, he saw a man in the shadows next to the neighbor's house, looking up at him." I pause and shift in my seat again to lean in closer to Mom so I can lower my voice. "He asked me if the stranger was a bad guy. I told him he wasn't because I didn't want to scare the wits out of him... but now I'm not so sure. I told the police, and they have it in the report. The problem is, we don't have a good description of the person, except that it was a 'big man,' according to Kyle."

Mom takes a deep breath, and her voice softens as she says, "It's good you told police about him, but I wish you had a better description."

"I know! Just that he was big. That's all I could get from a seven-year-old boy. I didn't want to press Kyle when he told me because I feared he would get even more frightened."

"Oh heavens, you must be so scared. The last couple of days I've noticed that he's been more reserved than usual and always looking over at you to make sure you're here. This man that he saw explains his behavior."

Her eyes meet mine as a tear rolls down my cheek. My innocent son shouldn't be running to the windows and reacting to scary, crashing sounds in his own home.

"When Kyle asked if I was mad about him not telling me right away, I told him, 'I'm not mad. It was just the neighbor from next door, coming back late from work.' What if it was the jerk from the city or some other crazy person? I can't see how he would have figured out my address this many years later. I never found out if he was the one who stole my ID badge, but since the police never caught him, I just don't know."

I visualize myself, a petite mom, going toe-to-toe with a psychopathic stalker. The result would be cuts, bruises, and screaming, just like my last attack—but this time I'd fight to the death to save my baby. *Maybe I need a gun?*

"You have a very strong sense of intuition, Betsy. You always have. Your son must follow suit." Mom leans in and wraps her arm around me, the same way she has a thousand times before.

Kyle's little blond crew cut and pale blue eyes are like his father's, yet I see a sweet, young boy, a person who's just beginning his life. He does, however, share my habit of looking over his shoulder and double-checking the door locks and windows. Something he inherited from me. His only concern should be playing, learning, and being a kid.

The tightness in my neck and upper back loosens up after talking with Mom. I get up and circle my kitchen island, dragging my left hand along the putty-colored granite, cradling the teacup with my right. I glance around the room, embracing the warmth of my home, accented with muted gray pillows, subtle teal textures on the couch, and soothing brown carpeting and hardwood. The plants in the corner by the patio door are thriving in the flood of light throughout the day.

"Mom, I love living here… in Westin Heights, in this neighborhood, and in this house. But I'm feeling unsafe. Just like I felt in the city after the attack."

"Honey, you have always been fearful since that man assaulted you. I think we should treat this threat as seriously as we did that one. We should tell your father about the letters," she says, her voice nearly a whisper. "And the man."

"What man?" my dad chimes in as he walks in the room cradling a small pile of brown gunk in his hand. Morgan is trailing close behind him.

"I'll fill you in when you-know-who leaves the room." I stick out my tongue and scrunch up my nose. "But, eeewwww. What *is* that?"

"It's Morgan's fake puppy poop, my dear." My dad chuckles with his signature belly laugh while shooting me a wink. "We got it from the joke shop in the mall. I'm here to admit that I'm exposing your son to my world of sick humor." He smiles at Morgan, who's already grinning from ear to ear, minus a front tooth.

My dad Cary has a full head of silver-blond hair and mahogany eyes—such a stark contrast to my little Morgan with his curly, black hair and deep, curious blue eyes. When they're together, they don't look related at all, but their sassiness aligns. He looks more like my aunt Ellen, curls and all.

"Just keep it G-rated, Pops," I order, offering a pleading grin.

"Have you seen the phony vomit your son and I left in the bathroom? We've kinda misplaced it."

Morgan runs through the kitchen, still wearing his school outfit splattered with paint, to find Barney, who is standing next to me. He loves that dog just as much as I do. With his luscious, cashmere-soft coat and fluffy, long ears, Barney is one good-looking animal, if I do say so myself. But more than that, my dog has been my best friend for ten years. It's a shame the poor guy always gets blamed for Morgan's practical jokes.

My parents always tell me I've met my match in Barney, from our love of long walks on the beach near our house in the morning to how I talk to him about Steven when the tears are flowing—even though he can't answer me. I have a strong sense of connection to him, almost as if he understands every word I say and promises to keep my secrets. When things get back to normal, I want to learn more about dog whisperers and how they tap into a dog's thoughts and actions—it's fascinating.

My father has met *his* match in my tiny fair-haired mom, Karen, with her quick wit, energy, and sense of adventure. They're always on the go, traveling, hiking, taking classes, and solving crossword puzzles. Since Dad's heart attack a little over a year ago, they've been following a structured daily diet and a brisk walking program—giving even us older "kids" a run for our money. With the events over the past two days, I should get moving with them again, in case I need outrun a crazy man.

My cell phone rings. "Hold on, Dad, let me grab this. Hello?"

"Mrs. Ryan," a familiar voice starts. "This is Principal Osborne from Kyle and Morgan's school. Do you have a second?"

"Sure, what is it?" My digital watch illuminates 4:00 p.m. *I hope Morgan didn't play a prank on another student after school again.*

As I wrinkle my forehead, my mom looks over with raised eyebrows, hoping to find out who's calling and why I seem concerned.

"Someone must have come in today after your sons were picked up and dropped off an envelope with your name on it. Ordinarily we wouldn't think anything of it, but it just seemed odd that it just showed up on the receptionist's desk." He pauses, waiting for my signal to continue. I'm frozen. I can pierce the silence on the line with a pin. My voice has stopped dead. "We haven't opened it, but would like you to come in and pick it up from the front desk."

His chilly tone signals to me that he hasn't forgotten the time he hit on me at the school holiday party. I shut him down immediately. I didn't have my wedding ring on because I was working in the kitchen all day, so he must have assumed I was separated from Steven. Even though my husband doesn't attend school events or parent-teacher conferences, I found it rather unethical and odd that an administrator would hit on a parent. I was certain that somehow word had gotten around that Steven had some sort of fling with his secretary, so he must've assumed... to this day he acts odd around me as if I was the one who led him on.

"Wow, uh... um..." My throat dries up, and my hands sweat. Dizziness takes hold of me as I set my teacup on the counter and grip a chair for balance. These notes keep flying in like fireworks. Bam, bam, bam.

I motion to Mom and Dad and cover the phone while I lean my elbows on the counter for balance. "Can you guys take the boys to your house for some dinner? I'll be over later. I need to take care of something first—it's about another letter. I'll fill you in when I get back."

"Sure, sport," my dad says. He and Mom gather the boys and head to the door, but he looks back at me, studying my body language and raising one eyebrow, a curious look on his face. I give him a thumbs-up to ease his concerns and blow the boys kisses as we wave goodbye. Barney trots over to my side and looks up at me as he leans on my leg. The heat coming from his body warms me from the inside out.

"Well, see, that's the thing," Mr. Osborne explains. "We never get deliveries for parents here. No one was expecting it, and it's just not customary for us to be collecting mail for you."

"I have no clue why another... I mean, why would an envelope addressed to me come to the school, delivered by someone I don't know?" While I wait for his response, I make my way over to the sink to rinse out my empty mug. I'm not about to explain my recent stalker threat to him. The fewer people who know about it the better. Could Mr. Osborne be the jerk floating around our house? He knows a lot about our family, where we live, and he definitely has an ax to grind.

Out the window, dark storm clouds roll in, blotting out any sunshine in sight. The forceful rustling of the leaves outside reminds me to double-check the latches on the windows once more. *There's my paranoia again!*

Maybe this envelope is from another parent? *Stop kidding yourself, Betsy, you know darn well who delivered that note: the obsessive stalker.*

Pressing, Mr. Osborne continues, "All that into consideration, please, Mrs. Ryan, come to the school right away. Good day." The phone clicks off, and I roll my eyes. *Well, he told me, didn't he? Mrs. Ryan? Ha, he used to call me Betsy. How times have changed.* He needs to move on.

CRACK!

The booming thunder causes me to jump, and I almost trip over Barney, who's still standing at my feet. He's scared, too.

I grab my purse, apply pink-tinted lip balm as I slip on my damp loafers, and head toward the door, making sure I have my keys so I can quickly run to the car. I glance over and tell Barney, "Mom is going back out into the rain." He swallows a groan, then reclines on his fluffy dog bed and starts gnawing on his rawhide. I'll take that as an *Okay.*

━━━━━━━

Half-walking, half-running on the polished floors—because there's no running in the school hallway after all—I draw in some air as I approach the front office, making a mental note on my to-do list to join my parents on their fitness walks.

"Here you go." The school secretary hands me the rain-sodden envelope, looking up at me with flushed cheeks, smiling apologetically. "Thank you for coming in right away, Mrs. Ryan. I'm sorry we had to make you come back today, given the horrible weather."

"No problem-o," I lie. "It's no big deal. Sorry to bother you. I'll tell them to deliver it to me next time." Throwing around fibs when it's related to my safety and security is justified today. I flash an awkward smile and dart out the door, successfully avoiding contact with Mr. Osborne. As I rush back down the hall, the flyers posted on the bulletin board whisk up and down on their thumbtacks.

Who would leave this note? Of course, it was the stalker. But why leave it at my sons' school? I clench my teeth and fight off a mixture of heat and shivers as I hurry back to the shelter of my car, stepping over fallen branches and acorns.

The perspiration wells up in my armpits, joining the rain spots and tears from earlier today. *This stalker can try to mess with my head, but when he gets my kids involved, then he's poking the bear—the frightened, ferocious Mother Bear, no less.* I'll wait until I'm sitting down in my kitchen to open this envelope. I don't want fury to drive me home.

I stare, unblinking, at the road ahead, trying to figure out how I can share this with Steven. I hope to have more answers about these notes before he comes home from San Francisco in a few days. He doesn't need another reason to get upset, especially after our fight about a possible move to the West Coast. One of many fights these days. Sometimes life is easier when he's on the road. There are fewer disagreements, and I don't have to prepare elaborate meals. As a chef, it's nice to eat mac-and-cheese and sliced apples for dinner, on occasion.

I understand he can't pick up and leave to come home and wonder who wrote some mysterious notes, but the load of carrying the worry about the baby and a stalker is more than I can handle. I'm trying to believe that I'm safe, but given the fact that we don't know the identity of the stalker means the police can't make much headway on my case, which leaves it up to me to figure out who would do this. No, I decide; telling Steven can wait.

───────

I let out a long, desperate sigh and collapse back into my reliable leather chair, dropping my handbag to the floor. The soft blanket falls to join my purse as Barney runs over with his Pooh toy and curls around my feet, making the throw his resting spot. "Hey boy, do you want to go out?"

Chuff, snort. He drops his toy to look up at me. I imagine him saying, *Yes, Mom. Let's go potty!* I shoot my dog a quizzical look, tilting my head, wondering, *If he could talk, would he say that?* He wags his tail and walks to the door.

Barney is very attached to the little Winnie the Pooh stuffed toy Kyle gave him when he was a toddler. One day I heard Kyle say, "Barney, I want to give this to you." I swear I saw the dog nod his head, but I didn't think much about it. I find it funny how animals and children communicate despite a "language" barrier. I smile at the chubby bear and remember the A. A. Milne quote—one of my favorites, about promising to be braver and smarter than you seem and think.

Maybe keeping this in mind will help me stop looking over my shoulder and think straight so I can push out the fear—I can't let this stalker harm us. As I shake my head, I grab an umbrella and head out for a walk. "Let's go potty outside, Barney." Rain, here we come again.

I jiggle the excess rain out of my umbrella, set it down, and grab a towel to dry Barney's paws. *Please wait, puppy.* He's patient while I get the job done. We connect eyes as he licks my chin. He loves to be petted, scratched, or rubbed in any way, even to clean mud from his paws.

"There ya go, big guy," I mumble, patting his back to let him know he's done. "Now, Barney, let's look at those rotten notes again and see what we're up against." He seems to nod in agreement and follows me over to the kitchen table. I push the plantation shutters closed to shield from prying eyes and get down to business. I often wonder if other people talk to their dog like I do—and if they do, I wonder if they wait for a response.

"Okay, so the first envelope came last night. After our post-dinner walk, I found it taped to the side door, remember? That was the gross one about 'watching me.'" I twist my face in disgust. "Then envelope number two arrived at my doctor's office this afternoon, and that's the one where the creep said he wants my baby. Who does this guy think he is? Ugh." Barney chimes in with a *chuff-chuff.*

Trying to temper the uneasiness in my stomach and shield Barney from my distress, I continue to use a Mommy singsong voice, much like when he was a puppy. He responds favorably to it, and it brings my tension down a notch.

"And now, today, envelope number three lands at the school office. Let's open it together—this guy deserves detention!" Looking down at Barney, I see him shift his weight and then sit at attention while I open the envelope.

It's remarkable how Barney's anticipation matches mine as I start to open the seal. I wish Steven had that same patience with me. Lately, he's too preoccupied to notice me the way he did when we first got married over twelve years ago. I remember when he was so proud of the elaborate meals I'd create for hundreds of people, but now he barely notices if the dishes are done. I used to blame it on his long hours at work, but these days, I'm not so sure.

With both elbows on the table, I prepare myself for the next mental blow to the gut. *It can't get any worse than what he's already written.*

It turns out I'm wrong.

"Okay, this one is horrible. Barney, you will not believe it. It says, *I'm watching the boys.* What the heck! Who has the time to run around town and track pregnant women and their children?" Again, my maternal instinct kicks in to protect even my dog, from the face value of what I'm reading and saying— but a cold wash of tremors dances over my skin. I grab my wool cardigan from the back of the chair and slip it on.

As I fling the note across the table, I raise my voice, trembling. "This is the *last* straw!"

Barney backs up two steps, then takes an erect seated position again, and continues to keep an eye on me.

Bang!

"What was that?" Not expecting Barney to answer me, I look to him anyway, as we then direct our attention to the banging noise outside, almost as if someone slammed the side gate. I tiptoe slowly across the thick, brown area rug, over to the window, and peek through a small slit in the blinds. Barney moans and runs to curl around my legs. He's shaking. "What is it, boy?"

I wish I knew what he was thinking and what caused that noise. The storm may have stripped some of the bark or old branches from the tree on the side of the house. I can check later when we go for our walk. I see nothing outside, but that doesn't stop the goose bumps as they go all the way up to my neck.

"Maybe two deep breaths will help, but breathing won't stop a madman, that's for sure. Barney, let's hope the tree is our only threat at this moment. I don't feel like going outside to confront anyone right now. Do you?"

Tap-tap-tap.

A jolt of sudden jitters. The knock at the side door causes me to jump. Step by step, Barney follows my lead as we go to see who's at the door. I see my former landscaper, Freddie. His green baseball hat hides his long, black ponytail and shadows his pitch-black eyes. The lack of his signature smile pushes my pulse higher as I place my foot by the bottom of the door to prevent him from pushing it in—and slowly unlatch the bolt lock.

"Hey, Freddie, what's up?"

"Mrs. Ryan, do you know of any neighbors who need landscaping?"

My guilt for firing him and switching to a larger landscape design company, headed up by Antonio, over a year ago, bubbles up as I search for something to say. "Freddie, I asked everyone on my block. I noticed the Swansons are using your service, right?"

"Yeah, but I need more work." His fixed expression accentuates his need.

"I understand. Let me see what I can do. By the way, how did you get inside my locked gate?"

"The key."

"Oh, you still have my key?" *What if he made copies of it? I must change those locks.*

"Yeah... here ya go." He hands me a tinged version of my once polished key—it has seen its share of mud and grime.

"Thank you, Freddie. I'll send out another note this week. Anything else?" The hammering in my veins clouds my hearing.

His eyes narrow in on me. "No… but why can't I work here again?"

His cold stare and rigid stance forces me to repeat myself. "I told you, Freddie, my husband wanted to go in a different direction and work with a larger company who could also install our hardscapes and fountain. I hope you understand." I fake a glance at the clock on the stove. "Oh, shoot, I almost forgot. I need to take a call in a few minutes. Can I let you go and circle back later if I know of anyone who needs your service?" My crooked grin doesn't encourage him.

He bows his head then raises it again with eyes narrowed and utters, "Thank you."

I watch him leave through the side gate and listen as it clicks locked. I shut the door and flick the lock.

"Barney, that was a close one. He seemed really agitated." *Add Freddie to the list of suspects, and get a locksmith to change the side gate lock.*

The throbbing in my ankles forces me to sit down at the table again. I look around my kitchen and adjoining living room, finally fixating on a spot near the ceiling, wondering, *If my former landscaper is the stalker, would he really knock on my door? Is he that gutsy?* Upon closer inspection, I realize I'm staring at a spider weaving a thread around a tiny fly. Horrified by the sight, and the symbolism, I get up and grab a few tissues to rid the murder scene from my kitchen.

Not sure what to say, I wait, looking down at Barney, hoping he has an opinion about what just happened. All I get is a *woof.* I need to hang out with more human friends.

"I wish Steven were here, Doggy Boy, he'd know what to do—or at the least he'd be able to protect us. That's one thing about him, he's a bruiser." My chest tightens and a cold disregard rests on my skin as I think about my husband and if he's having lunch with anyone pretty, right now. I never used to be so insecure, but I guess one "innocent" kiss between a husband and his secretary will do that do a person.

As soon as I reach down and feel Barney's soft fur between my fingertips, the pull on my shoulders subsides. "We need to sort this out, buddy. I don't like having to manually slow down my heart rate every five minutes."

He wags his little butt in agreement. It's nice to have someone who agrees with me for a change.

What's my connection to this stalker, and what would motivate him or her to do this to me? It couldn't simply be because I fired someone who works in my yard, could it? In detective shows, the bad guy always has a motive, whether he's seeking revenge or has his own maniacal reasons for plotting to kill someone. Kill someone? What if? *Oh, for heaven's sake, Betsy, get a hold of yourself. Don't jump to conclusions!*

I wish somebody could give me the answers and push this incessant pulse of panic out of my nervous system. I start to walk around the living room to fluff and rearrange the pillows on the couch. *Oh, and I've been meaning to restack those magazines into a neat little pile, too…*

Out of the blue I remember *Murder, She Wrote,* my favorite mystery television show growing up. I watched the reruns, but the show is timeless.

The show's star, Angela Lansbury, played the lead character, Jessica Fletcher, a murder mystery writer. Each episode would present a police investigation surrounding a killing, and since Jessica was an expert at writing murder mysteries, they'd always consult with her for clues. At the end of each episode, she'd plunk on her old-fashioned computer, writing the mystery story of the current crime she'd just helped solve. It was a great concept and so satisfying to watch her help decipher the cases each week. We knew some poor soul would get whacked, but Jessica would make us feel better through her wit and charm—not to mention save the day.

If Jessica were a real person, she could come here and help me piece together my unanswered questions. She'd see the big picture and have it solved before the second commercial break... but never mind Jessica! I pull my mind back to the present. *I've got to think. I've got to be strong. I've got to stay focused on reality, not some TV character solving crimes in under an hour. I don't know anyone who would stalk me, so I'll continue to pay attention and look for clues.*

If all else fails and someone chases me, I could always run next door to my friend Misty's house. She would protect me. Even as a petite, single mother with a silky red ponytail, she doesn't seem to freak out about anything at all. Maybe it has something to do with her having a black belt in karate and being a registered gun owner.

Courageous or not, I need to call the police again so they can add the most recent threat to the case file. I can take bravery lessons from Misty another day.

Barney whines and jumps around like a puppy as I start to dial Mom and Dad's home phone number.

Hoowwwll, aroof, aroof!

"Oh, BAR-ney," I say as he jumps on my legs and scratches on my pants. I stop dialing the phone. "What's up? We just went out." He runs to the side door and scratches it as if he's trying to tell me something. On days like this, I wish I could speak dog.

"Okay, let's go outside." I try my best to believe Freddie isn't perched, ready to pounce, but I also want to keep my voice calm for my pet while I shrug on my damp raincoat. Looking over my shoulder and around the area in front of me, Barney follows as we leave the security of our nest.

"Mom has to go meet the boys," I remind him as we head out the side door, intending to get things done quick. The ridges of the keys in my hand give me a moment of trust that my home is secure. I lock the door *and* gate, checking each latch twice. My pepper spray is in my pocket.

Barney has been my sweet dog with a humanlike personality since he was eight weeks old. He came into my life right after my attack in the city—when I was having trouble getting pregnant again. Steven understood that the pain of losing a baby and then not being able to get pregnant again was a heavy burden on me. He knew I needed a different "baby" to care for while I waited for nature to take over. He agreed to my pleas, contacted the breeder I had been in touch with, and came home with the cutest puppy I had ever seen. "It's great mom practice," he said with tears in his eyes, "with your new best friend." It's easy to fall in love with your husband again when he makes such a thoughtful gesture. I smile at the memory.

———

"C'mon, Barn, Mommy has to go." I pull the leash toward the side gate, hoping to signal him to move along, though we need to keep our walk close to the big oak tree in our side yard. A sudden chill, surrounds me, as I look down to see Barney's mouth full of something that probably shouldn't be there. "What *is* that?"

Reaching down, I pull a limp, wet, dead bird from his mouth with an envelope attached to it. "Did you get this... dead bird... and envelope next to our tree?" My bottom lip quivers. "Oh, my God, that poor little creature—and right next to our house!"

I drag Barney the few steps back to safety through the gate and towards the side door. Then I place the tiny, limp bird on a patch of earth next to the door before entering, and bring the envelop inside.

I wash my hands, unleash Barney, and give him a treat, then wipe the stream of tears from my cheek. I search the depths of my mind for an explanation. Could Freddie have left that dead bird? He was just here. Oh God, who would kill an innocent little animal and then attach an envelope to it? That sick bastard! And now I have *four* envelopes. *I need to call the police again. I know they'll think I'm crazy.* The evidence is the same, just different words—horrible words, just no proof of who this person is.

"It's a regular sob-fest for me today, Barney. I know you don't understand why I'm crying so much, but this crazy person has me terrified. I don't want him to hurt you or the boys."

I blow my nose and bend down to hug my dog, extra long. "Big boy, I need to leave, but I promise I'll be back soon. Keep an eye on the house for me, and stand up to any bad guys." He stands still, at attention, and watches me leave, just like a little soldier. Scooping up the envelopes and slinging my purse over my shoulder, I race out the door to my parents' house. *I'll read the fourth threat when I arrive.*

The short drive to my parents' home seems to take forever. The twists and turns in the road catch me off guard. While waiting for a red light, I figure out what to say to the police when I call them back. I glance down at the passenger seat to see that the fourth envelope has little bloodstains on it from the poor, helpless victim. My heart fights a cold rush, magnified even more by the chilling fall wind that's swirling around today.

Just wait, Betsy, I urge my impatient self as the light changes, and I hit the gas a bit too hard. I'll share the new envelope and one from school with my mom and dad; they'll know what to do.

I've always considered their house as my home even though I love the suburban lifestyle and home Steven and I have created together, regardless of the bumps along the way. Nothing feels more secure and safe than the familiar family pictures, artwork, and household items, or aromas like Mom's chili or peanut butter cookies. I wonder if Kyle and Morgan have that same connection to our home, which I've worked hard to make special during my time as a stay-at-home mom. Who knows when I'll go back to work again.

It may be sooner than Steven thinks. I miss it. During stressful times in my life, I really miss my old colleagues. We talked about everything the world threw at us, just like group therapy. We were a strong trio. After I went on maternity leave, Mrs. Cranston said my job would be secure whenever I was ready to come back to work. As head chef in the kitchen, I was responsible for planning and execution of all social, philanthropic, and family events. Given their extensive outreach in the community, every day was filled with creative and delicious ways to expand my chef skills. The experience gained was invaluable. That was six years ago. I couldn't even imagine putting that chef coat back on right now. Aside from the fact that my belly would prevent it from happening, I don't think I could keep up with the long hours and heavy workload of the job… or Steven's nagging me for not being home enough. I'm sure all working moms get the same guilt trip, but it was a tough weight to bear.

As I drive past the hole-in-the-wall delicatessen I worked at as a teenager, near my parents' house, I continue to think back to my days as a chef—smiling at my accomplishments. A typical day started with early mornings at the fish and farmers' markets, the Spice House, and the butcher. Then it was off to the kitchen to check the calendar and start our prep work. My job was to ensure that the kitchen ran smoothly for a variety of events and the Cranston family meals. My talents were appreciated by major figures in our community, and it was a great-paying job. Ironically, the night I was attacked in Chicago, I had worked with Candy on a fantastic fundraising dinner to benefit women suffering from domestic abuse. That's crazy karma.

Our employers were the talk of the town, Chicago's very own socialite celebrities. Carter and Candy Cranston had twin daughters in high school. Their philanthropic work ranged from cancer research and the arts to pet safety and school fundraising. They had a spot on all the most prestigious boards in the city—and the social calendar to prove it.

Working in the Cranston kitchen also made me and my two coworkers privy to a lot of information about how the world of giving operates. One rare incident always sticks out in my mind. There was a heated discussion going on during a lunch meeting for one of Mrs. Cranston's charity boards, and one woman threw her blueberry tart at another member. Even from all the way in the kitchen, we heard a crash, a scream, and several women yelling over the sound of furniture being pushed around. We ran into the dining room and found a woman blotting blueberry stains from her mauve two-piece suit with her linen napkin. We grabbed some kitchen towels and club soda and offered to assist her. She was angry.

"How *dare* you throw a blueberry tart at me," she cried. "And my new Chanel suit! You'd better hope it comes clean! And by the way, I'll be sending you a bill for the dry cleaning." She stood up, pulled at the trim of her jacket, threw her shoulders back, and walked out—shrugging off the unseemly outburst. Then the food-throwing troublemaker ran out after her, and we could hear the yelling continue outside.

Nowadays, I'm head chef at 1632 Ash Street, our home. My bosses usually order chicken nuggets and kid cups, and come to think of it, they throw their food from time to time, too.

Turning my trusty maroon Lexus onto my parents' lush tree-lined street, I see red flashing lights ahead. As I get closer to their driveway, I realize it's an ambulance—parked right in front of their house. The heat rising in my body is more than I can stand. I need air. I fumble with the car door handle and run up the three stone steps to my parents' front door, nearly bumping into the paramedic leaving.

"What happened?" I manage to ask.

"Little boy, about five…"

"Yes, yes, what? I'm his mother!"

"Ma'am, he's okay," he assures me. "Just a slight fracture in his arm. We put a little cast on it. Plan on visiting your pediatrician tomorrow for a follow-up exam."

"A cast? Morgan, Kyle! Mommy's here!"

With a red marker, I write *M-O-M* in the center of the cast on Morgan's little arm. The letter *O* is a heart so he can remember how much I love him whenever he looks at it. I set the marker down and wrap my arms around his tiny body. With a quivering half smile, I add an extra pulse in my hug. He holds on longer, echoing my energy.

"Next time you boys decide to play tag in Grandma and Grandpa's house, try not to slip down the stairs, okay?"

He stares at me with his innocent blue eyes and says, "I know, Mommy. I forgot to put my shoes on, and my socks were so slippy. Grandpa told me to, but I didn't listen to him. Are you mad at me?"

"No, dear, but I want you to learn from this so the next time I remind you to be careful and not run in the house on the wood floors, you'll understand what I mean," I tell him, patting his shoulder like Mom used to do with me when I was young.

"Okay, I will, but can we watch now?"

While the boys sit on the couch in the living room, snuggled under a fleece blanket watching the movie *Homeward Bound*, I join Mom and Dad at the table in the kitchen. The movie's animal characters, Shadow, Sassy, and Chance, are scheming in the background while we grown-ups assemble and read over the four disturbing notes. The baby is still, letting me get comfortable on the wobbly chair.

"All day, I've been a nervous wreck," I admit after they've reviewed each one. "I look over my shoulder and jump at every single sound."

"I can't believe this, Betsy," my father says, flipping the collection of messages onto the center of the table. "The last note is so vile! *I will take your dog*. Who would write such a thing? And a dead bird, of all things! I don't always buy into your spiritual stories or explaining that things are just fate, but there's no denying this one." His otherwise good-natured demeanor is shadowed by outrage.

I glance at my dad then try to ignore his passive-aggressive criticism by looking down. The worn maple floors remind me of the years they've lived here and the memories we've shared in this kitchen: good and maybe not always so good.

Mom puts her hand on mine and draws in a breath. "Oh dear, I agree. We need to call the police again."

I look past the envelopes and over at my boys in the next room and nod. The thumping musical score in the chase scene with Chance and Shadow pulls my attention briefly away from the intense stress caused by the onslaught of notes. "After the first envelope, I thought maybe it was a bad practical joke, but the rest have been just plain scary. I want to call the police again, given this dead bird business. They need to figure this out."

"There must be fingerprints on them," my dad offers. "Or some other clue they can use to track him down, right?"

"I hope so," I answer, looking at the pile of threats that landed next to the full tissue box. "When they came to get my statement after those first two envelopes arrived, they didn't take them, but simply took pictures of them, which surprised me, but at that point it seemed like a hoax. The new notes should give them more to work with." I pause and rub my eyes. "You know, seeing them all together makes this threat so powerful. The words carry a lot of hatred and rage. Who did I offend in such a meaningful way to cause this type of response?"

"Honey, it could be anyone, from the city attacker to a person you met at school. We won't let anything happen to you," my dad says as he reaches for my hand and gives it a squeeze. "I have an idea. How about we follow you home and help get the boys to bed and spend the night? Then tomorrow while the kids are in school we can go and meet with the police and file another report."

"That sounds great." I sigh, shaking my shoulders to loosen them up, causing the chair to jiggle slightly on the bare floor.

My ringing cell phone interrupts us, the words UNKNOWN CALLER flashing on the screen.

"Hello?"

No response.

I widen my eyes and ask again, "Hello? Who is this? Who is this?"

"I'm watching you," a deep voice breathes. "Don't call the police—or you'll be sorry."

Click.

I stand, frozen, trying to register what I just heard. The voice sounds familiar, but I can't place it. It doesn't sound like Freddie, but it's someone I've spoken to before. With every muscle and bone in my body, I try to maintain balance to avoid collapsing onto the floor. My parents are staring me down, waiting for an explanation. "That son of a—he's watching us," I say. "And if we call the police, he says I'll be sorry!"

"Oh no!" Mom cries out as her confident posture dissolves underneath her oversized blue Oxford shirt. "What do you think we should do, Cary?" She sniffles, grabbing a tissue from the box on the center of the table.

"Let's get these kids home and into bed," Dad says as he pushes himself up from his chair, causing it to scrape on the floor. "I'll call the police right now. Forget the nut job. I'll do it so he won't be able to pin this on you."

I curl up in my soft bed and breathe out a sigh of relief, knowing everyone is sound asleep now that the police are gone. It was like playing musical chairs, keeping the boys distracted while the officers were outside interviewing me. They love getting ready for bed with their grandma because she asks them interesting questions about their day while they're getting their pajamas on, joins in on the teeth brushing, and tucks their sheets in snuggly after they hop in bed. Her captivating stories based on her world travels always lull them into sleep mode without hesitation.

I hope the extra presence of police cars driving around in our neighborhood will thwart any future threatening attempts from this guy. It's been helpful having parents who live close by. Dealing with the pregnancy, the stalker, and Morgan's arm has been a lot for one day.

I wish Steven had a better relationship with my parents. They have always been genuine and nice to him, but there's an undertone of edginess and attitude he puts forth in return. I know it's got to be hard for him, since his own parents passed away years ago, but that doesn't make it right. He has his sister, but she lives on the West Coast and doesn't make time to come visit us. That must hurt him.

Last Thanksgiving, I was happy Mom and Dad came over to help with dinner preparations, as chasing around two young sons can get frustrating. After thirty minutes of peeling potatoes and stuffing the bird, I watched Steven walk into the kitchen and start with, "How many people does it take to make a holiday dinner? I never recall *my mom* having a crew in the kitchen with her on Thanksgiving. Betsy, it's not your work kitchen!"

Heading toward the door, my dad swiftly stepped outside with Barney and Morgan to play catch, while Mom ran upstairs to fold laundry that didn't need folding. Since I had a horrible headache, I ignored his comments. I knew the stress of work caused him to overreact with me, but I refused to get caught up in a fight and feed into his tantrums.

Though I have seen them decrease lately. I guess when you turn a deaf ear to negativity, it diminishes, or you just don't care anymore. I can easily blame the way he acts on his work stress, but I sense it goes a lot deeper. I can't deny it any longer. Once he gets back, I'm going to suggest we get help and work through the things that cause us to fight. We love each other, but just don't see eye to eye these days.

Bah-boom!

A noise, like the one I heard earlier today outside the window, shakes me from my thoughts as I swallow a big gulp of lukewarm herbal tea. On cue, the blood starts surging through my veins.

"What was that?" I ask Barney. His ears perk up as if to say, *I don't know, let's check and see.*

I scramble out of bed, pulling my Winnie the Pooh pajama top—bought to match Barney's favorite toy—down over my growing belly. I tilt open the shutters and peek out. Only my dim bedside lamp is on, so if anyone *is* out there, they won't be able to see me, I hope. I scan the front yard but see no one. I look across the street to the neighbor's house and manicured yard, but it's also empty. If it's Kyle's stranger, he's nowhere in sight.

Maybe it's the crazy man from the threatening phone call, maybe it's Freddie, or maybe it's just the wind blowing the dangling branch. *Should I wake Mom and Dad? I need to call the tree guy this week and have them cut that branch down. It's a constant source of stress.* I reach in my purse on the floor next to the bed, grab my to-do list, and add, *Call Tree Guy, ASAP.*

I decide to wait a few minutes and let the butterflies in my stomach slow down. The baby kicks and turns because of stress or the fact that I just hurtled out of bed. I hope this doesn't indicate future nighttime waking rituals.

"Breathe," I command myself, inhaling through my nose and exhaling with a *haaaah* out of my mouth. The kicking ceases. It seems that Baby likes it when I take in deep breaths.

I settle back in bed with clouds of pillows and my down comforter surrounding me. I lean on my propped-up wedge pillow and grab a book to read, hoping to get my mind off the loud noise. Barney sits next to me, our bodies barely touching but enough to generate warmth between us. Together, we wait, listening. He's looking up at a spot on the ceiling. Maybe it's another spider homicide?

My mind wanders around the silence in the room to my parents' bed thirty years ago, a bed that had *way* too many pillows. *Their* dog used to hop up and get lost in the sea of fluff, like Barney often does now. I would watch my mom create a little moat and cocoon with the two larger, king-sized pillows while aligning the two smaller pillows at the head of the bed. The V-shaped top would allow her to rest her head just so. My dad, on the other hand, would use one flimsy foam one and be *just fine*. I can still picture their room. The pale blue sheet and pillowcase perfectly highlighted the gray paint and wallpaper scheme my mother had selected for their master suite. I've often thought she could have been an interior designer. Mom is so creative the way she can pull colors and textures together.

Dad would say, "Your mother's back acts up from time to time—maybe it's all that bike riding in Europe—so the doctor says she should prop herself up to give her support and relief."

One time I came right out and asked Mom about all the bedding, and she just laughed and said, "A ruffled mind makes a rested pillow, according to Charlotte Brontë. You know, Betsy, she's that British gal who wrote *Jane Eyre*."

"Oh, of course," I had replied, preoccupied with the mound of comfort before me.

Now, I hope my parents are doing okay in the guest room. I wonder if they, too, heard a banging sound? *Did I leave Mom with enough pillows? She's too polite to ask for more. Should I go in and check?* "No, it's after midnight. Let it go, Betsy," I whisper to an empty room as I rest my back against the fluff and fold my arms.

My head is throbbing, my back is strained, and my heart weighs heavy as I think about the empty space on Steven's side of the bed. But I'm thankful I inherited my mother's pillow affinity so I can sleep in comfort and avoid the unidentified sound outside and the pain from the events of the day.

Ring-ring-ring.

Rubbing the sleep from my eyes, I reach for the blaring phone on the nightstand, not recognizing the caller ID. I hope it's not another scary call. "He-llo?"

"Hey, babe, it's me." Ah, Steven's familiar voice. "Were you sleeping?"

With the back of my hand, I wipe off the drool on the corner of my mouth. "Oh no, not at all. I must've dozed off while reading. What time is it?"

"It's eleven o'clock out here, I'm calling from the hotel phone. Sorry it's so late, but we just got out of our dinner meeting. It's all good news. I'll share it with you when I get home in a few days."

"I can't wait." Luckily, he can't see me rolling my eyes.

"I wanted to let you know that I love you. Please give the boys and your belly a kiss for me, okay?"

"I will, I love you, too." I smile as I hear his voice, yearning to reach through the line and give him an "I'm sorry" hug. He doesn't mention the fight, which is a good sign that he's not mad anymore.

"I've gotta go now. The guys are going back down to the hotel bar to grab a drink and rehash the details from today's meeting. I'll talk to you tomorrow night. Everything good there, honey?"

Not wanting to expose my sudden rush of rage, hearing the words *hotel bar,* I quickly answer to avoid sounding jealous. "We're doing fine. I'm just sleepy right now. Go celebrate. You guys worked so hard on this merger. You earned it." *Was I convincing?*

He knows he should speak with me a little longer, but I understand why he wants to make the call quick. It's late, plus I don't want to let on that I'm freaking out over a stalker. Now is not the time to talk about it—it's complicated, especially at this hour. What could he do for me right now anyway? Sit and wait for another note to arrive? *I'll be fine with my parents here.*

"Betsy?" he asks again.

"Yeah?" I hear myself saying as I scrunch my face, hoping to avoid any confrontation. "I'm doin' great." My nose is flaring wildly, and I'm grateful he's not here to see. "The boys are great, Barney's great. We're all great. I'm looking forward to hearing the details of your good news when you get home. I'll talk to you tomorrow. Good night, Steven… love you." I hang up the phone and sigh as I squeeze the pillow close to my chest—some of the spiky ends of the feathers poke me through the pillowcase and my pajama top. I get the point.

"Barney, I hope I didn't hang up too quickly with Daddy," I admit. "But he was having *such fun* while we've been going through H-E-double-hockey sticks today. I just don't have the energy to tell him about our crazy stalker." I glance over and see my dog sleeping with his legs twitching, like he's chasing a squirrel. Then he stops and rolls over to his back. He's down for the count.

Back inside my cloak of bedding protection, I nestle in and restart my book. Heck, it's one in the morning and I'm wide awake… I might as well read for a while. I try to concentrate on the chick lit in front of me, even though my life is starting to look like a suspense novel.

Bam-bam-bam.

After dozing off, I'm shaken from my reverie again as I ask Barney, "What the…?" Growling, he scrambles to his feet to investigate the sound outside. Not far behind, I clamber to stand over my best friend and steal a peek through the shutters, again. The moonlight glints through the slats. This time Misty is standing in her backyard, throwing big pieces of lumber onto a pile. *What on earth?* I grab my cell phone and shoot her a text: *Whatcha doin' with all that wood this time of night?*

A few seconds later, my phone screen lights up with her reply: *Those crazy contractors messed up the bathroom rehab, so I'm hiring someone else. In the meantime, I'm getting rid of their junk. They can come get it in the morning—those jerks.* Her watch must be broken or she doesn't care what her neighbors think, but this isn't normal—not to mention creating a roaring sound causing me to jolt out of bed like a dart.

Okay, neighbor, I punch the letters on the keyboard. *But you know it's 2 AM. You scared the bejesus out of me! Please don't frighten me like that again, girlfriend!* My toes squish into the shag carpet, making a foot fist.

Deal. But don't be such a chicken, she replies.

Come over in the morning, after I take the kids to school, I text her. *Are you around then? My house. I have your favorite coffee!*

Sure! I'll just swing by after my kickboxing class and bring bagels and cream cheese—your fave! G'nite, she writes back.

Leaning on my headboard, my mind shoots back to the conversation I had with my dad earlier today. I hope, after we reported another note the police, they'll increase patrolling in this area. It's the best we can do until we know the identity of this crazy person.

Back under my mountain of covers, I slip back into my dreams—blocking out the fear—only for a few short hours.

I watch my boys climb the stone steps to meet the teacher at the entrance of the school, mingling with the other children their age. Patches of red, brown, blond, and black hair create a rainbow of natural colors, a veritable Monet masterpiece of tresses. Morgan is blithely swinging his left arm as if the cast were not even there—that child! Still, I can't help but smile when I see his teacher toss me a joint hello and goodbye wave as the children file in behind her. It's comforting to know they're in good hands, because today I am determined to track down this madman.

I scan the playground and down the street before I pull away from the curb. There's an out-of-the-ordinary white van parked across the street from the school. I drive ahead and park my car out of the way of the carpool line and wait. Pretending to look at my phone, I peer over my sunglasses at the rearview mirror. There's one man sitting behind the wheel, unmoving. To stay razor focused, I turn off the radio and tune my senses into the threat across the street.

I've never seen this vehicle here before, and for it to be parked across from the school, it signals a red flag. *Betsy, go over there and ask him what he's doing.*

I flick on the hazards button and slide out of my car, though I need to wait for a passing vehicle to get out of the way. The *whoosh* of the bus pulling from the curb indicates the last of the children filing into the school, which also means the crossing guard and the remaining group of teachers will be going into the school and out of sight by the time I get over to the van. Hurrying my pace, I teeter across the street and walk right up to the window of the van and firmly wrap my knuckles.

The man turns his face toward me, and I realize that I recognize him. Rolling down the window, my doctor's custodian Henry says, "Yeah, whadda ya want?"

Jerking my chin back over my collarbones I reply, "Uh, oh, hi. Hi, Henry, how are you?"

He blinks a couple of times then casts a skeptical look at me. "I'm good."

The silence between us is dense and detached. *Say something, Betsy. Ask him if he's the stalker!* "I came over to see if you needed any assistance. I noticed you were stalled on the side of the road and thought you might need a hand." *Good God, Betsy!* My nostrils are flailing wildly.

"I'm not stuck, I'm waitin'." Then he rolls up the window and looks the other way.

My eyebrows hike up and my lower lip drops. "Haaa!" Realizing I'm not getting any further with this conversation, I turn on my heels and storm back across the street and hop in my car.

While I'm fastening my seat belt, my phone pings. It's a text message from Mom. *"Hey Honey, we tried to call you but it went to voicemail. We understand you're scared to death about this stalker but trust we're here for you. We locked the doors behind us this morning. We have appointments later but we'll check in afterward. Love you."*

I'm glad they checked in. Last night, Dad seemed very agitated after the police left. I can almost imagine how he'd react if he witnessed this guy's behavior just now.

Could the stalker be Henry? This interaction didn't get me anywhere, but it seals my belief that he's a lot ruder than I thought he was. He may have been in the middle of something, but I was surprised by his curt response… and then to roll the window up on my face? I'm going to add his name to my ever-growing suspect list since he showed up somewhere unexpected, like Freddie.

Knowing I can't do much else with Henry, I return my thoughts to what I'll share with Misty when I get back home.

I've known her since the day we moved into our Ash Street abode, almost ten years ago. Our hairstyles were longer and our makeup more dramatic. Our day-to-day lives were different then, too—less stressful. With only Barney to round out our still-tiny family, Steven and I were the cute, new couple next door, just starting out. No fighting. Over time and through plenty of changes, my trusty neighbor has been a consistent friend, a sounding board, and fashion aficionado. But we've always had boundaries.

Today, that will change. Sure, I've cried and complained to her, but never have I let on that I envy her or that I need her help—which I require now more than ever. Because earth-shattering or not, those pink slips are turning my life upside down. And I think my plucky neighbor will have some useful ideas.

Misty got divorced right after the birth of her second daughter, Samantha. Her older daughter, Abby, was just a year old, and she found out the hard way that her ex, a powerful, wealthy CEO in the city, was a no-good cheater. She got a hefty settlement in the divorce. He had been having an affair with his secretary and living in a high-rise apartment on Lakeshore Drive, with a lake view, five nights a week for goodness knows how long. Sounds like television drama. When Misty caught him there with the girlfriend one night, it was an ugly scene—she used her karate moves on him. It was rather entertaining to see his black eye the following week. I called her right away and made a joke about what a brute she was. She put up a good front, but I know it was hard on her.

Her now ex-husband doesn't come around much anymore. I can't imagine going through a divorce and raising two children under the age of two on my own. To this day, I don't know how she does it.

My friend rolls with the punches, gets back up on the horse, and continues to motor on—not skipping a beat. I've learned this about her in bits and pieces over the years. We'll meet for wine on the patio, or coffee talk after school drop-off, but she never gets down to the nitty-gritty. Misty never shares her deep, dark secrets. Instead, she's guarded about what she's willing to offer up.

I, on the other hand, will spill the beans after a single glass of wine. My co-workers, Richard and Heidi, always used to tease me, saying I'm a wimp. Many nights after work, they'd tie one on and I would say, "Oh, look at the time—I've gotta go!" or "Gosh, I'm just so tired." After a while they figured me out. Misty had me pegged as someone who doesn't drink much the week she met me, and quite frankly, that's fine with me because it's nice to know my friends realize who I am. Knowing that my dad had some issues with drinking, I'm not willing to tempt fate. I'm fine drinking club soda!

At home, I fill the copper kettle on the stove, set out some precision-cut fruit, and place fragrant flowers on the table for my guest. I take my time to create harmony to tie in with the soft hues on the teacup. The arrangement should always blend in with the décor, not dominate it, I remind myself, as I lift the stems out of the vase just a little and reposition them, fluffing the greens. No one flower wants to be the loudmouth in the setting. Focusing on my love of flowers helps distract me.

The doorbell rings as my spunky neighbor slides through the open door. Her black yoga pants and purple Nike sweat jacket covers her workout clothes, but you'd never know she just worked out because her skin is flawless and fresh. She pops into the kitchen, exuding boundless energy—she's one of those "life is a bowl of cherries" people despite her past hardships. Quite her opposite, I'm the bowl of pits today. I pull at my top to cover my belly as I wipe and re-wipe the spotless countertop with the worn, yellow sponge—then fumble to return it to the holder inside the sink. Misty sees right through me, of course. Thanks, stalker!

"What gives, Goldilocks?" Misty cradles her mug of lukewarm coffee in her palms as she takes a sip. Her light pink nails are manicured perfectly.

Stalling, I get up to reach for the extraordinary display of fruit I'd assembled before her arrival, and casually reply, "Oh, you know…"

"Yeah, I *do*, but what *aren't* you telling me?" she interjects, raising her eyebrows.

"You know! I mean, what? What do you know?" Tilting my head, I look at her and scrunch my eyebrows as I place the silver serving spoon down next to the uneaten fruit rainbow.

Determined to get me to open up, my ally leans in and whispers, "Steven. Is he acting up again?"

"Oh… no, that's not it!" I respond. "But what have you heard about Steven?" I ignore my stomach grumbles to lean in and find out more.

"Betsy," she starts, placing her hand on mine. "I hear you guys fighting all the time. It's no secret you're having problems. I see him coming home late, leaving early. I know the signs."

I lean forward and draw in a breath, not only because she hasn't touched the gorgeous fruit extravaganza I've prepared or commented on my lovely flower display that highlights (but doesn't scream) *look at me,* but because I feel she's tiptoeing over the assumed red boundary line we drew in the sand years ago. This is not the topic I'd been planning to cross the line with, at least not today. "What fights? We just talk loud and…" I pause and retreat. "Well, okay, if you must know, Mr. Wonderful is pushing the San Francisco move thing again."

"Betsy, Betsy, Betsy…" Misty shakes her head.

"No! You need to listen," I snap. "He's not having an affair… at least, I don't think… We're fine. That's not what I brought you over here to talk about today!" I purse my lips and exhale a plaintiff little *humph.* A tiny flame is heating up in my belly, making its way upward. Another exhale puts it out. I decide to sit and listen to my friend.

Choosing her words wisely, Misty hesitates, takes a breath, and returns to the conversation, apparently attempting to soften my already-deep frown lines. "I'm sorry, it's just that this looks and smells so much like my pre-divorce scenario. I don't want to see you get hurt." She offers a genuine smile and takes a swig of her tea.

"Thank you, I figured that, and I so appreciate having you right next door. I feel safe knowing you're a text or phone call away. And we *will* return to the Steven conversation someday soon, but what I want to share with you is much more… well, it's crazy scary and urgent." The armor begins to strip from my heart as I prepare to tiptoe over the red line to join Misty in this new phase of our friendship.

"Put on your seat belt, girlfriend, you won't believe this…"

———

After hearing the sordid chain of frightening events, my friend gawks at me with her mouth hanging open. "Holy crap, Betsy! What are we going to do? I know what *I* would do—kick his butt—but what do *you* want to do? You have four stinkin' letters, a threatening phone call, and a dead bird? Come on!"

"I don't know!" I reply, throwing both my arms into the air. "I have to admit that at first I thought it was a cruel joke or something, but since that second letter came to my doctor's office yesterday, I just don't think so. I've talked to the police twice, but they have done little except take my statement and tell me to call if anything else happens. That's why I wanted to tell *you*, Misty. Plus, for your safety, I had to share this with you. You're a good friend. And it doesn't hurt that you can beat someone up with your eyes closed."

Pink flushes her cheeks as Misty changes the subject. "Okay, what do your parents think?"

"They're really banking on the police to sort this out. But I know I need a backup plan... and I trust *you* can help me with that."

She frowns. "Do you think there was anything to the fact that the janitor from your doctor's office was near your sons' school? Do the boys know about this?"

I shake my head. "No, I think it was a coincidence about Henry being near the school. I know he's a janitor, so maybe he works at a variety of different places. And I'm not planning on telling the boys anything about this. It would only scare them. Look, Misty, I'm worried. How would some stranger know how to reach me at my sons' school, or my doctor's office, for crying out loud?"

She glances out the window. "Have you considered your old landscaper, Freddie? Remember he used to flirt with you? Maybe he has a sick crush or something."

"Freddie?" Her mention of him surprises me, given that he had just shown up the day before. "Actually, he came over here yesterday asking me for more work. I didn't have any answers for him, but he really seemed upset. He still had a copy of my key, though he gave it back to me yesterday."

Misty frowns. "I know he works on the neighbor's yard, across the street. Maybe he's been snooping around and has been placing the notes?" Raising her eyebrows, she continues, "Didn't you say something about Kyle seeing a man over there the other night?"

The thought hits me like a swift punch on the arm, just like it did when he was here. "I never thought a person who worked for me and has spent time around my family for years would actually turn around and threaten me. We've always had a good relationship."

"But you fired him."

"When I fired him, I was crying. I had no choice. His work wasn't that good and we ended up switching to a more established, larger, and more reliable landscape architect team."

"Well, maybe he thinks otherwise. Good that you got that key back."

"How tall do you think he is?"

"I don't know, maybe six feet?"

"I'm going to add his name to my list of suspects. Whoever it is tall with dark hair. He must watch me—and has for a long time—and his knowledge about my schedule after working for us, that might explain the man Kyle saw late that night."

"If I ever see that stalker S.O.B, I'm going to blow his head off!" Misty declares. We nervously snicker. "If he shows up, you *have* to call me right away—I don't care if it's three in the morning. Speaking of which, was that why you were up last night texting me?"

"Misty, come on now, you know darn well you threw that wood around like nobody's business. You must've known you'd wake someone up."

She shook her head. "Wasn't on my mind. I just had to get that badly managed project out of my house. I'm starting over with a new contractor next week. But that's not important right now." She pushes away from the counter. "Either way, just call me if you have any issues. Sorry, but I gotta run. Let's talk later, okay?"

"Okay, that sounds good," I reply, getting up to give her a hug. "I have to make my way over to Dr. Deller's office for another baby checkup. Yesterday he didn't have time to do the ultrasound. I shouldn't be there too long."

———

The boys will love the uneaten bagels for an after-school snack; I wrap up the uneaten fruit for dessert later and place it in the refrigerator. It'll be perfect with a dollop of fresh whipped cream and a sprinkle of cinnamon on top. I'm a tiny bit disappointed Misty didn't notice my memorable display of food or flowers. She's always too busy to notice details, or to eat, explaining why she's so fit and trim. But for listening, protecting, and coming up with ideas, my neighbor is my number one go-to gal.

As I do every week, I thumb through a cookbook and make a shopping list for our weekly meals. I'm sure I can run to the grocery store right after my appointment. Always a chef, the meals must go on. Regardless of a madman stalking my family, we *do* have to eat. I hope the police pick up the pace on investigating the stalker so I can get my life back to normal.

Cooking energizes me and removes all negative thoughts from my mind. I get razor-focused on the food and everything else is a blur. It's what I need right now. Tonight's dinner with my boys will give me a quiet, little slice of alone time with them since Mom and Dad will be at a fundraising event for the Cancer Foundation. They love getting dressed up and going into the city for galas and plays, and tonight they're going to the Cranstons' annual casino party. Since I'm not officially working for them right now, I get invites to all their celebrations and fundraisers for free. Kind of nice perk; it helps to be associated with powerful people. *"You never know who has money. Always keep your eyes open for donors,"* Candy Cranston always says.

Steven has never liked going to their events. He calls them "phony" reasons to hang with the rich. When the invite arrived, I reached out to Candy to find out if my parents could attend instead, telling her Steven would be out of town. It was a fib, but now he really *is* gone for work. And I am glad that someone from my family will represent me tonight.

Candy and Carter were understanding when I took my leave of absence right before Kyle's birth, and have been continually accepting each year I extend it. At some point, I will decide between work and family.

Going back to work two days a week might be okay with Mom babysitting. I could take the train into the city after dropping the boys off at school, and she could stay with the baby and pick up the boys later in the day. She could start dinner, which I would line up ahead of time—or as the French would say, *prepare des aliments*—and I'd be home in time to eat with the family. I know there are culinary interns who are eager to work extra hours in the Cranstons' kitchen, so I could have everything prepped for them and ready for the evening events, and catch the Metra train home to Westin Heights. *Mom helps me at home, and the staff picks up the slack at work.* Something to think about after this dog walk; the doctor's office awaits my arrival.

———————

Barney's walk is a shortened version of our ordinary routine, but I know he senses my urgency to get out the door to the doctor's office. "Come on, furball, Mama has to pee again, can you believe it?" He seems to understand my request, and following a light tug on his leash, he moves along. I capture his work in a blue plastic bag, tie it shut, and toss it in our covered trashcan by the side door, next to the bush. I remind myself to grab my to-do list when I get inside and add, *purchase some odor-free trash bags.*

I click the latch on Barney's leash and set it on the small entryway table. He follows me down the narrow hallway to the pantry, stuffed with canned goods, boxes of cereal, nuts, baking supplies, and his favorite—dog treats. Over the years, Barney has figured out, success with the doo-doo bags equals a trip to the snack-filled pantry. The aroma of gooey, chocolate chip cookies baking in my double oven often lures him to the kitchen, too—but no people food for him.

As I sit in the small powder room, I happen to notice the paint cracking between the trim and the light-blue painted wall: another item for my to-do list. As Barney slinks, in between my legs and the maple cabinet, to steal some petting, I glance down and discover that I'm spotting. *This can't be happening!*

"No! No!" I cry, as I shoo him out of the bathroom to nudge the door closed. I struggle with the tangle of my undies around my ankles while I wobble back to the seat and try to catch my tears with a fresh piece of tissue. Sitting, I examine the situation and see what appear to be large clots. "No! It's too soon!" Tear droplets are hitting my thighs like a leaky faucet.

I clean myself up and rush to grab my cell phone and a towel, then settle on the couch to prop up my feet, hoping to stop the spotting.

"This isn't my first rodeo," I whisper bitterly to Barney while dabbing my runny nose and moist eyes with the edge of my sleeve. *I need more tissues.* With three losses under my belt, one after the city attack, and another being a painful D&C procedure where they had to remove the partial miscarriage, I know what could be in store as I dial the doctor's office. I realize I'm further along this go-around, but it's better safe than sorry.

"Yes, this is Betsy Ryan. R-Y-A-N."

I'm tapping my heel on the edge of the couch as I wait for the receptionist to slowly spell out my name. Are there that many people coming to this office that she can't remember me?

"Donna, it's an emergency! I'm spotting, bad. I need to talk to Dr. Deller, now. Please!"

"Okay, Betsy. I'll check. If he's in with a patient would you like to speak to Dr. Hildebrandt instead?" she cheerily replies, almost as if this wasn't *her* first rodeo and this is normal.

"No, thanks, I'd prefer my own doctor. Can you just go get him?"

"Sure." Donna puts me on hold and the background music plays in my ear. Maybe she doesn't remember my other miscarriages? Although she's known me for years, how could she know about those life-scarring moments when I crawled under my bed in misery, wanting to stay there for days? *Good God, hurry up, Donna!*

"Hello, Betsy?" My doctor's familiar, soothing voice echoes through the phone. "How are you feeling today? I hear we're having some issues." His calmness washes over me and regulates my heartbeat.

Catching my breath and slowing the heel tapping, I say, "Yes... I'm alarmed right now. The clots were large and substantial, and I know it's too early to go into labor. I don't want to get off the couch and trigger an early labor!" I hope he can keep up with my rambling. "I don't want to drive knowing that I'm spotting, just in case it's an indication that I could be in labor. I know we talked about bed rest last month, but since everything seemed to be going okay, I really thought I was out of the woods." I take a second to breathe in and exhale, then I continue, "I have no way to get there because Steven is out of town and my neighbor isn't home. Should we just cancel for today?" As if sitting upside down will hold the baby in its place, I run my feet up the side of the wall, reminding me of a yoga pose I've never liked doing.

Again, my doctor replies taking his time to explain, "Okay, Betsy, let's cancel your appointment today, but I'll swing by to check in on you after my next patient. Should be less than an hour. Will that be all right?"

Smiling to him, even though he can't see me offer my thanks, I nod my head. "That'd be great! I think I'll feel better just having you come by."

"Sounds good. Do you want to leave the key under the rock by the side gate so you can stay on the couch?"

"Oh, thank you. I would've called my parents to come and check on me but they're on the other side of the city right now. I agree it's best that I cancel my appointment, and thank you for agreeing to swing by." My voice slows down—and the pumping blood follows suit. "Thank you. It means a lot to me."

My doctor clears his throat and says, "It's no problem, Betsy. I want to pop in and see you just to make sure you're okay. You know I don't do house calls often, but I have no problem swinging by on my way home. I'll see you soon."

Knowing my doctor will be here soon gives me a strong sense of security about the baby—but not so much about leaving the secret key hidden under the rock again. *I should be fine in the middle of the day.* I almost believe myself.

Trying to get my mind off the spotting and fear of triggering early labor, I shift my thoughts to hoping *this towel catches anything slipping past the panty liner—avoiding any stains on the couch. I'd hate to have it cleaned with all those stinky chemicals.*

I rest my head back on the couch and wiggle my butt into a more comfortable position, then call Misty. I fill her in and ask if she can pick up the kids later and walk Barney when she drops them off. Without hesitation, she says yes; the tension in my chest releases a little more. I wrap myself in a soft, tan blanket and doze off.

A snore reverberates in my nostrils, causing my eyes to open. Shaking my head, I regain composure and blink off the blur as my eyes adjust to the daylight. I reach for the side of the couch to prevent myself from falling and notice Dr. Deller's eyes on me. He's seated in *my* tan leather chair with my favorite blue silk pillow next to him. In the background, I can make out the pastel flower arrangement on the counter. He's about the same age as my Uncle Herman, mid-sixties, around six feet tall, a little extra weight around the middle, but overall, in pretty good shape.

I push against the couch and rise in my seat as I say, "Uh, hi. Sorry, I guess I fell asleep. How long have you been here?"

He crinkles his eyebrows and turns up his lips. "Only a few minutes. The dog let me in." He follows my response to his joke. I squeeze out a small grin as he continues. "I've been trying to wake you." Barney is sitting straight up on the floor next to the couch as if to protect me. He looks past his short, black nose, sniffing for danger.

Ever since he was a puppy, Barney, like Steven's first dog, Benny, has followed our simple commands, like retrieving a stick or signaling when he needs go out. I credit the hard work we put in at the official new-dog-owner training classes. We would practice our drills in the park and go over commands every day. He always follows instructions and then comes back wagging his tail and circling us, waiting for a good butt scratch or tasty treat.

Since Steven agreed to give Barney to *me*, I took it upon myself to do all the training. My dog soon learned who was the Alpha Mom. I wore the crown, Queen of the Kitchen, after I would bring home large paper bags filled with stock bones from work. I loved taking him on long walks throughout the tree-lined parks and to the desolate beach at sunrise. We'd sit waiting for the big orange ball to pop up from the east side of Lake Michigan, to make its way up into the sky—causing us to squint. Then he'd run up and down the beach, kicking up sand and grabbing stray sticks. Steven installed a flexible doggy hose by our side door for when we'd get full of mud or sand on our walks so we'd never have to worry about making the house dirty again. It makes getting muddy a lot more fun.

"If it's okay, I'd like to run to the bathroom and check to see if the spotting has stopped."

My doctor replies, as I tippy toe past him and slip into the powder room, "I agree, I was just going to suggest that."

After a thorough check, I'm pleased to share with Dr. Deller, "No additional spotting, doc."

"Perfect. Since I'm here, I can take a quick listen to the baby. Off the record, of course."

Just as Dr. Deller approaches me, Barney stands up on all fours and glares at him. No growl, but a stern *look*. What *is* it that's bothering my best friend? I thought he'd remember my doctor from the last time he came to the house, but Barney doesn't take his eyes off him.

"It's all right, Bud," I assure him. "He's making sure we're okay."

Dr. Deller pulls his shiny stethoscope out of his bag and positions it on my belly to listen to the baby. It's cold. He places two fingers on my wrist to check my pulse and then smiles at me and says, "The baby sounds fine."

Barney follows his every move with only his eyes then glances up at me for reassurance. Barely above a whisper I tell him, "Everything is fine." I wonder how many human phrases dogs understand? I'm guessing this pooch is above average.

"Betsy, since the baby's heart beat is normal, and the spotting has stopped, I don't believe you're in early labor. I think it was a false alarm."

The rigidity in my shoulders loosens, giving my cheeks a chance to pull to a smile. Something I haven't done much of lately.

"I suggest you stay horizontal for the rest of today and see how things are going by morning. Remember, Betsy, if you can't reach me for some reason, you can always contact Dr. Hildebrandt through our office."

"Thanks, doc. I know, but in an emergency like this, I'd prefer to see you." Trying to be polite, I extend my hand, inviting him to sit on the couch. "Would you like something to drink?" *I'm hoping not. I could use another nap before the kids come home.*

"Sure," he replies. "I'll go grab some water. Don't get up."

"Yeah, that's fine. The fridge is over there." As I finish my sentence he's already up and walking toward my kitchen.

For a fleeting moment, my arm muscles tighten again because he's acting very comfortable here, as if he knows his way around my house. Still, he's my doctor and I trust him, so I shake off the hunch.

"It's been such a crazy couple of days, I appreciate you coming by and checking on me. It reminded me of my last miscarriage—I felt so panicked."

"It's never a problem, Betsy. You are one of my preferred patients."

"You've been taking care of me for a long time, so you know the drill with me by now—always worrying..." I trail off with a little giggle. *I know I'm paranoid. But doesn't everyone else obsessively lock their doors, check the back seat of the car when they get in, or look over their shoulder when walking in a bad neighborhood?*

"I've seen you go through so much. I wish I could do more, but sometimes things are beyond our control and left up to fate." He pauses and catches my glance. "Do you ever feel like we can change our destiny?"

Blinking and turning to look out the window, I avoid looking at him for a minute. I'm at a loss for words. That's a deep question, and out of character for Dr. Deller. "Well... thank you for helping me throughout this roller coaster ride the past few years. And yeah, sometimes I think we have *some* control over what happens. But I believe it's God letting us *think* we have control while in reality he pulls the strings from up above."

"I didn't realize you were a religious person." He looks up to meet my glance again.

"We all have to hold on to something." I want to fill the lack of words with some sort of small talk, but I keep my mouth shut—it seems we've crossed the same red line Misty and I recently hopped over. I've never really had a deep discussion with him before, or even said more than three sentences, so I'm feeling uncomfortable. It's ironic how a doctor can help you through labor, miscarriages, and other personal medical experiences, yet not share much about his personal life. I want to jump back over the line to where we started—less awkward and more traditional doctor-patient style.

I casually look over at Barney for direction, wondering what kind of vibe he's picking up from my doctor. Not that he'd tell me, but his actions may indicate something. Barney must sense my angst about this conversation because he hops on the couch next to me, snuggling in and then turning a cold gaze on my doctor. Involuntarily, I massage his ears and scratch under his chin. He's my security blanket.

Dr. Deller keeps talking. "I gave up holding onto anything after my wife died four years ago. It seems like yesterday. I can't seem to get over it, so I put in extra hours at work." He looks down at his clasped hands resting in his lap and then back up at me. "I'm trying to keep my mind off things. Don't get me wrong, I've gone through the obvious stages of grief, but the hole in my heart doesn't want to close. I think that's why I take additional care with my special patients when there's a problem." We share a look of agreement.

"Loss is so painful, Betsy. I know you've lost three babies, and it's my job to make sure you and baby stay healthy." My doctor reaches for my hand and gives it a quick squeeze, then offers a small, innocent smile.

I'm not sure *why* I feel so uncomfortable. He's trying to help me... *or could he be attempting to catch me off guard? My intuition is bouncing around like a Ping-Pong ball. I don't know what to think!* Okay, this conversation needs to end. I really don't want to talk about my past losses. I'd prefer to focus on more positive things.

"Very true, thank you!" I reply. "Hey, I just realized my sons will be home from school soon. I have to call my neighbor to see if she can help out and walk Barn for me." *Okay, so I'm lying, kind of.* Nostrils flaring.

"I can take him out for you, if you'd like," he offers.

"I may have him sit here with me while we wait. He calms me down, but thanks. My neighbor really doesn't mind. In fact, she owes me." I shift my attention to Barney and scratch his belly. "It's been a long day. If you don't mind, can you show yourself out? I don't want to hurt the baby by getting up off the couch." I smile and hope he obliges.

He seems to register something in my abrupt reply as he says, "You're right, Betsy. I have to get going." At the door, he gropes awkwardly for the handle and leaves.

As the door clicks shut, I wait a minute or two and then do a swift tippy-toe run over and bolt the lock. Then I run to each of the wooden shutters and flip them shut. "What was that, Barney? Did you feel as weird as I did just now?"

"*Chuff-grr-rowf,*" he says, as if to say, "Heck yeah, Mom."

I flick a stray dog hair off my throw pillow as Misty howls, "Are you kidding me, Bets? How did the conversation get so odd in that short amount of time?"

"I don't... I'm not sure." *Maybe I'm not explaining this well.* "I mean, I had no choice. There was spotting and I panicked. I didn't want to take the chance and drive to my appointment alone so I canceled it, but he said he'd swing by here after work. After I offered him a drink, it was as if I'd opened Pandora's box or something." I pause as Barney shoots me a look, as if to say, *I didn't get a good feeling about that guy.*

I shift my attention back to Misty and continue. "Almost as if I let my guard down and he seized the opportunity to share his pain with me. I never really took the time to think about his wife's passing and how it impacted him. I have been so preoccupied with my pregnancies and miscarriages."

"That's sad about his wife, but why lay it all on you?" Misty frowns. "Maybe he thought it would make you feel better knowing that he had suffered a loss, too?"

"That's true," I concede. "But Barney seemed to get a strong sense of him. He acted almost as if he was protecting me from the doctor. God, I hope he's not the stalker."

Barney looks up at me as if to say, *Yes, Mom, I did.* I smile at him and then look back over to Misty.

"Did his conversation ever make you feel awkward before? Like at your appointments?"

I pause and think. "Not really. It's always been strictly professional, given that he looks *down there* quite often."

"Ew. Now I'm very uncomfortable." She laughs, grabs the dog's leash, and says, "We'll be right back, Goldilocks. You sit tight. I have some doo-doo to collect."

I really do have the best next-door neighbor.

Hearing Morgan and Kyle chattering with Misty's kids, Samantha and Abby, in the other room reminds me that I need to figure out dinner. I never did get over to the grocery store today. I accept defeat and tap the Domino's Pizza app on my phone to place an order for pizza, salad, and chocolate lava cakes...and a bottle of root beer, for good measure. As a chef, it's almost sacrilegious for me to order from a fast-food Italian chain, but given the circumstances I believe I get a free pass today. Plus, they *do* make yummy lava cakes. I have made hundreds of pizzas from scratch, sourcing plump tomatoes, fresh basil, and mozzarella... it's laughable that I'm relying on an app for dinner.

"I love Domino's," Misty says, as she peers over my shoulder, unclasping Barney's collar from the leash. "Wanna split an order, like usual?"

"Yes, ma'am. I already put it in."

"Remember to get a bottle of Sprite, too."

"Done. Now we just need to feed the pup and we're all set for dinner. We can count our calories and fat intake tomorrow."

"Cheers to that, neighbor."

I watch Misty as she walks into the boys' playroom-turned-office to share the dinner news with the kids. Kyle does a fist pump, while Morgan, Abby, and Samantha jump up and down in circles, cheering, happy that they get to have a fun pizza night together. I take a mental snapshot to save this image in my mind, forever. This is what motherhood is: memories with friends.

I've had so many mixed feelings over the past few days, and as much as I hate what's happening to me with these damn envelopes and the baby, I'm thrilled that my friendship with my feisty little neighbor is growing and evolving. Our children get along great and we moms really do have a lot in common. I join Misty and our children in a group hug. The kids give us toothy grins and smiling eyes.

Working my way back to the kitchen, I crack open a couple of shutters to let the last light of the day seep in while I switch on a lamp. From the corner of my eye I notice that my side gate is wide open—and, I realize as a wave of adrenaline courses through me, with an envelope taped to it. I call Misty into the room, trying to maintain my composure, but my knees buckle and I fall to the floor with a thump, right in between the couch and the table.

"Betsy! What the heck?" Misty runs over and squats down to help me back on my feet. "What are you doing on the floor? Kids, go play until dinner gets here!"

I'm whimpering, pointing to the window. "The envelope. Please, no more."

Misty helps me over to the couch and then runs fearlessly outside into the twilight to grab the note on the fence. She runs back into the house and rips it open. Her face turns the same shade of white as the envelope as she reads the message.

"What does it say?" I ask, as she pulls the door shut behind her and runs over to me. She gulps and turns the paper to face me. In the familiar scribbled print, it reads, *Did the bleeding stop?*

I look at Misty, wild-eyed and shaking.

"Breathe slowly. Okay, it'll be okay, girl. Just take a minute. I'm so confused, though, because I locked the gate after I took the dog out and there was no envelope when I came in. So how could this be possible?" She shakes her head.

"I don't know," I say, voice shaking, "but we must call the police again, Misty. He must've jumped the fence when he saw you come back inside, or maybe he made a copy of the hidden side gate key before I removed it? I should get the lock changed right away—it's on my to-do list. Can you slide that shutter closed?"

She runs over to the window and to do just that. "I'm calling the police. After they come by, you and I should make our own plan, too, including calling that locksmith. We have to be ready for this fence-hopping creep if he shows up again."

After settling down and locking the doors and windows, Misty agrees with me that we'll call the police, and while we're waiting for them to arrive, we'll eat our dinner. Feeling helpless, I take a minute to acknowledge and appreciate having Misty here with me. The tension throughout my body seems to slip away, knowing there are two of us to defend our children, if we must. Looking on the bright side, if there is one, I get to sit down and enjoy a tasty cheat meal with Misty and the children. The only thing can I do at this point is stay seated and relaxed. I'm hoping the stalker is long gone, at least for tonight.

Tonight's fast-food feast is just what I need, and baby seems more relaxed, too. Pizza and root beer are my favorite diet cheats aside from Ben and Jerry's Phish Food with sliced banana and whipped cream.

I sit quietly at the table while Misty cleans up after dinner, and try to shift from a place of intense fear to consciously focusing on something positive. I love being in my kitchen. My chef's kitchen, in French known as *la cuisine aménagée*, is the heart of my home—and the place for one of my true passions. When we built this house, I told Steven it had to have all the elements and spaces that a professional kitchen could offer, which explains the ample counter space, walk-in pantry, and extra freezer. My friends and family love to see me work my magic in my favorite room.

I am determined to chase the most recent note out of my head as I continue to recall memories of family, friends, and especially food, and how they give me comfort and joy—and since we eat the stuff three or more times a day, why shouldn't it be special and memorable? I remember being a young girl, lying on my bed looking at the ceiling, mentally writing out lists of foods that I wanted to try. I'd look through my grandma's cookbooks, deciding what we'd have for our Sunday family dinner each week. Her beef tenderloin roast, complete with roasted carrots, potatoes, and onions, always topped my list. Most kids my age didn't enjoy the foods I liked—I was different. I tasted all kinds of cuisine, from French, Italian, and Greek, to good old American apple pie. I took pleasure out of working in the kitchen by my grandma's side—scallions and all. She taught me how to make a *roux* or *mirepoix* —a soup stock; and in high school, I joined the cooking club to continue cultivating my dream. In the morning before school I would join her and don my apron to practice my knife skills and perfect my grip so I could chop garlic with ease, slice onions paper-thin, back-slice peppers, and rock-chop parsley like a pro. I know she's looking down on me, cooking up a storm.

After high school, I graduated from Le Cordon Bleu in Chicago with degrees in culinary arts, patisserie, and baking. My first real job was working at the Ritz Carlton in Chicago as a *commis*, or basic chef, under the direction of the *chef de partie*, Frederick Berteau. He was tall and thin with dark, slicked-back hair and a pencil-thin mustache. I learned the responsibilities of the food stations and ranges, and how to manage day-to-day operations. I was a quick study and in time moved up the chef ladder.

These days success comes in the forms of serving as room parent, carpool line coordinator, and baking for class parties. I'm definitely in a culinary career holding pattern.

I can't worry about that tonight. Right now, we moms have a different kind of "cooking up" in mind, while the kids are safe, playing in the other room. While the police do their job, I'll brainstorm with my neighbor to gather more clues about this madman's agenda.

Feeling fueled after dinner and ready to meet with the police again, I grab my phone and the pile of envelopes containing the pink notes, and snap pictures of them. I learned that trick on an episode of *Law & Order: SVU*. I don't want the police to take them as evidence and then leave me with no proof of this stalking. I remember once I wanted to contest a speeding ticket but had misplaced it; I had such difficulty pleading my case. Now I always try to be prepared and cautious. Tonight, shouldn't be any different.

The first time the officers showed up they didn't take the original envelope. This time I will insist further that they investigate where the notes originated. I'm sure they'll want to pull fingerprints or other clues.

This reminds me of what the character Edna Mole says in the Disney movie, *The Incredibles*, "Luck favors the prepared." Last year Steven and I were watching the movie with our sons (while munching on way too much buttered popcorn) when I heard the line. It's a motto I've lived by since, and yes, now I can say I live my life by a quote from an animated movie—and from bad experiences in the past. Whenever I quote Edna, my husband just rolls his eyes and says, "Are you kidding me? You're citing a Disney character for safety?" Why not? Always be ready for what might happen. I often wonder if I had used my pepper spray that night in the city, if things would've been different. I may not have lost my first baby! Live on the defense, not the offense. Experience in this case, explains the top-of-the-line security system with video surveillance we had installed last year. You can never be too safe or well-equipped.

A light bulb goes off in my head, and I sit up from the comfortable position I found. "That's it! Misty, help me stand."

"What is it, Betsy?"

"With all the commotion, I forgot about the surveillance videos. I can't believe I didn't think of it sooner. Where is my head?" Misty squints, so I continue. "It's *so* unlike me; this stalker must be distracting me so much, causing me to forget things. When the security company installed the alarm system in the house, I included the video feed option."

"Of course!" Misty says, shrugging her shoulders as if to say, *Why didn't I come up with that myself?*

I waddle directly over to the desk and pull open the drawer. "Now, where did I put the login information? I thought I taped it to the bottom of the drawer. I never thought I'd need it living in *this* neighborhood, but… oh, here. Luck favors the prepared."

I grab my laptop and sign into the security site so we're able to download the files to my desktop before the police arrive. I want to give them everything they need so they can catch this crazy man. Since I've had no legal issues with the police in this village, I'm not sure how they handle stalkers—or to what extent they can fight them off, except for filling out that form they talked about the other day. It isn't every day that a guy tapes threatening notes to a person's door, causing them to fight for their life.

"Here we go, username… password… this goes back seven days."

"Let's hope we catch him on the footage."

"Misty, look at this," I say, waving my hand to the screen. "There I am with Barney leaving for a walk. Now I'll fast-forward it… there. See it?"

An accomplished twinkle inside spurs my excitement to continue down this path of investigating. I see a man wearing a dark jacket, ski mask, and boots. I can't see his face.

She leaps up and throws both fists into the air. "Is that the guy? He's big, maybe six feet tall."

My mind jumps to the night ten years ago when that horrible man killed my baby. He was about the same height. I try to push the thought from my mind, but the parallel is too similar not to bring it up. "Yeah, but the mask doesn't help identify him—much like the jerk that attacked me in the city. What is it with these guys and ski masks? Can you see anything?" I narrow my eyes to get a clearer look. There's no way it's the same guy… right?

Grabbing my laptop, Misty says, "Let me see that. Look! Right there. He's opening the gate and putting the note on the side door with his left hand. Who is left-handed that has a key to your gate and house? Did the attacker in the city use his left hand when he came after you? It's highly unlikely he's moved to the northern suburbs with all of the soccer moms, Betsy."

I wonder while rubbing my belly, hoping the baby can feel the heat of my loving touch through the skin between us. "Maybe it's the guy who installed the new locks on the gate, or someone from the landscape crew? A few people have the front door key—Steven's assistant, the pet groomer, and the cleaning service. But my God, Misty, how did he get the key to the side gate?" I hold my forehead with an open hand. "I've only given it to my parents, you, and the landscaper. I keep very close tabs on who has entrance to my property. Perhaps he found the key that Steven insisted we hide outside, in case we ever needed it? I know it's still there, so he could have easily put it back after copying it."

"That's the only logical explanation. He must've found it."

"Regardless. I want to snoop around to find other clues. It's not that the police are unable to do their job, but they're at a standstill so far, until we can identify who the stalker is. I need to keep searching. It'll distract me from having to constantly look over my shoulder."

"I agree, Betsy. And even though your video doesn't give us a good glimpse of his face, I was thinking we could compare it with the footage from the light post security cameras along our street."

"I completely forgot about those little cameras they recently installed! I know they've used them in the city for a few years, and it's cut down on crime. Unfortunately, they didn't have them ten years ago when I could've used the footage to identify my attacker."

Shaking her head, Misty replies, "I never thought I'd live to see the day when, even in the 'safe' burbs, we are being watched. Times are truly changing."

"They certainly are. I'm not sure how we'll get access to that video footage, but it's worth checking into at Village Hall." Chuckling I continue, "At first I thought it was to catch us moms speeding to and from school pickup or to the grocery store, but now I have a different opinion."

"I know. I can't tell you how many times I've driven faster than the speed limit around here. When you go over to the village office to peek at the surveillance tapes, delete any footage you see of me speeding."

"Shut up! That's what I was going to say."

"Well, great minds think alike."

The doorbell chimes, and Misty runs to answer it. "Betsy, you stay sitting. I'll let the officers in."

It's the same two young officers as before, reminding me again that I'm getting older. *After this baby is born,* I'm headed straight to the cosmetics counter to purchase wrinkle cream. Maybe I'll get Botox *and* a tummy tuck, too. The way things are going with Steven, who knows? I may have to start dating again.

The lanky man in front of me—only twenty-five years old—has his notepad open and a bead of sweat dripping off his left brow.

"Another note arrived," I say to the officer. "As I told you the last time you were here, Officer…Flaggler, is it?"

"Yes, ma'am."

"I don't know who placed the notes, but they all have the same type of paper and writing. I also have digital files of my security videos I can email you. I can't be certain the phone call was from the same person, but I just assumed…"

"Mrs. Ryan, we *will* add this new information to your original complaint, and look for other leads," he says. "I'll take the letters for fingerprints and other testing. You can email your video links over and we'll add them to the paperwork. If you have an immediate threat or see or hear something suspicious, please call us right away. Do you still have the card I gave you the last time I was here?"

"Yes, I have it over there in my desk. I understand you're doing the best you can." *No, I don't. I wish they could do more to solve this!* "You should talk to my children's school office to find out if they have a description of who delivered the note there, as well my doctor's receptionist." I jot down the information and hand the scrap of paper to the officer, "Here's a list of who I know has a key to my side gate."

I don't know if it will help, but I must try. I realize it must be difficult to pinpoint an unknown person delivering crude notes to a suburban mom, but for cripes sake, there must be *something else* they can do.

"We'll talk to them," Officer Wilson, standing beside him, says in a softer tone. "If we unearth any clues I'll contact you immediately. Keep your eyes and ears open and get in touch with us right away. Thanks for this list. We're just a phone call away… Oh, and remember to stay off your feet." She's tiny, with noticeable strength in her legs, torso, and arms. Her silky, black, shoulder-length hair is pulled back in a neat ponytail. Who says chicks can't be strong cops?

"Okay," Misty and I chime in. While still seated, I shake hands with the officers.

Misty walks the officers down the hall and to the door. After they leave, she closes it gently. "Well, that went as expected." She quirks her left cheek, causing the side of her mouth to smirk. I lift my attention from the lit screen in front of me and nod in agreement, then turn my focus back to the computer to search for the Village Hall website. I need take matters into my own hands.

"Tomorrow, I'll take the kids to school and then run over to the village to find out about their security cameras," I explain. "I understand that without substantial eyewitnesses, the police can't make much headway, but I have to keep trying."

"Do you think it's a good idea? I mean, you were flowing like a river just a few hours ago and now you want to play *CSI: North Shore?*" Her comment causes me to giggle.

I shrug. "I'm fine, but I appreciate the reference! The medication Dr. Deller gives me helps prevent pre-term labor, he says."

"Then why in God's name didn't he give it to you before the other miscarriages?"

"It's a newer treatment."

"Oh, so you're a guinea pig? Do you trust him?" She dips her chin and raises her eyebrows.

"Honestly, Misty, I do trust him, but there's a nagging pull in my gut, warning me about something related to him or his office. I just can't put my finger on it right now. He's really trying to help with the baby. He reminds me of my dad. Honest, sincere."

"Ex-cuuuuse me, didn't you say that you felt a creepy vibe around him a few hours ago? What's changed?"

"For one, I feel better—not so panicked. I'm sure I overreacted. And two, I believe he's so incredibly sad about his wife," I say, looking down at my belly. "His grief touched me. It's encouraged me to try and repair my fractured marriage. At least my husband is alive, and there's an opportunity to talk things through with him and find out why he's been acting stressed and angry lately. I can only imagine what it would be like losing a spouse and not having the opportunity to have things settled and be at peace."

Misty's cold look reminds me to tread lightly around the subject of husbands. "Okay, but don't talk like that to a divorcee." I feel bad. She is the kind of person I can trust and don't have to watch what I say when I'm with her—one who wouldn't hold it against me if I say something stupid, like I just did.

Barney is pacing back and forth across the living room floor, trying to get my attention. He must sense that Steven hasn't come home and he's worried, or he may have to go out again. I ask Misty to take him for another walk and help me get the kids to bed. I owe her, big time.

━━━━━━━━

Later that night, just as I get settled in bed, the blasted phone rings. "Hello?" I whisper into the receiver.

"Hey babe, it's me. How are you and the boys doing?"

"Oh, I'm okay. I had a little bit of spotting today, but the doctor checked me out and everything seems fine. How about you?" *Remember, Betsy, not a word about the stalker. He shouldn't have taken that flight to San Francisco. He should have stayed home to work through everything before he left. Dropping the ball on me about moving, the night before he leaves? Who does that? I know he'll feel terrible once I do tell him about the stalker, but maybe I don't want to deal with him being home right now. I'm safe with my parents, Misty, and the police.*

"Spotting? Are you sure everything's okay?"

"Yes, the baby's fine."

"Okay, I trust your judgment, but listen, I just spoke with your dad." There's a warm sincerity in Steven's voice I haven't heard in a while. "I didn't want to start our call in an alarming way, but he told me about the pink notes and threatening call."

"I'm fine, Steven. I'm sure it's just some prank, honestly." Nostrils flare. I'm not sure why I still feel the need to fib to my husband. I guess I'm still angry and don't want to face this truth with him. I give in, "When are you coming home?" *Did I come across helpless? Do I even care what he thinks? Yes.*

"Well, that's why I'm calling you. After I talked to your dad I told my boss I had to fly home for a family emergency. I'm at the airport right now, waiting to board my flight. I should be back early tomorrow morning."

"Oh! Really?" A once-lost rush of warmth stirs inside for the big lug. "That's great because truth be told, I'm kind of scared and could use your big shoulders to support and protect me." I just spilled the beans. And, was I flirting with my own husband? "I didn't want to bother you during this important time for work, and honestly I didn't think it was a threat until more notes started arriving," I hear myself gush. "I have the police, my parents, and Misty here to help me, honey. I thought it would be fine. I'm sorry I didn't tell you sooner." I stare at our wedding picture over on the dresser, remembering how happy we were. I know we can get there again. A thin smile finds its way to my face.

"Don't you worry, babe, I'll make sure everything is okay. Oh, that's my flight. I'll see you when I get home. Love you."

Dreaming is something I do well. Since the first time I became pregnant, I've started to understand this mother's intuition thing more clearly. My awareness heightens, I experience coincidences more often, and I imagine things and then they happen. I've heard this phenomenon is common when women are expecting, but to experience it firsthand is miraculous.

Tonight. I'm dreaming that Barney and I are having a practical conversation while sitting together in my room on the hardwood floor. Barney's voice is like a twenty-year-old college guy as he warns me, "Mom, I smelled something very familiar on those pink notes—a scent that's been around you other times."

Dreaming, I respond, "Oh Barney, what are we going to do?"

"I don't know, Mom, but I'm bummed about that dead bird. I know the bad man did it so he could get my attention."

My dream continues as I ask Barney if he thinks my doctor has anything to do with this mystery.

"Mom, I know the doctor is a helpful man, but I feel unsure about him—there's some smell near him."

I nod, still dreaming.

"Mom, I miss having Dad around. What I mean is, I like my belly rubs and walks with you, but they're different with Dad—more boy-like." He leans in so I can scratch behind his ears.

Roooww, roooww, roooww!

Half awake and trying to blink the blur from my eyes, I hear my dog barking in a very agitated way while pacing back and forth next to my bed.

Now fully awake, I roll over a mountain of pillows and realize the phone is ringing. The red glowing numbers on the bedside clock indicate it's 5:45 a.m. as I blindly fumble for the phone situated next to it.

"Mrs. Ryan?"

A voice I don't recognize. What's wrong? I hope it's not the stalker. "Yes?" I reply, my response barely above a whisper.

"This is Officer Jon Meacham at Good Faith Hospital. I'm sorry to say your husband has been in an accident."

Rubbing my sore eyes and brow, I choke on the words, "Steven? What happened?"

"The doctors are working on him now," he says. "You should get here as soon as possible."

"Is he okay?" My voice becomes increasingly stern, but I don't care.

I hear a deep exhale on the other end of the line. "They brought him in unconscious. We won't know until he gets out of surgery."

Trying to register what I'm hearing, I reply, "Uh… Should I come to the hospital…or…I mean, what time will he be out of surgery?"

"Ma'am, I think you should come now, just in case…"

"In case what?"

"Just please come to the ER, as soon as you can."

Knowing they'll be awake getting ready for their morning walk, I quickly text my parents to come over right away. I scramble out of bed, almost tripping over Barney, who is crouching down, scared, on the floor. There's not a doubt in my mind that he understands something bad is happening. I take a few seconds to squat down and squeeze him tight and lovingly. Now sitting cross-legged on the cold floor with tears welling up in my eyes, I tell him, "Everything will be okay, puppy. I'm going to see Daddy."

Sitting in place, Barney curls up on my lap and starts licking my leg. He snuggles in between my knees, pawing at my arm. Our gaze locked. I know we are sharing a connection that is much stronger than most people could ever imagine. Is it my imagination or does my dog feel my pain? Maybe he's trying to comfort me during this horrible experience? It's possible I'm still dreaming and I'm wishing for a personal connection with my dog to help me cope. I look him straight in the eyes and say, "I wish you could understand me—the actual words I'm saying. I'm so worried about Steven."

He studies me with deliberate attention then starts to wag his tail, jumping his front paws up and down.

Caught completely off guard, I nudge myself closer to Barney and hug him tighter. A reassuring embrace I need right now. The look we share tells me all I need to know. I believe he's going to stay by my side and protect me from whatever happens for as long as he lives. At least, that's what I think.

Before heading downstairs to update my parents and get to the hospital, I lean in and give my dog another extra-long hug and say, "Thank you, Barney, I love you."

Thankfully, my parents live close by. The relationship we share is very symbiotic. They're always here for me; I need them right now. I can't lose my husband *or* my baby.

"Thanks for coming over and agreeing to help with the boys this morning." We exchange quick hugs as I continue, "The boys are still sleeping, but when they wake up please feed them, grab their backpacks, and get them to school. You can tell them I had a morning meeting and I'll pick them up later, okay?"

I pause and catch my breath and continue what I know is rambling. They know what to do. They've done it hundreds of times. My panic about Steven seems to be showing itself in an odd, overly talkative way. "Please don't mention any of this to them. Also, Mom can you feed Barney and make your awesome Grandma Pancake recipe for the boys? Save one for me."

"It's no problem, honey," Dad responds with a sympathetic smile. "Once you get any other details from the hospital, remember to call us. Now get going."

"I'll pray for Steven and don't worry about the boys, I'll get started on my recipe right away and wrap one up for you to eat when you return." Mom replies with a supportive smile.

Whenever I would get extremely stressed or worried, my Mom would come to the rescue with *her* grandmother's secret recipe of paper-thin crêpes—love from the kitchen. She called them Grandma Pancakes, complete with warm syrup and a dollop of whipped cream on top. My great-grandmother brought the recipe with her when she arrived in this country from Sweden. I used to roll them with a fork, stuff a piece of crispy bacon in the middle, and eat it like a hot dog. Instantly, my Mother's love from the kitchen would make everything seem better. Now, I can focus all my energy on my husband, because I know my boys are in good hands.

I've always disliked hospitals. I appreciate what they offer the masses, but I associate them with illness and death and that "particular" smell: industrial strength cleaners, medicines, and oddly unhealthy food. This hospital is no different. Smells aside, this one is quite nice as far as hospitals go. I know because I gave birth to both of my sons here, in the new women's wing. It's a state-of-the-art facility with shiny, high-tech equipment and a clean, modern décor throughout the halls. Medicine has come such a long way. Now they even have medication to help moms-to-be avoid going into preterm labor. *Let's hope they work.*

Dressing while you're half-asleep can be risky business. I glimpse at my outfit in a window as I'm rushing down the hallway and chuckle despite my heartache and anxiety. Pink Lacoste polo (in place of my Pooh nightshirt) and teddy bear pajama bottoms with brown Ralph Lauren sneakers—no socks in sight. What in the world? Why didn't Mom or Dad say anything? I guess we were a little distracted this morning.

I speed walk past reprint paintings of mountains and trees on the walls to the ER's reception desk, arriving out of breath. I mumble something to the person there about needing to find my husband, Steven Ryan. She informs me he was moved and gives me directions to the ICU check-in desk near his room, three floors up.

In the elevator, I share the space with a gurney carrying a young child with a broken leg. It's clear she's medicated. Her little brown eyes, peeping through her brown, wavy bangs, have that starry gaze. Her mother is clutching the side rail of the moving bed, wiping her sniffling nose with the tissue in her other hand. *This,* is why I don't like hospitals.

Steven is in intensive care. Meanwhile I'm also in need of intense care—mentally, emotionally, and physically. We are quite the pair. I brace myself for Steven's condition and approach his room, escorted by the nurse.

I watch him in the hospital bed, slowly breathing in and out, so helpless; his tan, strong arms move rhythmically with each exhale. The purplish-red bruises on his face and the stains of blood in his hair indicate the accident was serious. No one has taken the time to tell me what happened, but clearly it could have been fatal. I'll have to get a full report from the doctor when I see him.

I decide to get silent, block out the external sounds, and hone in on Steven to see if I can pick up on anything in his subconscious—now that I know women are very intuitive when they're pregnant, I figure it's worth a try. In meditation class, people are always talking about how intuition works. There's always a first time for everything. Focusing this way will help me cope and maintain my composure.

I close my eyes, open my heart, and clear the clutter in my mind for what feels like a very long time—just breathing. I've seen psychics on television communicate with people through their minds, so it must work.

Silence.

Steven.

Betsy?

Can you hear me?

I can hear you! I think.

Your heart is beating, fast. The baby is here with us. She's beautiful.

OH. MY. GOD. I can't believe my thoughts. I can actually hear and feel him in my heart. The butterflies whirling inside give me the sensation that I'm floating, filled with momentary bliss. Eyes closed, I sit as still as possible, clutching on to this fleeting moment while my rigid grip on the chair keeps me grounded. I don't want it to end. Is this what it feels like to be in the presence of angels?

Suddenly, someone drops a metal tray off in the distance, shaking me from my meditation. My eyes pop open and adjust to the blurry background of blinking lights. My mind races with hundreds of thoughts, questioning where I am and who is here with me. *Whoa, what did I just experience? Was I imagining what I heard—making it up?* Also important, did he just say, *she?*

Wait—I *was* communicating with my husband! Like a chocoholic looking for another candy bar, I desperately close my eyes again and try to recreate the miraculous experience once more. I have so much to ask.

This chair is uncomfortable. The nurse's station is making too much noise, and I'm starving. Ugh, I can't do this. How did I do it before? Maybe I need to *not* try, to get back into that weird, floating place. This is so foreign to me. How do those psychics do it on television? I used to think they were phony, but *I* just did it. I must try again.

"Mrs. Ryan." A doctor in a white coat taps my shoulder. Dr. Abbot, his tag says. "Do you have a second?"

I stand to meet him and shake hands. "Of course."

"I've been taking care of your husband, Steven, and I wanted to get you up to speed."

"Yes?" was all I could muster. At this point I want to get the story directly from Steven—or whomever that was talking in my head. *Hurry up, doc.*

"Steven experienced several internal injuries due to the taxicab accident…"

A cab? Why didn't he let me or Dad come pick him up at the airport? We should have offered. Hindsight is 20/20, I guess. I visualize a huge Mack Truck smashing into his yellow cab.

The doctor clears his throat. "Mrs. Ryan? Did you hear me? I said, I'm keeping him here under observation in the ICU all day. Currently, he's unconscious, although we didn't discover injuries to any major organs. The deep lacerations on his head and body were tended to, so be forewarned that he looks pretty banged up. Until the swelling in his brain goes down, we need to just be patient and wait. He's being monitored around the clock. I will contact you once we know more. He's heavily sedated, so he won't be waking up anytime soon."

"Okay. Thank you, doctor. I'm just going to sit here with him a little longer and then head home." I write my information down on a piece of paper. "Here's my cell phone number and email. Please contact me with updates." I reply quickly so he'll leave me alone with Steven. My heart is pounding with the prospect that I will hear him again. I'm craving more silent interaction—at least some form of communication with my husband. I need to know that he's okay.

Dr. Abbot walks away, his stethoscope springing with each step as it dangles around his neck—the tool that confirms life. It must be arduous for doctors to deal with families of sick people, delivering bad news day in and day out. It takes special people to take on the roles of healers and doctors.

In the stillness, the throbbing in my back and calves takes center stage, while the cold space around my heart fills with more hope than it has in the last twelve hours. The *hum-buzz* of the machines around me creates a backdrop for a private connection with my spouse. The white noise blank canvas will give the words spilling out of our hearts a page to land on and take shape.

Silence.

Steven, I'm here.

Silence.

Honey, it's me, and our baby.

Silence.

An hour passes in the dimly lit room with no further connection. My butt is numb, and my eyelids are getting heavy. I could turn on brighter lights but don't want to draw attention to myself. Maybe the first time I connected with Steven, my mind was playing tricks on me? I look back at the many times I've nonverbally communicated with Barney about whether he wants to eat or go outside, or not, without even thinking about it. I wonder if this is similar?

The force of my sigh propels me to push myself up from the chair and walk away. I'll try this again later.

Betsy! I love you. Steven's whisper stops me.

Leaning back on my heels, I pivot and jump back in the chair. I get in a square meditative pose, one I learned in meditation class, and begin my balanced breathing. I close my eyes and pray. *Dear God, please don't let this turn out to be my imagination. I need to communicate with my husband. I do love him, despite our problems. I want our marriage to work.*

The vanilla-colored walls in Steven's room are devoid of windows and fresh light so I rely on the blinking screens for illumination. The beeping machines remind me I'm in a place where your name and favorite color don't matter. It's about curing disease or prolonging a dance with death. Impersonal or not, this room is sustaining his life. The gentle wisp of his breath is steady, as he says, *My girl, Betsy.*

I'm here, Steven… please let me know if you are going to be okay.

I don't know, my love. I'm very tired. I don't have the energy to move my arms or legs right now.

Silence.

The sandbag on my heart is more than I can bear, but I'm hopeful that tomorrow will bring good news and more communication with him.

"Dad, Mom, I have something to tell you," I announce, as I enter the side door of my house—a door Steven and I stepped through together so many times before—an entrance to our family and our home together.

We spent over a year and a half going back and forth on the layout and size of the rooms; and negotiated paint colors and trim. After living in a rental home a few blocks away, we were eager to move in and add to our family of three. Our sweet puppy Barney was the perfect child. We've celebrated birthdays, anniversaries, and even losing a tooth or two. A collage of memories, define what this home means to me... to us.

"What is it? Tell us." They reply almost in unison as they leap up to greet me. I'm guessing many years of marriage have that effect on people. When you're married to a person for so long you start to take on their characteristics in some ways. I almost think they've started to look like each other. Now they dress alike in the grandparent uniform: white T-shirt under the requisite button-down shirt, with khakis and white sneakers. It's the perfect traveler's outfit, too, which suits their love of adventure these days.

"First, thanks for waiting here for me," I say. "As you know, Steven is still in the ICU and unconscious." I can't believe I'm saying this about my husband. Just last night I was flirting with him, hoping to patch things up. Now, he's unconscious in the ICU.

"What did the doctor say?" Mom is always so direct and to the point.

"Dr. Abbot told me he'd know more later today, but they didn't find any damage to any organs, just swelling on his brain due to the accident. He's being monitored by machines around the clock with the staff all nearby. But Steven told me he could hear me and that he loved me... I mean... I felt that." My face turns red as I realize how crazy I must sound.

"What?" They have fixed expressions as they pull out chairs to join me at the kitchen table, a table Steven thought would look great in our adjoining living room/kitchen area. A table I thought wouldn't fit; I was wrong. I was mistaken about many things when it comes to my husband. Was this God's way of giving me a glimpse into what life would be like without him? Like in *A Christmas Carol*, when the angel takes Scrooge around town to see how he's impacted other people's lives—to see how he could change. Well, it worked. I could change; heck, I *am* changing. I'm trying to talk to my dog and transmit messages to a comatose husband!

Taking a huge breath and getting centered for what I know won't be an easy thing to describe, I exhale and begin. "Guys… to clarify, let me explain what happened this morning that, I think, is related to my communication with Steven."

The look on their faces indicates they're at least willing to listen.

"I've discovered that Barney actually understands me. English, I mean…" They continue to stare at me, gaze unchanged. "Just this morning, after the call from the hospital, I felt such a strong connection to him. I believe he comprehends much of what I'm saying and feeling. He replies with the typical tail wagging and dog-type sounds, but I know he comprehends more."

"Wait. Stop." I can't tell if my dad is being serious. "Can you back up that sentence and explain further? People don't talk to dogs, Betsy. Get serious. You have a husband in the ICU. Shouldn't you be focusing on that?"

"Dad, I understand all of that, but there's nothing I can do about Steven except sit and wait." I wiggle in my seat and shift my focus from his narrowing eyes to Mom's more sympathetic gaze. "As far as Barney goes, I'm just telling you what I'm experiencing. Maybe it's the stress of the stalker, the accident, or the threat of losing the baby. I'm not completely sure. All I know is that my dog seems to react to specific things I say to him, and it's somehow connected to what's happening with Steven—I think triggered by the chain of events over the past few days."

"But—"

My dad tries to interject, but I continue. "At first I decided that it was just my *wishing* that he understood me, but then at the hospital, it happened with Steven, too. I understood him. Maybe it's different than what's happening with my dog, but both situations seem like ESP."

They stare at each other for a moment, not saying a word, until my mother finally turns to me and says, "Go on."

"After I spoke with the doctor, I sat quietly in the room and began zeroing in on Steven. Out of thin air, he told me, in an inside-my-soul kind of way, that he could hear me and that my heart was beating quickly—which it was—and most of all, our baby was there with us and *she* was fine."

"Oh, my goodness, you're having a girl? That's wonderful!" Dad jumps off his seat to come over and hug me—forgetting about his frustration with me earlier. Right now, he doesn't care because he's having a granddaughter. Mom, who shares his enthusiasm, leaps up to join in the hug. After a couple of minutes filled with smiles and cheers, we sit and get back to the story.

"I was excited about my baby girl and wanted to pinch myself to make sure I wasn't dreaming. But then it was quiet again, almost as if the weird connection with our souls broke off. I thought I was making it up or maybe the trauma of his accident actually did trigger my subconscious mind, and now I have this unusual gift."

Since they haven't laughed me out of the room yet, I continue. "I sat there for another hour trying to communicate further, but I got nothing. And then just when I had given up and was leaving, he sent another message to my soul. He told me he loved me."

"Wow, that is some story, Betsy," Mom says finally. "It must've felt extraordinary communicating with him like that."

I'm not sure they understand what I've just experienced, but they're trying to respond positively. Just like they've done my entire life. How could they understand? Washed with frustration, my heart chills like a glass of cold water is flowing over it—an ache that doesn't leave. I want my parents to realize what I've just experienced, and I want another chance with my husband. I need to work things out. Why is it that when we're on the brink of death, we finally start to become humane towards each other? Except for Mom and Dad, of course. They're the only two people I know who can get along after over forty years of marriage.

The Cranstons, on the other hand, always bickered at work. Sure, they loved each other, but bicker, bicker, and bicker. I could hear them from my workstation in the kitchen. It was annoying. Steven and I bicker, too, and it's just as annoying. Interesting how this tragedy has shined a light on that aspect of my relationship with my husband. I never really looked at it that way. I grab my *to-do* list from my purse and add *Stop bickering with Steven* to the top line, and I also add *Fix the cracked paint in the powder room* lower down the list. Steven is a priority right now.

"Betsy, I'm not sure what to say about that soul business right now, but I want you to know that Steven has been an important part of our family for a long time and we love him. We will pray for him."

"Thank you, Mom, I appreciate you saying that."

"Honey," my dad chimes in, "I want to let you know this morning when we were having breakfast with the boys, they mentioned the police were here last night." He waits for confirmation I don't offer up right away. "What happened?"

Mom and Dad listen and watch, intent on making sense out of every word I say, while I fill them in on what they missed yesterday—the spotting, Dr. Deller's visit, Misty and the pizza party, the new pink slip, and, oh yeah, the police visit.

"This stalker business *has* to stop, Betsy. What did they say?" My dad slams his fist into his open hand. He didn't have anything else to say about my communication with Steven, so I'm not going to bring it up again. I have bigger fish to fry.

Knowing that my father is angry because I didn't share this news with them sooner, I quickly reply, "They said they'll see what they can do, which won't be much given we don't have any physical descriptions of the stalker's face except for what's on the video from my surveillance camera. It showed he was wearing a mask, is left-handed, and his approximate height, but that's it."

The three of us share a frustrated sigh as I continue. "The officers took the envelopes to the station to see if they could pull any fingerprints or other clues from them, and they told me they would interview some of the neighbors to see if they saw anyone poking around."

"There has to be someone in this neighborhood who saw this guy grabbing your hidden key or jumping your fence." The lines on my father's forehead crease deeper.

"I was planning on going over to the village today to see if their cameras caught anyone on tape, but now with Steven in the ICU on top of everything else, I haven't had time. I'm sure the police have already checked them, but I want to double check."

Dad asks, "Did you tell your doctor about the notes while he was here? Or that you received one at his office?"

"No, I didn't even think of asking, I was more concerned about the baby when he was here. And until I know for sure that the staff in his office are off my suspect list, I don't want to fill him in, anyway. My main concern while I'm there is to make sure my baby girl is being taken care of."

"Oh Betsy, I hope your intuition is right... a granddaughter, just imagine! And Steven, well, he will be fit as a fiddle before long, I'm sure of it." Mom makes everything all right. She always says that fiddle phrase when someone gets sick or has an operation. I remember when Dad had his heart surgery, she would shake off tears and say, "Your father will be fit as a fiddle before you know it, mark my words." And he was.

"By the way, have you guys talked to Brenda lately?" I change the subject to my sister to lighten my emotional load before I leave to run some errands and pick up my sons at school. "Last I heard she was in Africa, photographing animals for some magazine."

"Not a peep. I got a text message from her when she was in Tanzania two weeks ago, so I'm due for another text or call from her soon." Dad reassures me, "I won't tell her about Steven, unless it's bad news." He quickly adds, "Which it won't be."

Little do my parents know, last year Steven hit on Brenda at our holiday party. He was a little tipsy; she wasn't. She doesn't drink at all, so when her brother-in-law hit on her, it was disgusting. A week later, on New Year's Eve, she canceled on our family party. Mom and Dad were upset, but I knew something was up. I went into my room and called her, and after endless prodding, she spilled the beans about the unwanted flirting episode. She assured me nothing happened and he'd put a fire extinguisher on it immediately after she told him to back off, but still, it was awful. The heat that rose from my stomach spurred the green-eyed jealousy monster. My resentment from that incident lasted for quite a while, but then I realized nothing happened and eventually I got over it. Steven knows it hurt and he hasn't gotten drunk or tried anything like that, at least that I know of, since.

I love my sister and I miss her, especially right now. At least I have my parents here for me.

Together we leave the house through the side door and double-check the lock.

I blow them a kiss. "I'm taking Barney with me to run some errands and get the boys. I'll call you later."

———

Carpool pickup line is always a dream. I listen to the radio, something I don't get to do often, and enjoy privacy in my Lexus' extremely comfortable bucket seats. When Steven bought me this car, he was so excited about all the research he'd done on what would be the safest and most reliable vehicle, at least according to his findings in *Consumer Reports*. His top pick was my Lexus. As a busy suburban mom, I need giddy-up—and this bad boy had it. Plus, I love the back cargo hold with the extra space. As I sit in comfort, I realize there have been many Lexus moments with Steven. He's thoughtful and caring. That side of him gives me hope he, too, will want to work on our fractured relationship.

Barney adores this car as well. He loves riding around with his head sticking out the window. I look over and see him sitting in the passenger seat, panting with his doggy smile as he pops his head out. Together we watch the kids file out of school. It's warmer than it has been in days, so most of the kids are carrying their jackets and hats. We crazy moms—yes, I admit it—seem to always think they need their jackets, hats, boots, gloves, and scarves if the temperature dips below fifty degrees. In the sea of children, Morgan and Kyle bob over in our direction as I start the ignition. "What should I tell them, Barney?" Not expecting him to answer, I look over at him anyway.

Without hesitation, he replies. *Ra-Roo Roo Ruff.*

Catching me off guard, but not as stunned as I should be, I smile at him and scratch behind his ears, then push the unlock button for the boys. If dogs could laugh, I would guess Barney is doing that right now—with his tail wiggling and mouth wide open.

As the boys get in the car, they call out, "Hey, Mom." Kyle takes over the questioning. "How was your meeting?"

"It was fine. How was school? I hope it was awesome!" That's the best diversion I've got. I want to avoid discussing anything about Steven with them. They're too young to handle it; if they were to see him in the hospital, they'd have nightmares for weeks. Steven looks like one of those guys beaten up in those action movies he loves to watch. *The story will be, he's still out of town. Got it, Betsy?*

"Fine, fine," they reply. *Fine,* Barney wags.

I casually turn up the radio, and sure enough a song about getting signs from angels comes on the radio. I look over at Barney, then back at the road. My best friend looks at me almost as if he's admitting that he's chosen this song specifically for our ride home, and flashes a big, toothy canine smile.

Dear God. I love those boys and that dog. Would it be out of the question to wish for Steven to heal, a safe pregnancy, AND the ability to talk with my dog?

Thankfully, we only live a few minutes from school, because I can barely see the road through this waterfall of tears. On the sly I grab a tissue from the sun visor and blot my face as we pull into the garage, hoping the boys are too preoccupied with their conversation to notice. The lyrics about sending an angel play on.

Barney, my angel, stands by us.

Like every day, my sons place their backpacks on their cubby hooks in the mudroom, then take off their shoes and wash their hands before going into the office/playroom to work on homework and play. I'm glad I've successfully passed along these habits that will serve them for years to come. Plus, I don't want school germs entering my home through the side door. My holistic and protective approach to health—where healthy food and preventative medicine reigns—seems to anchor me most of the time, except for pizza cheat nights. *But what good did it do for Steven earlier today?*

A wave of pregnancy exhaustion and fear for Steven hits, directing me to the closest chair. Luckily my phone is within reach.

"Misty, hey, it's me," I begin as soon as the other line clicks on. "I wanted to let you know Steven was in a horrible accident early this morning, and—"

"What? How did it happen?" Her reaction is a mix between a squeak and a shout. "When, where? Oh, my God, Betsy, what can I do? I'll be right over." The line goes silent.

I know I've been leaning on her a lot lately, but what else am I supposed to do? Friends help friends, and now that we've crossed over the red line to the point of no return, I have nothing to hide from her.

Zipping through our connected fence door, she runs from her sliding patio door to mine. When we built our home, I told Steven I wanted a secure, six-foot-high solid wood fence around the perimeter of our property. Not long after Misty and I became friends, we added the doorway, connecting our yards.

Like a breath of fresh air, my superhero neighbor swoops in to save the day. She lets herself in through the back door with her key, to find me walking over to the counter finishing off the last bite of some cheddar cheese and a cracker. I wipe my mouth with a napkin, then toss it in the trashcan, and cross the room to join her by the couch.

"Thanks so much for coming. I seriously don't know what I'd do without you." We share a mutual smile and tight embrace. "Before I tell you about Steven's accident, I was wondering if you could stay here with the boys while I run an errand?"

Nodding in agreement, Misty says, "Sure. Now, what's up with Steven? I'm all ears."

"The doctors say they'll give me an update later, so what I'm about to confidentially tell you is *all* I know." I lower my voice so the boys don't hear me talking. "I also have something rather unusual to share about my experience at the hospital and with Barney…" I pause and our eyes lock into an understanding. We sit for a quiet moment and then she says, "Do tell," as she leans forward, elbow on knee as I begin to give her a detailed recount of the day so far.

———

I'm waiting in silence for a minute, which seems more like an eternity. Finally, Misty voices her thoughts.

"Betsy, I am so sorry to hear about Steven. I'm sure you'll be at the hospital a lot over the next few days, so remember you can count on me. He will get through this," she says, grabbing my hands and giving them a squeeze. "He's a strong man... healthy, young, in good shape."

"Agreed, but the doctor wasn't so sure. The crazy thing is, when I could understand Steven, he seemed so, so... gentle. Unlike how he's been treating me lately."

"Really?"

"He's a good, kind person, but he's also had a dark, moody side. And God only knows what he does when he's traveling. But this version of Steven was more sincere—innocent and loving."

"Well, when you're in a serious state, sometimes you shed the darkness and lean toward the light," Misty says. "I know you're spiritual and accepting of the fact that angels exist, but do you think an angel was working through him?"

"Not to be ironic, but again, God only knows. Seriously, I'm talking to my dog—who I think understands me—and sharing thoughts with a husband in the ICU. I just pray they can help him, whoever they are. I look up and around the room, almost thinking I might see an angel or ghost floating around.

"They will heal him. Just have faith. In the doctors and the angels." Her supportive smile gleams.

"I hope so... I really do have to get going, but I'll bring something easy home for dinner. You and the girls can join us. Hopefully tonight's meal won't be as dramatic," I say, thinking of last night's note incident. "I'll be back in a little while. Thanks again."

As I leave the house and lock the door, I look carefully around the yard, at the gate, and over to the garage, making sure no one is watching me. I scan the road outside my side gate to see if there are any street cameras on the poles. I count two. When I go to Village Hall tomorrow I'll see what their surveillance tapes have.

When we first moved here, the neighborhood welcome packet touted how safe and secure this village was, just twenty-five minutes from the city, but a world away. Now, I'm not so sure. Downtown, you had muggings and random attacks and violence, but as you drive north on Lakeshore Drive, life is supposed to become rosier, safer, and less stressful. When they printed their brochures, I'm sure they never imagined that this madman with pink slips would be coming to town.

My first quick stop is back at the doctor's office to give a urine sample and let Dr. Deller double-check the baby after the spotting incident. Donna is, as usual, painstakingly slow checking patients in for our visits with Dr. Deller and Dr. Hildebrandt. She always confirms if our address, insurance information, and status is up to date. I know it's her job, but quite frankly it's kind of annoying at this point. I was just here earlier this week. I guess not everyone is on Betsy time.

"Oh, hello, Mrs. Ryan. How are you feeling today?" she asks. That's a loaded question, which at this point only my attentive dog, my ICU-ridden husband, and I could begin to answer honestly.

"Fine, thanks. Is he running on time? I've got to get back to my sons at home." Hoping this will nudge her along a little bit.

"Sure is. Hey, I'll be right back," she says. "I have to run to the stock closet and get some more office supplies and then give this file to Dr. Hildebrandt. The nurse will call you in a few minutes." She hands me a small cup. "You know the drill." As I grab for the cup, I see a small stack of pink paper sitting on her desk. Squinting, I shake my head and continue to the bathroom, looking over my shoulder, half expecting to see a madman following me. *Knock it off, Betsy. It's not that unusual for a women's health practice to have pink paper. It's ironic, but not out of the ordinary.*

Peeing in a cup is never a fun thing to do, and being almost eight months pregnant makes it even more difficult. I aim the best I can, but nine times out of ten I get urine running down my arm, barely filling the cup. Luckily, I always seem to get just enough.

It's funny—we weren't going to find out the sex of the baby this time around because we didn't want to jinx it. We just wanted to have a healthy baby, regardless of the gender. Why then, did Steven *tell* me? Was it my imagination? Did I make it up? Wishful thinking? Continuing to silently sleuth my situation, I pull up my black leggings and straighten my floral Zulily maternity tunic. I scrunch up my brows as I realize a drop of pee landed on my Tory Burch flats. Figures! You can dress me up, but you can't get me to pee straight.

I imagine our little girl running through the yard with her own miniature version of my cream-colored designer flats. Her hair is in a pink bow, matching her fancy purple dress, like Mommy. Her brothers chase and tickle her as she plops to a sitting position. They circle her and protect her. She's their baby sister. We are a family. *Soon. I'll have a daughter soon.*

Back in the waiting room, I'm left alone with just *People* magazine to keep me company. Flipping through the pages, I see an article on celebrity moms who have "Bounced Back After Baby." Who are they kidding? I've had two kids and that weight is *not* coming off in just two months. I'd love to know what kind of drug or surgery they get, because this mom would love to bounce back that fast. I'm a real mom and chef who loves to eat and I'm not planning on starving anytime soon.

"'Scuse me." A man's voice pulls my glance up from my reading. It's the janitor, swooping past to empty the trash bin that's now filled with little cone-shaped paper cups, which we moms become all too familiar with during these regular pee-checking visits. "You waitin' for the doctor?"

That's odd. I wonder why he's asking? I reply, "Um, yeah, Dr. Deller." I watch him nod and walk away. He's a tall, dark-haired gentleman, a man of few words, which makes me wonder why he was so rude to me the other day. He casually goes behind Donna's reception area, empties the trash there, lingers to wipe her monitor with a green microfiber cloth, glances around, then proceeds to the back area by the exam rooms. That's even more odd. I would think he could do this after business hours. Well, I guess I *am* the last patient of the day. I remind myself to stop being so paranoid. In my mind, everyone's a suspect.

———————

It's always awkward to be in the stirrups. The OB-GYN visit is one I've gotten used to over the past few years, but the cold chrome footholds don't do it for me. Then there's the latex glove with that cold petroleum jelly stuff. It feels so intrusive, so impersonal. Dr. Deller always diverts his eyes from mine while I keep my eyes trained up at the ceiling. The poster they've positioned up there is of a grassy knoll filled with flowers and butterflies. The sky is blue, and the lake reflects the hills in its glassy surface. I guess I'm not the only one who needs a distraction from this position.

"Well, my dear, everything looks fine. Thank you for coming back in to get a thorough exam. Yesterday was more of a social visit—but let's keep that off the record. I know I shared a lot with you, and I hope I didn't make you feel uncomfortable," he says after a moment of checking.

As I respond, he peels off the latex glove and tosses it into the red biohazardous waste bin.

"Yes, sir. I've been very well-behaved..." My voice trails off as I look down to the floor, suddenly choking back a shuddering sob.

"Oh no, Betsy, what's the matter? Listen, your baby is doing just fine. This little bun in the oven is finishing up and should be born on time, no more complications."

It's funny, or maybe ironic, but at this point, I feel like I already know this in my bones. "Thank you, doc. I really do believe you. But it's not that. It's Steven. He's been in an accident and is in the ICU... I was there earlier today, but he was unconscious so I left." I feel my jaw clench as I think of my husband unconscious in the hospital bed. "I'm actually going to head over there again because I haven't heard from the doctors yet."

He widens his eyes, causing his forehead to deeply crease as he softly replies, "Oh, I had no idea. What can I do to help?" He rolls his stool closer to the exam table. "I could go over there and check in on him, if you'd like?" At this moment, I appreciate what he's trying to do for me. I'm also grateful that he was there for me yesterday, and now he's willing to check on Steven. Who does that? I feel the tension in my brow relax as I shoot him a grateful smile. I may have misjudged my doctor. There's no possible way he's the stalker, but what is this nagging pit in my gut?

"That is so incredibly generous of you, but I don't know. I'm worried the stress of all of this will harm the baby. I've been trying to get quiet, meditate, clear my thoughts, and just breathe."

"That's a good idea, Betsy." He lowers his voice as he shares, "When my wife was in the hospital, I used to go there and sit quietly with her, hoping and praying for some connection." Looking out the window and then returning his gaze to me, he says, "I used to sleep in the chair next to her bed, and I swear... I used to think that she would talk to me, in my mind, through my dreams."

I try not to let him see the shock on my face as he continues. "She would tell me that everything would be okay and that God is good and is here with us," he confides. "I could feel that she was protecting me."

Sitting there, unaware that my jaw is hanging open, I listen and nod. The similarities and odd circumstances send waves to my stomach, and heat rises in my face. It is possible that Steven *and* Barney really *are* communicating with me, in their own ways. The overload of this information causes my head to spin. I grip harder onto the side of the exam table as I pause, wondering if I should... here goes nothing. "Well, doctor, I have a confession to make..." I shift my weight to my elbows. "...I, too, have had a similar experience, with Steven, and with my dog, Barney."

"Are you kidding me?" His face lights up, like I've affirmed everything he's been wondering about for years. "Like what?"

"No, I'm not kidding! In fact, this morning when Barney started to react to what I was saying, I thought I was going crazy."

My doctor nods in agreement. "I can only imagine."

"Then, when I picked up my sons at school, he wagged his tail and reacted just as I was thinking about how the song on the radio was sending me a sign."

"That's some dog, Betsy."

"Tell me about it. I keep thinking maybe it's my imagination, but there was no denying, he's been trying to get my attention for quite some time. I guess I've been so preoccupied with my life that I didn't see the signs."

"Well, why would you? It's not exactly an everyday experience, having a dog directly respond to specific situations like that."

"Exactly. But when I was at the hospital this morning and my husband communicated with me, I couldn't dismiss it. It was true, it was happening—with my husband *and* dog, to some extent. I don't get words from Barney, but I imagine what he *would* say, and it feels like it's generated from his thoughts. I know it sounds crazy."

I'm starting to see my physician in a totally different light. I no longer feel uncomfortable sharing deep, personal things with him; instead I find myself craving to hear more about his experiences with his wife. How did he know it was real? Why did it happen to both of us? Questions I want to ask him, flood my thoughts as I make my mind up about Dr. Deller. I'm sure now that he can't be the stalker—and yet, I still have this gnawing feeling about this office.

"Do you think you ever had this type of interaction with Barney and Steven on this level before and just didn't realize it?"

I push myself up so I can sit on the exam table to continue our conversation upright, and pull the flimsy paper over my lap. "Yes. In fact, as I think back, I know of at least two or three other times where Barney was trying to get my attention, but I never put the pieces together." Once, he was pacing back and forth by the back door, moaning. I decided to check the backyard and discovered Morgan, stuck in the swing, hanging upside down. I rushed out to unhook his shoe while Barney ran alongside me, barking.

There was a time when he started howling nonstop at midnight. Steven ran downstairs and noticed that our garage door was open. We suspected that maybe the neighborhood teenagers used their parents' garage clicker to open the doors along our alley; there were two other doors opened, too. I don't know how Barney knew that, but he did. Unfortunately, our detached garage isn't hooked up to the alarm system.

I also recall Steven and I having strange yet similar thoughts with each other. One day I was thinking about calling him at work, and the phone rang and it was Steven. Another instance happened when I was craving ice cream during my pregnancy with Morgan, when out of the blue, he brought my favorite flavor home after work. We never added up the many times this happened with us. We would always chalk it up to the fact that we're an old married couple. This thought brings a twinkle to my eye and flutter in my heart.

My doctor smiles and starts telling a story about a time his wife and he joked about how they must read each other's mind, wondering if they were secretly separated at birth or something. As he's talking, I can't help but drift in and out of the conversation and begin to think about other circumstances in my life where I had the ability to think of things before they happened, or when I'd imagine someone and they call—it's on my mind now, every second. And how could it not be? It's a whole new universe I've stumbled upon by accident—an existence that might protect me from the madman on the loose.

Zeroing back in on my conversation with my doctor, I nod and agree that our stories are similar, knowing what it's like to communicate on another, more spiritual plane. Guilt riddles me as I acknowledge to myself that I've been selfishly thinking of my own internal stories, but he doesn't seem bothered.

"Well, Betsy, it looks like we share a special, blessed gift," he says. "If you don't mind, would you please keep this between us? I have some nosy people around here and I'd prefer not to have my business talked about. Dr. Hildebrandt isn't as religious or spiritual, and this kind of talk might bother him. And who knows about the office staff? People can be very snoopy."

"You should know me better than that by now," I say with a soft smile, shifting my seat to get comfortable, still clinging to the paper covering on my lap. "I would *never* share anything private that we talk about with your staff. I'm very thankful I have someone who can relate."

He smiles, and I hesitate. "My question is, how do I proceed with Steven? Do you think I should keep trying to communicate with him like this? Or should I let him heal and rest and see if he reaches out to me first?"

"I think you have to wait and see how things go when you head back over to the hospital."

The knock on the exam room door causes us to jolt and shift our glance toward the door.

Dr. Deller says, "Hello? Come in. Yes, Dr. Hildebrandt. How, may I help you?"

"Hi, Mrs. Ryan. Doctor, I'm sorry to intrude, I just wanted to let you know Henry and I will be leaving in a few minutes. Donna just left, and she asked me to let you know."

"No problem, thanks. We were just finishing up. Mrs. Ryan will be leaving shortly, but I'll be here a bit longer. Thank you."

My instinct shoots pains in my belly. Not labor pains, but nervous stomach pains, like seagulls are swooping in circles inside me. I need get out of here. I can't breathe.

"Ooh!" I whimper in fear.

Dr. Deller turns to me. "Betsy, are you okay? Is it the baby?"

"No, ah… I'm fine," I lie. "I have to go." I struggle to get my pants back on and quickly run out. Henry and Dr. Hildebrandt are nowhere to be seen.

For the millionth time this week, I run and try to catch my breath as I propel the palm of my hand onto the elevator button. I need to get the heck out of this building. I could take the freight elevator just through the hallway door, but this route is faster. I push the little black button a second and third time. Finally, the doors open to an empty elevator. I enter after furtively looking down the hall to make sure I wasn't followed. The blood surging through my veins feels like I'm running a marathon. That would be quite a sight. Here I am running across the finish line, fighting off bad guys and holding my bouncing stomach.

The incredible urge to get out of that office has me baffled. I don't understand why I'm getting these feelings. Maybe I was picking up on something in the doctor's office and my body was warning me about it? Maybe a comment Dr. Deller said, or Dr. Hildebrandt's entrance, or the janitor walking by? Or perhaps I'm just losing my mind and having a nervous breakdown. Either way, I need to get out of here.

While waddle-jogging to my car, I scan the parking lot, left then right. Still no one is following me. The parking lot is nearly empty this time of day aside from a few scattered cars.

I start the ignition and grip the steering wheel as a scream surges from my lungs. No one can hear me, but the baby squirms. Her feet tuck as if she were a gymnast doing a trick.

"Whoa. Okay, baby. Breathe," I say. "Emmy Grace. That's your name, you know." Talking to her in a calm way eases both our nerves. "Yep, Mommy knows you're a girl now, so I'm going to call you by your name." Another scan of the parking lot shows I'm still alone. There's no one in sight.

The sound of my voice seems to send a relaxed energy to my belly, and my little girl settles down. It settles me, too. I imagine her breathing, gurgling, maybe even blowing bubbles from inside. I'm sure she can feel the pounding blood through my veins starting to slow down—but *her* sense of tranquility brings me back to center. She's not going anywhere; she wants to meet her brothers, Morgan and Kyle, on her birthday.

There's very little movement in the parking area as I make the short drive out of the lot and turn onto the street. While sitting at a traffic light, I suddenly remember that I need to bring cupcakes to Morgan's class party tomorrow. Today just keeps getting better and better. Why do I always sign up for these things and then forget? I never used to forget things at work. Still, I welcome the distraction from the stressful event at the doctor's office and turn the car in the direction of the closest grocery store. I know I don't have time to bake today. Some chef *I am*.

Jockeying for a parking spot near the grocery store can be tricky in this little suburb near Northwestern University, Steven's alma mater. It's almost like parking in downtown Chicago, but with less traffic and cheaper parking meters. The streets are lined with traditional university buildings denoted by white wooden signs in black or purple script, an overflowing coffee shop with a green awning covering a few metal coffee tables outside the door, and a large smattering of students and bikes. This is life in this suburban gem. We are so lucky to live here.

Baby and I enter the gourmet grocery store and instantly take in the array of eye candy, aka, Food Paradise. Each square inch of this store screams wholesome, delicious, and beautiful organic food. Chefs like me appreciate the high quality and are willing to pay the extra cost for our families. The entry displays contain flawless apples and pears lined up in perfect rows, facing us, best sides up. Walking between the aisles makes me feel like I'm an imaginary character in a video game with her princess daughter in tow as she glides through the mountains of brilliant colorful candies and treats; but in this case, it's vivid produce—known as treats to some.

Moving past the highlands with its rainbow of food, we are then transported into the lowlands of bakery town. I think back to the days after graduation from culinary school when I wanted to work here. I later changed my mind because I didn't "want to work where I like to play." Crazy as it sounds, I still relish coming to this supermarket as often as possible, if just to get a midday retreat from reality. I don't want to spoil my secret escape just down the road. So here we stand, waiting to be taste-infused amongst the freshly baked breads, gigantic muffins, expertly decorated cakes, and piles of cookies.

Okay, Emmy Grace, which cupcakes look the best to you? I ask the question, but don't really expect an answer.

I scan the elaborate, multi-level displays of carbs for the winning container of childhood satisfaction. Like speed-reading, I grab one box after another, discovering what ingredients are in each. Even though we're at a gourmet shop, it's always best to check the labels, a habit I've been training my own kids to do ever since they were toddlers. We would make a game of it and now we use the *Nutrition Detectives* program of label reading and ingredients list evaluation. Primary school-aged children really dig that kind of interactive stuff; plus, it gives us a reason to "play store" with all the empty boxes, cans, and bottles.

Kick-Roll-Shove.

"Whoa, Emmy! What's the dealio?" I ask quietly as she does the wave inside my gut.

I like to have these imaginary conversations with my pregnant bellies. I ask questions, and if they don't kick, shove, or roll, I fill in the blanks for them. I believe it's the beginning stages of getting to know their personalities. Each of my successful pregnancies has followed this ritual. I like to call it "private Mommy time."

"Oh, so you like these pretty pink frosted cupcakes, do you? I see the frosting is colored with beet juice and sweetened with Stevia. Perfect choice, my little princess helper." I talk to my baby in a singsong style, like I did with Kyle and Morgan, hoping she understands me. I have the feeling, after a day like today, she probably does. "Good choice in cupcakes, lovey. Now let's go grab some premade food from the deli counter for dinner and then it'll be off to see Daddy."

———

Conveniently, the store is down the road from the hospital, so the drive doesn't take long. I'm hoping to get there before the end of visiting hours.

Ordinarily I love driving down this stretch of road along the lake. I can take in the rousing whitecaps of the waves hitting the beach and the clear blue skies that meet the horizon at the lake's edge. In the fall, the tree-lined streets are splashed with vibrant orange, red, and yellow leaves, and come springtime, the daffodils and tulips really light up the melting snow with pink and purple highlights. The homes along the route come in all shapes and sizes, with manicured lawns and quaint, little rock gardens—altogether showcasing the perfect place to raise a family.

But today I'm focused on Steven's health.

As I pull up to the curve where the streetlight meets the corner and the hospital sits, my stomach starts to knot and develop a dull ache. Baby is a little jumpy, too, as we proceed through the light just around the corner and into the visitor parking lot. This time of day, close to dinnertime, it's easy to find a place to park at the hospital. Lucky for us, it's also close to the entry door. As I put the car in park, my phone pings, indicating a voicemail message. As I listen to Dr. Abbott's message, he says that Steven is still unconscious, but he seems to be in stable condition. At least there's no more bad news, right now.

As I begin to place my phone back in my purse, it rings. I check the caller ID; it's Dad. "Hey, I'm glad you called. Boy, do I have an update for you," I say.

"I'm all ears," he says.

"I just left the grocery store, but while I was inside, Doctor Abbott must've called me because I just picked up his voicemail. He said Steven is still unconscious, but he seems to be in stable condition." I hear Dad let out a big sigh of relief. "Thanks for coming over to relieve Misty of her babysitting duties. How are the boys? I'm sure they're starting to wonder if something's up—or if they still have a mom."

"Well, they know you're still their mom, and no, they don't think anything is up, at least from what I can tell," he says. "We've been distracting them with lots of things since we got here, including some new pranks with Morgan. Don't worry, though, Barney isn't involved this time. We weren't sure if you'd have any time to think about dinner, so your mother and I took them to that new healthy hamburger place in the mall. Is that okay?"

It was more than okay. I appreciate that they serve hormone-free meat and source their vegetables locally, but mostly, I love that my parents get the whole organic thing— and the fact that the apple doesn't fall far from the tree. I can still share the meal I picked up at the store with Misty and her daughters, anyway. "Oh, sure, that's great. Thanks!"

"How about you give me the *Reader's Digest* version on the rest of your latest update, because I'm about to get my butt whipped in Monopoly Jr. over here."

"Not much else to tell, except that Dr. Deller was able to communicate with his wife before she died and my baby girl is now communicating with me through cupcakes. By the way, would you mind calling Misty to tell her I won't be home with food for another hour or so? If she wants to eat without me, tell her it's okay."

There's silence on the other end of line. "Whoa, lots to take in there, kiddo," Dad finally says. "We'll have to talk when you get home. Just don't let this craziness get to you. You're an Anderson at heart, and we come from strong stock. I'll fill your mother in... she just told me to say hello to you, too. Be careful."

"I'll be careful. Tell Mom hi. I'll see you guys soon. Kiss the boys for me." My chest muscles release some of the tension after talking to Dad.

———

This hospital is always so busy. I often wonder if our country is getting sicker or perhaps the medical care system is more improved and therefore more people are getting things fixed.

Watching the doctors and nurses scurry about from room to room and in and out of the elevator reminds me of Dr. McDreamy from one of my favorite TV shows, *Grey's Anatomy*. The character, Derek Shepherd, can play my doctor anytime. The actor, Patrick Dempsey, is just so incredibly surgeon-esque. Just thinking about those dreamy eyes brings a smile to my face. I can honestly say that if Dr. McD asked me out on a date, I would say yes. That's not to say I'd kiss him or anything, but oh, to be close to that lush head of dark, tousled hair, accented with just a touch of gray, and that slight indication of a beard. Mmm-hmm!

"Excuse me, ma'am. May I help you?" I turn to see a young, blonde nurse in baby-blue scrubs—the same color as her eyes. She's all of twenty-five years old, fresh-faced and eager.

"I'm here to check in on... visit with... see... Steven Ryan. I was here earlier today. I'm his wife."

"Certainly, follow me. You know visiting hours are until 8:30 p.m., and only two visitors are allowed in his room at a time."

"I understand. Why? Has he had any *other* visitors?"

"Oh yes, his brother came in a little while ago. In fact, you just missed him."

I feel the baby kick as my lungs begin to ache. "He doesn't *have* a brother," I say, suddenly terrified. "He *doesn't* have a brother. Do you understand?" I've gone from relaxed breathing to hyperventilation in a matter of seconds.

"Take a deep breath, Mrs. Ryan," the nurse calmly says, clearly not understanding the implication. "Let me get my supervisor."

As soon as she walks away, I start to walk over to his room, but a security guard stops me in my tracks. I try to explain who I am, but he's not hearing it. Temporarily agreeing, I plop in a cold metal chair, searching for answers as I watch her run over to the nurse's station. There's a slight commotion as another woman runs to get one more person, maybe a lead doctor or something. I take a deep gasp of air to send oxygen down to Emmy Grace while I tap into her loving energy to calm myself. I'm sure this is some mistake. That's nonsense. He doesn't have a brother. I bob my head from left to right, trying to get a glimpse of the hospital room they won't let me enter—Steven's room.

A woman hurries over to me. Her nametag says, *Shirley Bowen, Head Nurse, ICU.* "Mrs. Ryan. I understand you're concerned about the person who came to visit your husband this afternoon?"

My cheeks are beet red. I don't even need a mirror to tell me all the heat has rushed to my face. Why aren't they getting it? "That's exactly what I'm saying. Don't you ask for ID or something before you let them into this place? Does anyone have a description of him?"

"Ordinarily, they check your identification at the front desk on the main level like you did this morning," she says, "but that doesn't mean people can't lie about their relationship to the patient. If it were a hospital employee, we wouldn't check that, either. They have ID badges and come and go throughout the hospital based on the type of badge they have. We can ask the check-in desk if they have a description of him, but ordinarily that's not something we'd do. However, we *will* check into this right away."

"Okay, good, because the last time I checked, my mother-in-law didn't have any other sons before she and my father-in-law passed away a few years ago. Steven's only sibling, Sarah, is in San Francisco," I say. "I'm really concerned about this. Would it be possible for your staff to allow only a specific list of visitors to his room?" I'm not about to get into my stalker situation with this woman. Everyone's a suspect, and I don't know whom to trust.

"Absolutely. You can get me that list when it's convenient. Now, feel free to go see your husband. I'll let the security guard know you're on the approved list of visitors."

———

Sitting in silence next to my still husband gives me time to collect my thoughts. I try to breathe slow, calming breaths and prepare for all that could occur, everything—health, death, and taxes. I never thought I'd have to think about what my life would be like without my husband, but in times like these, that cold, stark reality hits home. Let's hope he gets through this quickly.

He is wearing a pale blue hospital gown that partially covers the complicated twist of tubes and wires connected to the deluge of machines around his bed. It's more than I can comprehend at this moment. The beeping, buzzing, and humming make the space between us even colder and more impersonal.

"Oh, honey, I wish things were different. I wish you weren't in that bed, unconscious. The boys miss you, and I miss you. You've been out of town so much lately that we've been moving on with life, each day… Oh, did I tell you that

Morgan fractured his arm? He's fine. Don't worry." Shaking my head and grimacing, I whisper, "Also, do you have a brother that I don't know about?" Levity is all I've got right now.

I wait, motionless, but all I hear is white noise. The absence of his response is rather eerie, making the stillness more evident. Nothing can prepare you for an event like this; it's almost surreal.

Trying to get comfortable for any length of time in a hospital room chair is like trying to take a quality nap on an airplane. It's simply not possible. Anyone who says they can is lying or just overly tired. You can kid yourself into thinking that you're getting good sleep, but I've learned that sleeping in a chair, much like trying to sleep on a red-eye flight from San Francisco to Chicago, is simply inhumane.

This has always been one of my many disagreements with Steven. I want to take a nice mid-morning flight, which includes lunch, beverage service, a movie, and a light pre-landing snack, and then head home, shower, and relax from our trip. He, on the other hand, wants to leave at night, *sleep* on the plane, and then arrive in the morning to hit the ground running. He's not taking into consideration the fact that even if you could sleep for those four-and-a-half hours of flying time, that's nowhere near enough to function when you land; instead, you end up exhausted, smelly, and cranky. Your breath will taste like old socks and your once-pleated trousers will be a wrinkled mess. Too often we try to kid ourselves into thinking that we can powder our noses in the bathroom prior to landing and make ourselves look presentable. Not! I don't see how

Steven can make that trek several times a month. To each his own.

I find a somewhat reasonable position in the boxy chair to get quiet and clear my mind so that I can try to check in with Steven. I need to continue our conversation and find out more details about his condition. I wish the medical staff had shared more information about his accident. I know they are focusing on his recovery, not the "hows" and "whys," but I need answers.

Thirty-minutes pass without any semblance of communication from my husband. Aside from Emmy's wiggles, it's quiet on the hospital front.

Whispering, I say, "Come on, Steven. Where are you? I need you right now. *We* need you right now. Please tell me something."

Silence.

"How did you get into the car accident?"

No response.

I think of the day I met my husband. For years, I longed to find the perfect guy—going to bars, parties, on blind dates... no one ever really "rang my bell," or if they did, they *broke* my bell. Then one day I ran into the library to do some cooking research. As usual I picked out my favorite, *The Flavor Bible*, a cookbook on seasonings—one way too expensive to buy. While I was sitting at one of the ornate oak tables, thumbing through the pages, a handsome guy came over and sat down beside me with a pile of books. I couldn't help but notice his gorgeous head of blond hair and tan, muscular arms. His purple-and-white Northwestern sweatshirt rounded out his all-American collegiate look.

Focus, Betsy, I remember thinking, my face flushed. *You have a meal to prepare this evening and you need the right spice combination.* But instead I just sat there, fantasizing about him wrapping those strong arms around my waist, pulling me close for a gentle kiss on my...

"Excuse me," he said quietly, interrupting my daydream.

"Um, yes?" God, he was cute.

"Can I ask you a quick question?" he asked, as he leaned on the edge of the table. Boy, I wished I were that table.

Caught off guard, I mustered, "Oh, uh, sure. What is it?"

He caught me off guard again when he asked if I would have dinner with him. I eagerly accepted. He continued by saying, "Great, I'm new in town and am kind of tired eating dinner with my cocker spaniel, Benny. Don't get me wrong, he's great company, but he's lacking in verbal skills," he said. "I moved back here from San Francisco and would love to get reacquainted with the Windy City with a personal tour guide. I used to attend Northwestern."

He was cute *and* smooth, I told myself, but I worried that I might be a targeted bimbo or weekly challenge for this guy. At that point in my life, I didn't want another bad relationship, but I *did* love the idea that he had a dog. I wondered if Benny liked women who cooked delicious food and offered the leftovers to any lucky dogs that happened to be hanging around?

I didn't know at the time I was getting ready for my last first date, and the first with my future husband.

I remember how happy and infatuated we were back then. The sun was shining. We were young. I was so skinny.

Interrupting my musings, I silently hear Steven finally respond.

Betsy? I'm here.

"I'm right here, honey." I try to speak softly to avoid alerting the hospital staff. I don't have time to explain how my unconscious husband is communicating without words.

Truck.

"Truck? Was your car hit by a truck?" Searching for answers, I stand over his bed looking down at the man I love, blinking away the tears, fighting against the sobs that are getting caught in my throat. I see the man I've created my home and family with, the man who is supposed to be with me forever, protecting me from the cruel world—from the stalker. He once vowed no other man would harm me like the attacker years ago. I need him now.

He seems so small and helpless at this moment, his muscular build not as predominant. I, on the other hand, am trying to be the strong one. *Super Betsy!* I'm dealing with the stress of the mystery pink slips and calls, Morgan's broken arm, and the pregnancy. Some unknown force seems to be working through my psyche at this moment. I feel almost superhuman, even though I'm a sobbing wreck from time to time. I'm starting to find an inner strength I never knew existed. I've heard stories about mothers who've lifted cars after their children had gotten stuck under them. I'm not so sure about lifting a car in my condition, but I do feel galvanized to act against the man who's threatening me and my family. I must remember to add *Get myself a superhero cape* to my to-do list.

Motionless, Steven breathes in, out, in, out. Anyone watching us would never imagine that he is silently communicating with me, like this.

Yes, it was a truck. It came from out of nowhere. In this state, Betsy, I don't feel any pain, but when I look down at us, I see myself and know that in my physical form, I must be very uncomfortable.

My inner thoughts are razor-focused on Steven, rather than broadcasting them out loud to the ICU and the hallways beyond. I rest in my hard-as-a-rock chair again, close my eyes, block out the world, and imagine my words so I can clearly respond. *I'm so glad that in this state, you don't feel any pain. But when you wake up, I kinda think you'll feel differently.*

That's my Betsy! Always cracking jokes—very funny.

I'm not trying to be funny, though. I'm trying to be realistic. *What are we going to face when you wake up? Will you be paralyzed? Internal injuries? That's what I'm thinking. But most importantly, I want you to wake up.*

It's not time. I must wait…

Wait for what?

Silence.

Oh, for God's sake, Steven. I don't like playing twenty questions. Why can't you just make this easy on me and fill me in from A to Z? I have been through a living hell the past few days while you've been gallivanting around San Francisco—and by the way, I have my suspicions

*about all the extracurricular activities that may or may not have been
going on.*

There, I said it. I continue. *I don't mean to sound mean or
uncaring, but this whole situation has me so upset... I just don't trust you
anymore, Steven. There have been way too many incidents with
unanswered questions, and Misty says... Oh, forget it. I need to go.*

*It's okay, honey, you need to process this and get through the pain.
I'll be here for as long as I can. Good night.*

Silence.

It's difficult to have a conversation, much less an
argument, with your comatose husband. It doesn't have as
much *kick* as when you scream it and get it off your chest
when he's awake. On the other hand, the words flow quickly
and you say much more than you intended.

Feeling like I didn't get as many answers as I was hoping
for, only more questions, I hesitate before I leave Steven's
room. I'm hoping for one more transmission to express my
regret for getting upset with him, but it's really no use. It's
almost 8:15 p.m. and visiting hours will be over soon. Plus, I
should get home to see my sweet little boys. What am I going
to tell them?

———

As I walk in the side door of my house, I check my fear,
anxiety, and recent revelations about Steven at the door. I want
to come in thankful to my parents, snuggle-kiss the boys, and
say hello to Barney.

"Mommy!" the boys cheer.

"I'm glad to see you have your pajamas and slippers on.
Have you read your bedtime story yet?"

"Grandma and Grandpa let us watch a cartoon while we
waited for you to come home so *you* could read to us," Kyle
reports.

Kyle is a couple of inches taller than his younger brother
and rail thin in a sporty sort of way, especially compared to
Morgan's more solid body type—thanks to weekly karate

classes. I can thank "aunt" Misty for introducing him to martial arts, which have really helped bolster his confidence. I remember the first time he saw her practicing drills—he was instantly enamored and wanted to find out more. Like love at first sight, Morgan couldn't get enough of the jumping, kicking, and learning the respect and dignity of such a time-honored sport—focusing on mind, body, and spirit to discover his little champion within. I should join him just in case I need to kick my way out of an attack, sometime soon.

———

Reunited with my tan leather chair, I let the throw pillows envelop me in a long-awaited hug. I must have inherited my mom's fascination with pillows—as if there was any doubt. Looking around my family room and attached kitchen, I feel relieved that Mom took the liberty of tidying up. Sometimes it's hard to keep the house clean with kids and a dog running around all day, but one of the things we love about our Craftsman style home is the open layout that leads to the patio and yard. A yard we use to entertain, play, and even cook. We love that the barbeque is situated close to the door so we can grill throughout the cold Midwestern winters. The enclosed yard boasts two mature maple trees bordering the patio, both of which offer shade on sunny days and the boxwood bushes that line the cedar fence on the property's west side give the yard a manicured look. Many squirrels call those lush, green bushes their playground regardless of Barney's daily protest-and-chase runs. My yard really does give my home a protective feeling, but these days no trees or bushes can shield a stalker's eyes.

Taking their positions on either side of my lap and the baby bump, my two love bugs cozy in to listen as I read aloud from *The Giving Tree* by Shel Silverstein. When I was a little girl, Mom would read this or one of his other great books, like *The Missing Piece,* for hours. We'd cuddle up on the couch, perfectly adorned with color-coordinating pillows, and enjoy epic story time marathons. I never wanted them to end, and to this day I savor story time because I know there will be a time when they won't want to sit on my lap or read a book with me. If cultural history serves me correctly, hopefully they will come back to Shel and our other favorite authors when they become parents themselves—but let's not get ahead of ourselves.

"Okay, kiddos, story time is over," I finally say. "Let's go upstairs and brush our teeth and hop into bed. We have a big day tomorrow." Or at least *I* have a big day tomorrow, talking to dogs, unborn babies, and my comatose husband... but who's keeping track, and by the way, *who* is it that's trying to kill me again?

As I try to figure out how to explain today's events to my parents, I nibble at the little pink hangnail and cuticle of my thumb—a nervous habit I've had since I was in grade school. Mom's anxiety often displays itself in bouts of cleaning, which she's doing right now. Today it's the magazines on the nearby coffee table. We've already established that we're going to wait for Dad to come back from walking Barney before I get into the latest installment of "Betsy's crazy life."

I'm glad Dad brought a flashlight for their walk, just in case he stumbles upon a skunk during the excursion—or worse. I wait anxiously for him to return. I know it's time to face the music and release this pent-up anxiety, to be more productive and clearheaded about possible clues related to this stalker. Like a big red balloon filled with too much water, I imagine myself bursting into a million little crimson pieces, water everywhere.

"Mom, I know you're worried about Steven and the stalker, and I promise I'll tell you everything I can about that, but I really need to process it all with a living, coherent human being." No offense to my furry best friend and comatose husband, but I need my mom right now.

Although she's excited about the idea of a granddaughter, my mom is distracting herself from the idea that her daughter is communicating with her husband in a coma—or maybe her nerves are about the stalker—or both. Now she's taking out the window cleaner and scrubbing Barney's nose prints from the knee-level surface of the patio door glass while we wait for Dad to come back with the dog.

Finally, Barney runs in and jumps up on my knees, noses my hand, and then attempts to lick my cheek with his long, pink tongue. I've always had a sweet spot for my boy and his kisses, and now I need them more than ever to help stabilize my nerves.

Mom is watching me from the corner of her eye as she quietly returns the window cleaner to its home beneath the sink and then pivots to score two points in the trash can with a balled-up piece of paper towel. She raises both arms, fists clenched, mouthing, "Yes!" and walks toward the kitchen table.

The Anderson clan seems to operate on the theory of sitting down to discuss problems. Then, once armed with solutions, we tackle them head on. Ever since I was in grade school, I remember my parents taking this approach, and though my sister and I loathed the idea at the time, we always ended up prevailing in whatever challenge we were faced with. This team concept was something my dad picked up along the way through his career as a television executive. These roundtable discussions we've had over the past couple of days have really helped me cope with the reality that someone could possibly be trying to kill me. Like a pregame pep talk, I feed on "Coach Dad's" strategy and Mom's support and know our plan of action will keep me safe.

Dad throws Barney a good boy treat, then walks over to the refrigerator and grabs the lemonade to pour himself a glass before we start our discussion.

"Ladies, does anyone want something to drink?"

"No, thanks, Dad."

"Honey, grab me some water, then come sit down so Betsy can start our meeting."

Holding back a snicker, I send some loving energy Mom's way. I appreciate how serious she's taking this threat, all the while maintaining our "family meeting" tradition.

"I know I've thrown a lot at you guys already today," I say. I'm continuing my efforts to distract myself from the inevitable truth of my current circumstances. "And by the way, thank you for taking the boys to dinner."

"Of course, Betsy," Dad begins. "This stalker business— and now Steven—you shouldn't have to handle this alone. We're always here for you... even though I know technically we weren't the other night, which reminds me, I've been wanting to thank you for giving us those tickets to the gala. Your mother and I really had a great time."

"I'm glad." I smile, happy that at least *someone* is having a good week. I welcome the brief diversion from our task, as it keeps me rooted in the reality that life will go on, regardless of this madman's plot.

"Betsy, we really did love the evening, thank you for the generous gift. Candy and Carter were so kind to us. They asked all about you and the kids, of course, but I also made sure not to mention Steven or what's been going on around here. I did tell them you're missing your work, but that you're not going to make any decisions about coming back until after the baby is born."

My head shoots up as a twinge of interest sparks in my gut. "Really? Did they seem okay with that?"

"I think so. In fact, Candy pulled me aside and said they miss your special touches in the kitchen. They're fine with Richard and Heidi because they've been there for years, but the new chef—Kelly, is it? Anyway, she's just marginal at best—at least, that's the way Candy put it."

"Really?" I can already see myself swooping in to grab my old job back. I'll focus on that one later. That's going to be an argument with Steven, but I've never missed our arguments as much as I do now.

"Now, dear, let's get down to business. Will you please tell us what is going on with Steven? Surely by now the doctors have given you more to go on, right?" She pauses, noticing the tears that have sprung to my eyes at the very thought of Steven. "Oh, honey, I know this is hard on you, but it's also hard on us because we worry about you, Steven, and the boys. And right now, your father and I are putting up a front for them, and you know how much I hate fibbing."

Really, Mom? "I know, and I'm sorry for making you do something that you don't feel comfortable with, but we *have* to protect the boys." I draw in a breath and continue. "On top of everything happening, while I was waiting in the car after my appointment, I remembered Morgan's class party is tomorrow so I had to run over to the grocery store to get cupcakes." Thinking of my youngest son puts a happy grin on my face. "Then once I got back over to the hospital, they claimed Steven's *brother* had just left." I pause to let that sink in.

"Huh? Steven doesn't have a brother," Dad says, blinking.

"I know, Dad. I lost it with the nurses. They were as surprised as I was, but not nearly as upset as I was. They agreed to limit his visitors immediate to family members only—with ID. I have to say, I can't help but worry that this so-called brother is actually the envelope man who's been stalking me, which might explain why I've been getting a sinking feeling, warning me."

"But how in the world would some stalker know where Steven was?" My mom sits upright in her seat and clenches her teacup in both hands, like one of those stress balls.

"It's clear he's been following me around and researching things about my family. And if he's been around me, I wouldn't be surprised if he eavesdropped on conversations I've had, too." I tremble when I think about some madman being only feet away from me at any time. "You never know, he could be watching us right now," I whisper. "For all I know, he could have bugged my house."

The three of us fall silent, instinctively looking up at the corners of the room, at the softly lit lamp next to the couch, then all around us. Where could a bug be hidden?

"So," Mom says in her feigned chirpy voice, changing the conversation—going along with the fact that there might be a "bug" device in the house, "Tell me about Barney."

Briefly smiling at her willingness to go along with my "bug" comment, I continue. "Well, that's the thing. When I was upset after the hospital called me the other day, I swear he understood something bad had happened. Remember that time he warned me about Morgan getting stuck on the swing in the backyard? He was warning me about something important." I know how crazy this sounds. I'm surprised they haven't tried to convince me otherwise.

Barney, seated at my feet, shifts his gaze from the floor to my face and looks me directly in the eyes. As if he's smiling, he responds, *Garroof.*

"See what I mean?" I stare at Mom and Dad as they almost drop their jaws into their respective drinks of choice. I think they're starting to understand what's going on between my furry friend and me, and how it's related to my communication with my husband. "The same thing is happening with Steven. He's able to communicate with me. Today he told me about his accident. His cab was hit by a truck."

"Oh, no." My mom gasps. "That's probably why he's unconscious."

"Yes. He didn't, however, know about the person who came into his room."

"Okay, so where do we go from here?" Dad pauses, running his fingers first through his silver-blond hair, then drumming them vigorously on the table, apparently both thinking of an answer and waiting for one. I can tell Dad wants to help me solve this stalker problem. What father wouldn't? But since we still have no idea who is doing this to me, we're chasing our tails.

"My thought is, let's just go about our business… I'll call the hospital in the morning to see if there's been any progress. And if I can get Steven's subconscious to give me any additional information, I'll fill you in."

I start to feel the cold thawing inside as the stress tapers down simply from the act of discussing everything with my parents. Our seated table talks really help.

"In the meantime, let's just do life. Get the boys to school, and remember the cupcakes, you know…" I trail off, pointing to the phone and the corners of the room, as if *he's* listening, "…not worry about the threat. I also have an errand to run tomorrow morning at the Village Hall, but that shouldn't take long," I add, giving Mom a nod and a wink, to make sure she knows what I'm referring to.

Mom whispers in Dad's ear; I suspect she's telling him about my plan to look at the video surveillance tapes. He nods in acknowledgement, meets my gaze, and winks. I smile back and give a thumbs-up. It would be ironic if someone was videotaping us, when my system should be videotaping *them*. There I go, using my humor as a coping mechanism again. It's not funny, but it's all I've got to hang on to for now.

Curling up with a good book in bed is always food for the soul. I do it every night to escape into someone else's story. Tonight's installment is again the chick lit from the other night, a diversion from my own personal drama that really is stranger than fiction. My eyes skim the page, taking in the author's elaborate settings, descriptions, and required details of the lead male's muscular physique. I float into the imaginary world, escaping my obvious predicament, as my eyelids flutter, fighting off sleep at 11:00 p.m.

A few hours later, I awake, heart pounding. I push myself up to a seated position among the mounds in Pillow Land. The red glowing numbers on the clock read 3:04. The house is silent. The boys are sleeping. But now I'm wide awake. "That dream was so real. *Was* it a dream?" I'm talking to my dog, sound asleep on his back, upper limbs flopped open on the other side of the bed—Steven's side.

Trying to dissect the contents of the dream, I get quiet and attempt to recreate it in my mind. I close my eyes, assuming my memory will work better, and with calming, rhythmic breaths, I start to wind down into my quiet place deep inside.

I'm walking into a building—the police department—I'm taken aback, since I was planning to go there tomorrow. Maybe it's my mind setting things up? I follow the steps in my memory of the dream to see where it takes me. Now I'm looking at a poster of wanted suspects that could possibly fit the description of the stalker.

My dream continues outside the station, where the wind is blowing especially hard and bits of grass, scrap paper, and leaves are flying wildly about in a circular whirl, like water going down the drain. I grasp the sides of my sweater and pull them together as I push on to reach my car. There's no place like home, I sing quietly.

As I look up, I see a man wearing a black mask standing by my driver's side door. Our eyes meet as I dart across the street to get away from him. His eyes follow me, only turning his head to track my steps into the coffee shop across the street—a coffee shop I have visited dozens of times before when not dreaming. I disappear inside.

If my heart could jump out of my chest, it would right now. The coffee shop is filled with customers, so no one really notices me come in. I bob my head to the left and right, then run into the bathroom and hide. Crazy, the things you can do in dreams.

Sitting on a toilet in a locked stall becomes my hideout for the next several minutes. Oddly beautiful light-beige subway tiles make their way up the side of the wall to hip height, meeting a light brown-swirled wallpaper that covers the top half of the wall. The stall doors are a light pine, accented with chrome-locking mechanisms. They really put a lot of thought into this ladies' room, I think. I'll have to go back and check it out, for real, tomorrow.

Finally, my dream self seems to regain confidence and I storm out of the artfully designed ladies' room and back through the crowded coffee shop. I peek out the window and see that the wind has died down and the leaves and slips of paper are back to their original spots on the ground.

Suddenly I see a street sweeper come by, picking up the wind-blown trash and throwing it back in the garbage cans. The man who is driving the sweeper hops out, and with his microfiber cloth, walks right up to the window where I'm standing to wipe it clean. He lingers for a second, studies my face, and then hops back into his vehicle. I stand, frozen.

I snap back to consciousness.

Baffled, I grab a pillow and hug it to my chest. I can feel the little ends of the goose feathers poking through the crisp, baby-blue Egyptian cotton sheet. My faithful protector is still asleep next to me, whimpering and pretending to run in his sleep. Maybe he's having the doggie version of the nightmare I just had? He looks like he's smiling, however, so it's safe to say that rabbits are probably part of his dream.

The Village Hall, where I plan on getting to the bottom of my videotape mystery, is situated on a tree-lined street in Westin Heights. If someone didn't see the small white sign with black script identifying the building, they would think it was just an ordinary, historically preserved North Shore mansion, not a functional government building. It's one of the many ways the village planners have gone out of their way to retain the small-town look and feel of the downtown area. They also limit the amount of nationally recognized stores, restaurants, and businesses, instead reserving space for small business owners to thrive.

The local community has really embraced what this neighborhood offers, which is evident in the bustling foot traffic on any given Saturday afternoon. You need a reservation to eat at the trendy Double Day Grill, especially if you want a sought-after outdoor patio table on a balmy summer night. There's no need to schlep into the city for dinner and drinks with other couples, given our own hip spots. I do take note, however, that our little downtown could certainly use a cute bakery or breakfast spot. Something to think about for the future.

This morning is less busy, but I still sense the energy of the place as shopkeepers up and down the street start to open their doors—several of which lead to kids' stores, a sure sign we're not the only ones to move north for family-friendliness.

The folks living in this area are educated and affluent and want a quiet community to raise their children—safe and sheltered from the dangers of the outside world. It's the perfect place for us. Once this stalker is caught, it will still be a safe place to live. I think he's specifically targeting me, not this neighborhood.

Waiting in the entry area of the Village Hall makes me a little uncomfortable, as I have no desire to explain myself to anyone who may pop in, even though there are plenty of normal reasons why I would come here. I could be here to pay my utility bills or a parking ticket, or maybe I just needed to pick up a block party permit. To be on the safe side, I stealthily keep my sunglasses on and pretend to be deeply absorbed in the intricate pattern of the Oriental rug until I can talk with Sandy, the secretary working at the desk. *Let's hope the guy from last night's nightmare doesn't show up while I'm waiting.*

I continue to admire my surroundings while I wait my turn. The reception desk is made of a solid, dark-stained mahogany wood, adorned with beautiful carvings on the legs. It fits right into the small-town charm of the building. The adjacent chairs are upholstered with a paisley fabric, and a brass trashcan and magazine rack round out the scene—such elegance for a government building.

Finally, she's free. "Hi Sandy, I know it's an odd request, but I was wondering if you would be able to grant me access to video footage from the surveillance cameras on my street?" Realizing that my request is pushing the legal limits, I shoot her a pleading look, hoping, because she knows me, she'll do this one favor for me.

"Hey, Betsy. I wish I could, but the police came by earlier to check them out and told me not to let anyone have access to the files." Her sincere smile assures me that she means business. "Is everything okay? I mean, I know it's none of my business, but given that we know each other and our kids go to school together... should I be worried?" Her perfectly cut blonde bob glides across her collarbones and frames her angular chin.

Looking down at my shoes, I push around a small piece of lint, avoiding her gaze. "I know, Sandy, but I thought I'd ask," I reply, as my eyes slowly rise to meet her stare. "I'm not sure if there's anything to worry about or not. I'm not sure you know what's on the footage, but there's been some crazy notes, and... anyway, I just thought I'd look at what you guys had on film because my cameras at home didn't show any clear images of the jerk's face."

Sandy's jaw is ajar as she blinks and whispers, "Oh, good heavens, Betsy. I am so sorry this is happening to you." She glances over her shoulder and continues, "You know, since you already have a copy of your own footage, what harm would it do for you to have a copy of what we have?"

My face slowly forms a sly grin. I lower my voice and slide her a slip of paper. "I promise I won't show anyone. Our secret is safe with me. Here's the date and approximate time."

"Let's quickly look at this before my supervisor returns," Sandy says, typing away on her computer. After a moment, she stops at a video featuring my very own side door from the perspective of the streetlight camera at the corner. "This is the only digital file I have from the night you're concerned about." Sandy turns the computer screen so I can get a closer look. Together we scan the footage, then suddenly she hits pause.

"Oh, Betsy this is terrible. Were you robbed or something?"

"Oh, no. He's been snooping around my property and leaving rude notes," I say, not wanting to tell her too much. "Trust me, you know I've already talked to the police and they're on it."

Nodding, Sandy says, "I'm sure they are, but you know things around here can move at a snail's pace sometimes."

"I know, so to be sure I wanted to see if I could recognize any of his features from your footage myself." It's confirmed: that's the dude haunting both my dreams and my personal surveillance tapes.

Sandy's deep hazel eyes glance around the room to make sure we're still alone. We are. She leans in. "Listen, ordinarily, I'm not supposed to email digital files to anyone, but … let's just keep this between the two of us. I'll email it to you from my personal address so there won't be a trail."

"Thank you so much, Sandy," I reply. "I know Kyle has really enjoyed getting to know Sasha in class this year." I glance at her computer. "It'll be our little secret. See you at carpool pickup!"

I smile modestly, but, in my mind, I'm doing a fist pump, cheering for myself because I negotiated with her and saw those recordings. Unfortunately, it didn't turn up much, but it proved to me that I still have a way of getting what I want from people. I don't know if it's because I hone right in and relate to them on some level or another, or if it's just because I'm a nice person… or maybe it's simply because I look sweet and innocent. I'm sure the baby bump doesn't hurt, either. Frankly, I think it's all those things, combined.

Sandy doesn't seem too nosy, but the fact that she wants to keep this between us is probably a good idea—I don't want to see any terrified grade school moms running around Westin Heights. When I get home, I'm going to go through this footage again with a fine-toothed comb and see if I can make further headway about this guy, especially since he's trailing me in my dreams, too.

My cell phone rings as I'm leaving the building. I check the ID: Caller unknown. It could be the stalker.

"Hello?"

"I know you are looking for the videotape of my visit to your home… don't even think about telling the cops about this call." Hearing his voice sears my soul.

Panic pours through my entire body, tightening my chest and throat. I'm barely able to breathe. "I can track your number, jerk, so don't think you're going to get away with this!" I scream into my cellphone and then angrily end the call as I quickly pick my way between the bushes outside the Village Hall's back door. At this point I'm getting very agitated at this creep's gall. Sure, I'm scared, but he's starting to get gutsy. What is his end game?

Hoping no one has heard me, I begin to walk-jog to my car, glancing frantically across the street and behind my vehicle. Kitty-corner to where I'm standing sits the coffee shop, much like my crazy dream; except in my dream, I was in the police station—where I need to go next.

Our quaint neighborhood police station reminds me of the '60s television series *The Andy Griffith Show*, which took place in the small town of Mayberry, North Carolina. I used to watch the reruns with my little sister on TV Land, and would often wonder what it must have felt like for Andy to be a widower. The show really was about nostalgia and a small-town feel, much like the police department in my village. I wonder what the inept but well-meaning deputy, Barney Fife, would say about my current stalker crisis?

I head into the station and approach the front desk to see if I can get any updates on my case. I'm determined to get answers.

"Hello, Mrs. Ryan," says the female officer at the front desk after glancing at my ID, then tapping something into the computer. "This is regarding the threats made against you?"

I nod my head and reply, "Yes."

"Okay, I see here that Officer Flaggler visited you at your home a second time. The investigation is ongoing, and they're working every possible lead. What brings you here now? Another threat?"

My heart strikes inside my chest like a drum as I attempt to regain the confidence I found at lunchtime. "I'm inquiring as to whether there are any results from the fingerprints they took? And, I also wanted to report that I received another threatening call."

"Okay, just fill out this additional statement form and I'll add this incident to the report. I'll alert the detectives working on the case to be aware of the latest threat. They'll call you for any other details they might need. According to this report, the fingerprints have been sent out to the lab, but the results have not been returned yet."

I nod. "And how long does that usually take?"

As I start filling out the statement, she replies, "The results should be back in about a week." I groan, more audibly than I had anticipated, as she continues, "Mrs. Ryan, I can tell this is upsetting you, but rest assured, we have a very good department here and we will do everything in our power to protect and serve you. Remember to give us a call if anything else happens."

Once they read that he just threatened my life if I tell the cops, they'll probably put my case on the top of the pile. I can still hear his disgusting, vile voice over the phone: "I know you are looking for the videotape of my visit to your home… don't even think about telling the cops about this call." I couldn't hang up on him quick enough!

Walking out of the police department, glancing over my shoulder, I start nervously whistle-snapping the theme song to *The Andy Griffith Show* as I visualize little Opie walking down the street with a fishing pole. What would Andy do in this situation?

I lean against a pillar outside of the police department building, one palm against the cool limestone, forcing myself to think about reality, not television. I shake my head in disbelief. It still doesn't seem real that this is my life right now. Steven is *not* going to believe it when he hears about all of this. Thinking of Steven gives me pause. I miss his big, strong, and safe arms around me and my pregnant belly right now.

As I focus my attention on my baby, I realize my stomach is growling. I need to feed this baby; we're both starving. I find if I divert myself with delicious food, everything looks and feels better, even bad guys in masks making threatening calls. I'm glad the new threat will be added to my file, building a stronger case for fighting this madman. I take a quick look behind me, and throw back my shoulders defiantly and head out to lunch. I *will* stay strong.

———

As a foodie, I'm very particular about where I purchase my food, and who prepares it, for that matter. I'm always looking at their presentation techniques, the way they incorporate the ingredients, and the overall taste. Being a discerning tuna critic, I always end up going over to Foodstuffs near Good Faith Hospital, where they have the best tuna salad in town. They're located on a picturesque little street with a flower shop that has gorgeous arrangements in the window, a bakery, coffee shop, a fabulous '60s diner, and a sweet little park that the boys love to visit when we're over there.

I love tuna at lunchtime, but the doctor says that the risk of mercury in the fish can be dangerous to the baby, so I've been avoiding it. The problem is that I've been craving it so much lately. The doctor says that if I'm craving it, I probably need more essential fatty acids or protein. So, as suggested, I opt for chicken salad, even though it's just not the same.

As I wait, I can't help but appreciate the cozy gourmet look and feel of the place. The white subway tiles; chrome shelving filled with gourmet spices, seasonings, and hard-to-find delicacies; the bookshelves, overflowing with fabulous cookbooks; and the baskets on the floor, filled to the brim with freshly packed containers of chips, crackers, and cookies—all prepared on-location.

The salad bar is stocked with the best add-ons for the perfect salad-on-the-go, and the deli bar creates incredible sandwiches and premade salads and entrées. This is where my passion for Courtney's Tuna Salad was born. The folks working there make this unique version of tuna salad so special—keeping customers coming back for more.

Sitting at one of the wooden community tables next to the soup bar, I place my little green shopping basket next to my feet and ravenously rip into my lunch, consisting of chicken salad and split pea soup, all so fresh and delicious. After a few minutes of focused eating, when I'm feeling supremely satisfied (minus the unsatisfied tuna craving), I wipe the corners of my mouth with my napkin, pick up my basket, and head to the cashier to pay for my other items. Thinking ahead, I grab a roasted chicken and a side pasta salad for dinner. I throw in two frosted sugar cookies for the boys' dessert. I'll settle for the leftover fruit in the fridge.

While walking back to my car with a satisfied belly and tonight's dinner in tow, *my cell phone rings. It's the hospital. I'm suddenly afraid to answer. I hope Steven is okay.* "Hello?"

"Mrs. Ryan, this is Shirley Bowen from the ICU. Steven's doctor asked that I call you."

"Yes, of course. How is my husband?"

"Please, Mrs. Ryan, come to the hospital right away. Steven's condition has changed."

I fast walk over to my car and quickly tap in Dad's cell number—straight to voicemail.

"Dad, it's me. Listen, I'm getting ready to over to the hospital right now. They called me and said I had to come over quickly. Can you and Mom go grab the kids at school and bring them home? I'll call you after I know more." My breath fades as I push to get out as many words as possible.

When Dad was rushed to the hospital last year for his heart attack, we were in shock because he was in such great physical condition. The doctor told us that years of stress and the regular consumption of alcohol had led to heart disease. We were lucky... thanks to his regular walks on the beach with Mom, the episode didn't end tragically. Now he's healthier than he's been in years.

My mom was very calm and seemingly in control on the outside, but I could tell the undercurrent of sadness and worry had enveloped her soul. She is his rock, and he is hers; it almost seems that when one of them feels pain, the other one feels it, too. They are one and the same. After many years of marriage, they have found their groove and are sailing through retirement—happy and adventurous.

Luckily, Dad's medical event ended without devastation. But, with every passing moment, I'm becoming less sure we'll have the same outcome with Steven.

———————

The hospital is busier than usual today, so I wait in line before showing my ID to enter the ICU wing. I can see inside the impersonal rooms filled with medical machines, that every bed is filled, occupied by patients—either comatose or close to it—and sympathetic family members by their bedsides. I head for Steven's room at the end of the hall.

It's empty. Tears burn my eyes and a lump in my throat has me gasping for air. Frantically, I dart over to the nurse's station to find out where my husband is.

The same blonde nurse comes over to me, a too-cheery smile across her face. "Oh, Mrs. Ryan, I'm glad you were able to make it in. Your husband is in surgery. Once the doctor is finished, he will come to the waiting room and give you a full report."

"Surgery? What surgery? No one has told me anything!" I push her arm away as she tries to console me. "What happened?" I feel as though my questions are falling into the abyss, unanswered. I don't want to be consoled. I want to know what's going on.

"From my understanding, we did call you as soon as possible," she says soothingly. "That is why you are here now. I do know that Steven was stable and then had a sudden medical issue with his heart. So, please head over to surgery and wait for him there."

Feeling like a cog in the medical machine, I follow orders, turning on my heel and walking away. Anger propels my steps faster as I push the double doors open to attend to my post in the waiting room—a forlorn wife, floating in despair as her husband's life lies in the balance. His doctor holds his existence in his hands, and the future is unsure.

Watching reruns of *The Golden Girls* on a small-screen television in a very stark waiting room is not my idea of an afternoon delight; it's nothing like *The Andy Griffith Show*. I'm not in the mood to look at the flimsy, previously flipped-through *Good Housekeeping* and *People* magazines on the wooden rack over by the wall either. Half of the pages have been ripped out or earmarked by a previous occupier of these seats, and quite honestly, I don't really care what Kim Kardashian is up to these days, or how to decorate my living room on a shoestring budget. What I want are answers. How did Steven end up having a heart issue, and more importantly, *why the heck is all of this happening?*

Inhaling deeply and clearing my mind while thinking of butterflies isn't calming me down either. Agitation is boiling inside my gut, and I'm ready to blow my top. I look for a distraction. Glancing out the window, I see the blue sky is painted with strands of nondescript white clouds. Farther off in the distance, I can see the wide, unbalanced trunk of an oak tree, holding onto an infinite number of hand-shaped autumn leaves, together forming a canopy for the families of birds that pepper its branches. Swaying along with the windblown limbs and stems, I soothe my consciousness back into a meditative state.

Air escapes my lungs. With a yearning moan, I beckon my husband.

I know you are in surgery right now, honey, but please, if you can, let me know you are okay.

Silence, then I hear him. *I'm here.*

Warm relief floods over me. He can still communicate with me! I'm so worried about you.

Don't be, babe. I'll be okay.

What happened to you?

Go figure—a heart attack. Thankfully Dr. Abbott happened to be in the room when the alarms went off. They rushed me into surgery, but they're almost done. I can see them down below, working to close me up.

They performed a bypass grafting... can you believe it? I never realized that I had severe coronary heart disease, Betsy. Who would think that a guy in my condition and at my age would have that condition?

My stomach plunges as he speaks. I can't believe this! Please tell me you're not going to leave this Earth. I can't bear the thought of losing you, Steven.

I trust I will be okay. Don't worry. Soon our baby will be born.
Silence again.

———————

Wondering when the doctor is going to come in and tell me what I already know, I get up to stretch. It feels good to push my shoulders up and back while stretching out my lower back. Twisting my bent arms from left to right finds the crack I am searching for in my mid-back as Emmy Grace readjusts in my belly. Feeling rejuvenated from my lengthy meditative time in the waiting room, I decide to check back in with the nurse's station. I already know I'll have to come with my tail between my legs and offer regret for my past snotty behavior, so I step forward to present my justification.

Then I see the doctor approaching. "Mrs. Ryan," Dr. Abbot says. "I was just coming to find you to give you an update on Steven. He's experienced a—"

"Heart attack. I know."

He lowers his head and peers at me with his blue slits for eyes over his glasses. "We performed a coronary artery—"

"Bypass grafting, I know." *Why am I being passive aggressive? This doctor is just doing his job. I blame it on the stress.*

Confused, Dr. Abbott butts in. "How did you know that? Did our nurses tell you? They couldn't have known that. It was a last-minute procedure." He shifts his weight as his left hip pushes out slightly. His small yet muscular build commands respect.

"Well, I just assumed," I offer, as I inconspicuously rub my lying nostrils. "My father had a similar incident last year." *Stop it, Betsy. This guy is here to help!*

"Whatever the case, he's resting in recovery right now, but you won't be able to talk to him because he still isn't conscious."

"I understand. Can I please just peek in on him?"

He checks his watch. "You can go in now, and we'll talk later when we know more."

"Okay. Thank you very much, doctor." I look over at the nurse who had been the subject of my earlier attitude and give her a nod and look that says, *I'm sorry*. She nods back and smiles.

"Mrs. Ryan. You have my phone number, but we'll call you if anything should come up," Dr. Abbot says as he walks away. I've heard that before. I hope I can believe him this time. *Stop it, Betsy. Direct your anger at the stalker, not the person who is taking care of your husband.*

Entering my house with a smile on my face has never been so hard to do. I'll continue to wear this mask of lies in front of my sons until Steven is stable enough where I can bring them to the hospital to see him—if at all. I'm not sure I want them to see Steven like this. Barney probably thinks I've abandoned him, except for the quick micro-walks I've been giving him lately.

After hugs, kisses, and updates on their day at school, the boys run off to their rooms to play and do homework. Kindergarten homework is primarily coloring or matching pictures with letters, but to Morgan, it's still "big boy" homework, and he takes it very seriously. Kyle, on the other hand, has assumed the position at my office desk for the past couple of months so he can "focus and work hard."

"Dear, thank you for your message. Now that the boys are out of the room, fill us in," Dad starts, holding a tall glass of lemonade, his favorite.

Mom is standing at the sink, rinsing her cup. "Yes, and by the way, I can't believe it takes this long to get fingerprint results back. I'm sure they're taking your case seriously, but I wish there were more aggressive action they could take on your behalf."

Shaking my head, I reply, "I'm not sure, Mom, that's just how things are done—red tape. That's why I've decided to keep focusing on solutions and try to figure out who is doing this on my own. Maybe then I can convince the authorities to speed things up." I clear my throat. "Meanwhile, I have an update on Steven's condition."

"Okay, so fill us in. Ever since your message earlier, we've been waiting on pins and needles." Dad places his drink down and joins me at the table.

"Steven has had a heart attack."

"Oh, my God!" Dad pauses and looks down at the table for a brief second then continues, "But he's so young! What's happening now?"

I know they're feeling the stress of Steven's medical condition and the stalker as much as I am, but I need to explain the out-of-the-ordinary occurrence I had with Steven today so they'll believe me. "I understand it sounds weird, but Steven intuitively spoke to me while he was in surgery."

I see my Dad's signature furrowed brow. I know he's taking this seriously. Mom is fixed on every word I'm saying.

"Now, hear me out. He told me that he had experienced a heart attack and that they were performing coronary artery bypass grafting surgery on him. Then when the doctor spoke to me after Steven was out of surgery, he told me the exact same thing."

"Well, I'll be darned. You *are* a psychic!" Dad laughs, a combination of disbelief and desperation. "I had my doubts, but that's incredible... but so, so sad for Steven. You must be worried."

"Yeah," I reply. "I'm still trying to take it all in."

"Well, don't worry, honey, I'll talk to him about the walking and healthy eating program your father has been doing since his surgery last year. He will be okay. I just know it. In the meantime, let's find out who is torturing you with these letters and that call, and do something about it."

"Correction: *calls*, with an 's.' I got a second call earlier today after I left the Village Hall to check out the video footage. The footage should have been emailed to me by now, come to think of it…" I shut my eyes and try to remember exactly what the voice said to me on the phone. "Anyway, on the phone he told me, *I know you've gone to the cops. I'm watching you.* I already added information about this call to the police record."

Dad jumps in. "Are you kidding me? How does he know this? He must be following you everywhere, at various times of the day."

Barney runs over next to my chair, where I nestle in with my big cup of hot caramel tea. He's making odd sounds, as if he's trying to get my attention. Reaching over to place my steaming mug on a coaster, I squat down to scratch him under his chin. He wiggles under my touch and then rolls over to get a belly rub. Giving in, I use both hands and stroke his soft, pink belly.

"There isn't anything I can do," I reply, as I stand up and grab my mug, and meet my parents over at the kitchen table. The late day sun glares in Dad's eyes as he shifts in his seat.

Taking another drink of lemonade, he offers, "Betsy, there is something we could do. We could call someone, like a security guard, to watch over the house, maybe even follow you around town."

I let out a weak laugh and look away, catching a glimpse of the bright sunshine flooding through my first-floor windows— grasping at snippets of joy wherever I can find them. I turn back to my father. "Do you know how crazy that sounds, and how expensive that would be? I do think the police are taking it seriously, but we also have to be on our toes."

Barney rolls over and paws at my arm.

"What is it, boy?"

Garrrooof.

A strong intuition zeros in on my mind, *the bad man was with Steven. Before the heart attack and when the doctor came to fix him.*

The realization numbs me. I slowly stand up, grab my father's arm, and squeeze my nails into his skin through his Oxford shirt. I look out the windows, turning my head left, right. No one is watching, at least as far as I can see. I let go of Dad's arm and run to check the door locks, one by one. My parents are now standing, watching me scurry through the house, stunned.

"What are you doing? What's wrong?" Dad calls out.

"A thought came to me that the stalker was in Steven's room before he had his heart attack. Perhaps the mystery 'brother,' who the nurses told me about. Guys, I *must* go back to the hospital and find out if Steven's thoughts can identify the man. Dad, let's go back over there. Mom, can you stay here and feed the boys and Barney?"

Mom replies with an exhaustive exhale, "Consider it done. Be careful." I'm sure she doesn't know what to believe about my intuition with Steven and the stalker.

While driving along the twisting road back to the hospital, Dad doesn't speak. My mind is set on autopilot; I could drive this route with my eyes closed at this point. The twilight haunts me with thoughts of the night and the unknown. Where is he lurking and why is he doing this to me? There should be some explanation. Could it be a stranger? He knows so much about me, though, so it must be someone I know… but who is it?

After pulling into the same parking spot I occupied earlier today, I grab my black patent leather purse, making sure it's zipped, and start walk-running toward the hospital entrance with my father right behind me. Baby gives a sharp little kick, pulling my attention down to my belly, and I gently rub the tiny foot through my skin to let her know I feel her. When I look up again as we near the hospital entrance, I find myself face to face with Dr. Deller.

"Oh, Dr. Deller," I say, surprised. "What are you doing here? I mean—hi. This is my father, Cary Anderson."

"Betsy, Mr. Anderson! Hello. I was just in a meeting with my partner, Dr. Hildebrandt, and a couple of other doctors, on the fourth floor. How is Steven doing?"

"Well, truth be told, not so good. He actually had a heart attack earlier, and has already had surgery."

My father is standing close behind me, almost as if he's holding me up and protecting me from any possible threat.

"I'm so sorry to hear that," Dr. Deller says, with a look of concern on his face. "You must be so upset!"

"Yeah, it's just… a lot to handle. The doctors told me earlier to go home and let him rest."

I decide to share with him what's going on with Steven. At some point, I need to pick a side and trust him or not. After all he disclosed to me about his wife communicating with him when she was dying, it's clear: he's the only one who completely understands what I'm experiencing with Barney and Steven.

"While I was at home talking with my parents, I got a strong feeling that something terrible happened to Steven, urging me to come back. Call it intuition or ESP, I don't know. Anyway, I'd like to hurry inside."

My dad is still standing behind me, nodding in agreement as the twilight starts to creep up behind us, painting a gloomy backdrop. I'm shocked and amazed that this is my life right now.

"Oh, my gosh! Given what you've shared with me about your recent intuition, it's a good idea to get back up to the ICU and check on him. Do you want me to come in with you and confirm this and see if we can get some answers? Sometimes hospital staff will be more cooperative with other doctors."

"Betsy, we should get in there." My dad gentle guides my arm as we move towards the door.

"You're right. Let's go. Dr. Deller, I think visiting hours are only for another hour."

"It'll be okay," he says as he leads the way. Dad and I file in behind him. "You're with a doctor, so hopefully we'll get answers fast."

Feeling more confident and secure with my doctor, Dad and I follow the curve of the sidewalk into the brightly lit entrance of the hospital.

"Hello, I'm Dr. Deller," my doctor offers as he steps up to the reception desk. "I'm here with my patient, Betsy Ryan, and her father, Cary Anderson, to see her husband, Steven." He hands over our IDs and his hospital badge.

"Thank you, doctor. His room is just down the hall." It's a receptionist I've seen before. "Mrs. Ryan, you remember where his room is, yes?"

"I do, thanks." I nod as Dad gently places his hand behind my back to continue moving me along. His shaking hand mirrors my worry.

The ICU is so eerie at night, with the blinking lights, hum of the life support machines, and the lack of audible conversation in the rooms. You could hear a pin drop, which fills me with thoughts of the many arguments I've had with my husband. I can hear the screams and doors slamming. We have a chance to make things right. He needs to make it through this operation.

We head into Steven's room. He looks so tranquil lying in his bed. I know he must be out of it, because I've slept in hospital beds before, and they are not comfortable at all. His usually golden skin is starting to look ashen as the hours and days pass with him still in this unconscious state.

Dr. Deller picks up Steven's chart, handily clipped to the end of the bed, and reads it to himself. With a look of deep thought on his face, he studies it, holding his chin in his hand. The warmth from Dad's body permeates me as we wait, glancing between my doctor and my husband, hoping for news from one and a sign from the other.

The room is deathly still, cold and impersonal. I wonder if I should bring flowers or a card or something the next time I come, just to soften the unemotional feel. In the corner is a wooden chair with ugly upholstery next to a rolling adjustable table that can be used by the patient, when or if they become conscious again. The trashcan next to the chair is empty, proof that family or friends have not enjoyed a snack, or anything for that matter, to toss in the bin during a visit. Maybe I should be staying here longer when I come to see him? It's just that I don't know what to do. After Steven stops communicating with me, my thoughts return to the stalker I'm tracking.

The door opens, derailing my rambling thoughts as we're abruptly interrupted by Henry, the janitor who works at Dr. Deller's office. I didn't realize he worked in this building, too.

"Oh!" he says, shifting uncomfortably and looking like he wants to get out of here, fast. "I didn't realize there were visitors. Scuse me." As he finishes, he is already wheeling his cleaning cart back through the door.

My mind is racing. Why would a janitor from my doctor's office building be working here, too? Or be parked by my son's school? And why, of all rooms, would he be cleaning up this one? It's quite the coincidence … or maybe it's not a coincidence at all.

"Henry, it's okay," Dr. Deller says. "Were you coming in just to empty the trash or clean up?"

"I'll come back later," he says and disappears.

"That's odd. Did you know that Henry also works here?" I ask Dr. Deller.

Dad chimes in. "Yes, that's peculiar, don't you think?"

He shrugs. "Not really. Since our office building is part of the large surrounding hospital campus, the custodial staff is shared."

"Hmm, okay," I sigh, not wanting to get into why I find this so fishy. I look at Dad and raise my eyebrows, indicating that we'll discuss this later.

"So, having looked over Steven's chart, I can confirm what you've been told already." My doctor reads from the chart. "He's stable, which is a blessing, but the surgery was a major one, as you know, so the best thing you can do for him now is to wait and pray."

"I have been," I say. "But how much can a person take?"

He puts the chart back and turns to me. "Steven is a strong person, but he'll need to be here for at least a few more days. In my opinion, it doesn't look like there's anything suspicious happening here. The doctors have been pretty transparent with their notes, so, at this point, I think they're right that it's best for you to go home, get some rest, and spend some time with your sons." He finishes with a warm smile and look of assurance.

I smile in return, trying to sound relieved as I say, "Thank you for everything. We're going to stay here for a little while. I'll let you know if I hear anything. I'll see you soon."

"All right. Betsy, Mr. Anderson, I'll be thinking of you. I hope Steven recovers quickly. I'll see you next week, Betsy."

There's no time to waste; as soon as we're alone, I close the door to Steven's room gently, so it doesn't make a loud click.

"Dad, if you don't mind, can I meet you at the cafeteria in about fifteen minutes? I want to sit quietly with Steven for a bit."

"Not a problem, I'll grab some coffee and read the paper. Take your time."

Alone, I dim the lights and settle into the ugly, uncomfortable chair next to the bed and mentally reach out to my husband. I zero in on him despite all the tubes and wires and the IV pumping in medicine to control his blood circulation and pressure.

Steven, it's me. I'm alone and want to check in with you. I know that the surgery went well. Dr. Deller checked your chart and says you're doing okay, but you need your rest so I won't stay long. I want to get home to the boys, but wanted to tell you I love you.

His quick response catches me off guard.

I knew you were here, honey. I could feel you, Cary, and Dr. Deller in the room with me. I'm doing okay, but I'm really worried about you. Your energy seems so drained.

Oh, Steven. it's so nice to hear your voice. I've been worried about so much. I take a breath. I'll get right to the point. I had a strong intuition that someone you didn't know visited you today before your heart attack. Is that true?"

I want desperately to ask about his so-called brother's visit yesterday, but I don't want to cause him any extra stress.

Honestly, I don't know. This whole accident and heart attack has really taken its toll, and I don't seem to have one hundred percent awareness all the time. When a strong energy of love is near me, I can identify the presence—especially when you directly speak to me. I did sense your fear when you came in the room. Please don't worry about me, just take care of the boys, baby, Barney, and yourself. I wish I could help, but I'm just so tired…

I sit silently receiving the response from his motionless body, lips unmoving.

Oh, honey, I understand; please don't worry. I am concerned about your health, but I know you're in good hands.

I realize that based on what Steven is sharing, he's not reading my mind, the way I thought. Instead, he's somehow picking up energy—positive or negative, my desire to communicate. Given this, I need to clarify what it is I'm trying to figure out when I tap into his consciousness. I realize that if I tell him the visitor could have been a threat, it could impact his health and healing.

I'm about to give up when he says, Betsy, I did pick up the energy of a man coming into my room earlier.

Who was it?

Someone I've seen before.

My heart begins to race. Wait, Steven, you're telling me you've seen this man before? Where? When?

Silence.

This is important! I beg him to hear me. I need to know who it was… Steven!

Silence.

Knowing that he's checked out for now, I try to get in one last thought before I leave. *I love you!* He needs to know I care about him.

Back at the house, we give Mom full details about running into Dr. Deller and my talking with Steven, as well as updates on his medical condition. We also share our suspicion of Henry and his barging in on us.

She lets out a vanquished sigh. "Betsy, I truly believe he should be the prime suspect because he's always lurking around. It just seems too coincidental."

"I understand, Mom, but I'm not totally convinced yet, and am not ready to rule everyone else out."

"Understood, dear."

Dad ends our update with Dr. Deller's expectation that Steven will slowly but surely recover.

"Well that last bit is good news," she says. "We need all the good news we can get because the boys are starting to wonder why he hasn't called them in the last few days. I keep telling them he's busy at work, but sooner or later, they won't buy that."

"I know, Mom, I have to talk to them about Steven. And I will. But what I'm most stuck on now is identifying this mystery man who's gone into Steven's room twice now. I can only assume this person is also the so-called brother. The hospital staff claim they ask for ID from visitors to the ICU, but I can't help but wonder if it's someone that works on the hospital campus, which would include the two adjacent buildings and the offices of Dr. Deller and Dr. Hildebrandt. The custodial staff works in several of the buildings on the medical campus, too."

"Honey, have you thought that, if it's not the janitor, then maybe your doctor is involved in some way?" Mom gets up from the kitchen table, stands for a moment, and then hastily crosses the room to make sure the side door is locked. "I can't believe we forgot to do that earlier!"

My eyes follow her, waiting for the follow-up comment.

"Look, dear, all I'm saying is that we have to consider all suspects. I know you like your doctor, but hear me out. You've got to admit that you've been his patient for many years.

Maybe he's developed some deranged crush on you. Cary, what do you think?"

"Karen, it's hard to know which one of these guys is the culprit."

I understand what she's saying because I do have a nagging hunch that something just isn't right with him or his office. I can't put my finger on it, though. Could my doctor, who has access to my personal information in his files, be stalking me like some sick and twisted teenager?

"Mom, I agree with you… but let's look at this for a minute." I motion for her and Dad to come back to the table and sit with me as Barney runs over and sits by my feet. I take a swig of my water and continue. "If, in fact, my doctor *is* out to get me, and has been sending me filthy letters that seem like they were written by a bunch of crude, shipwrecked sailors, then why has he also been so kind and sympathetic to me in real life?"

"Well, that's simple. If he's guilty, he's not going to let on, is he?"

Mom is the one who got me hooked on the television series, *Murder, She Wrote,* when I was younger. She has the same sleuthing skills that I picked up from the show. "True. But then what do you suggest I do? Just stop seeing my doctor a month before my baby is born? Give birth at home in the tub?" Barney *chuffs* in agreement.

For a few days, while I was pregnant with Kyle, I'd flirted with the idea of having a home birth. I researched doulas, birthing tubs, and doctors who would be open to that type of delivery. The idea was squashed quickly after I talked with another mom who'd birthed at home. The part about floating in a warm tub of water in a dimly lit room was enticing, but the thought of gut-wrenching pain without medication ruined it for me. Not having thought about that aspect, I came home and immediately told Steven that I had changed my mind. I gave birth in the hospital—with an epidural, thankfully.

"Honey, we know that's unrealistic. What your mother is trying to say is to be careful, that's all."

"Yes, be careful. But there must be a way to get to the bottom of this without you having to switch doctors. Perhaps while we continue to round up clues, you should act like everything is normal with him." Seeing Mom in "solution" mode is more inspiring than observing the stress in her body over the past couple of days. It's nice she's turning anxiety into action. I need to follow her lead. My father is her perfect wingman, always supporting her ideas.

"Everything *is* normal with him," I remind her. "At least, as of right now."

"I understand how you must be feeling, darling. Just make sure you always bring someone with you when you go from now on."

"Seriously, who has that kind of time, Mom? I go in there twice a week to check on the baby, or for my ultrasound—it's quite the time commitment."

"If we're not free to join you, I'm sure your friend Misty would go along," Dad says.

My mom nods her head in agreement.

The doorbell's chime interrupts our conversation as Misty uses her key to enter. "Hey, neighbor, how's it going in baby land? More importantly, how's Steven?" Dressed in a tight pair of yoga pants, a pink tank top, and a matching zipper jacket, with dewy droplets glistening above her lip, Misty could've just run over from the gym.

"Misty, I'm so glad to see you. We were just talking about some things. Why don't you join us for some tea while I fill you in?" I top off my lukewarm tea with a dollop of hot water from the kettle, add a packet of Stevia, and turn back to the conversation.

"Great," she says, "but do you mind if I get myself a water instead?" I nod as she grabs a bottle of mango-flavored water from the fridge.

"So, get me up to speed, folks. My daughters are at their father's house for the weekend, so I asked if they could stay an extra night tonight. I figured you could use some extra help around here."

"Oh, wow!" I suppress the urge to jump up and hug her. "Thank you, Misty. You're the best. Now let's get serious and kick some stalker butt!" A spark of excitement races through me. It feels good to be excited about doing something other than sitting around waiting to be attacked.

"Yes, let's. You, feisty little mama, you!"

Dad clears his throat, his brown eyes flashing *serious*. "Okay, girls, here's the plan. Mom and I will stay here late until Betsy and the boys go to sleep and lock up as usual. Tomorrow, when she goes to the doctor, Misty, you can drive her over there and stay in the car to stake out the parking lot while she's inside. With the staff and nurses, Betsy should be fine at the appointment. My concern is in the parking lot, because anyone could be lurking there in between cars or by the buildings."

My mom chimes in, "We have our eye doctor appointment in the morning, but we'll come straight back here afterward. Does that work for everyone?"

"I'm game to do anything, Mr. and Mrs. Anderson. I've always wanted to be a Secret Service agent." Misty assumes the shooting pose for added effect. Mom squints her eyes in distaste but doesn't voice her thoughts. Luckily, Misty doesn't notice.

"Fine by me. I'm happy to know I don't have to go over there alone." The spark of enthusiasm for our plan gives me hope and emboldens my belief that with their help, I can defeat this madman. "Misty, I'll drop the boys off at school then swing by and pick you up on the way to my appointment, okay?"

"Sounds like a plan," she replies. My new bodyguard gives a quick nod of her head and salutes me. Her dedication and energy is contagious.

Looking around the room at my security detail, tears of relief flood my eyes—falling quickly to my cheek, and trickling to the end of my jawbone, then onto my lap. There is no stopping this flood of emotion. Now that I have a chance of identifying this unknown enemy or preventing a potential attack, the release is overwhelming.

I peek through the slits between my eyelids, halfway amid sleep and reality. The pink, billowy clouds covering the rising sun remind me of cotton candy. Smiling, I roll over and see my loyal companion sitting on the floor, at attention, next to my side of the bed.

I imagine he's asking, *Mom, can we please go outside?* He tilts his head to the side.

"It's so early, buddy, go back to sleep. I don't have to get up for another hour and a half." I stuff the body pillow between my legs and squeeze my thighs together, forcing the feathers to retreat to both ends.

Resolutely, my dog stands his ground; the moan in his throat reverberates like an old door creak. He's not giving up. He must really have to go.

"Okay, geez!" Rolling over onto my side, swinging my legs over the side of the bed, my toes meet my slippers. Balancing baby, we pad over to the bathroom to let mama pee first, then get dressed quickly and brush my teeth. Since I'm up this early I decide we could use a real walk this morning, not just our usual in-and-out experience that we've been doing the past few days.

I slip on a loose pair of brown maternity yoga pants, long-sleeved T-shirt, and a baggy white sweatshirt with zipper pockets that should keep me warm. I'm thankful it still fits over my ever-growing bump. I slide my sneakers on and pull my messy curls into a ponytail at the back of my head, positioning it directly into the adjustment hole in my baseball cap. Next I glide a thin layer of pink lip balm across my lips, lather a layer of moisturizing sunblock over my face and neck, and zip downstairs with my pup, grabbing my house key and phone to text Misty.

I quickly send her a text message to see if she's already up and working out, and ask her to come over to my house in case the boys wake up while I take the dog on a much-needed long walk to the beach to regroup and get some fresh air.

She quickly types back, "Sure, gimme a couple of minutes."

Confirming on the antique grandfather clock in the hall that it is indeed 5:35 a.m., I know that I have a good hour before I should be home to wake the boys for school. It's Friday, which means they'll be raring to start the weekend.

A few minutes later, Misty locks the door behind me, ensuring my sons are safe and secure as I head out into the early morning light for a brisk walk with my buddy. I put my pepper spray in my pocket, just in case I need it. However, I can't imagine my stalker being up at this hour.

———

While we walk along the desolate sidewalk at dawn, I think fondly of how often Barney and I have enjoyed early morning walks to the beach—just the two of us and a random squirrel or seagull.

This morning, the beach is deserted and peaceful, but I keep Barney on his leash until I'm completely sure there are no other dogs present. He tends to be very protective and will sometimes charge at other animals, including innocent ones. I don't think I have the capacity to run and chase him down today.

The rising sun, coming from the east—the Michigan side of the lake—pops up slowly from what looks like the end of the earth, making its entrance for the day. The orangey-pink sprinkles float on the rippling surface of the water, reflecting on the dotted collection of boats in the harbor. The shiny rays of hope bring a new day.

The temperature near the lake is always cooler, with a slight breeze. I close my eyes to take in the fresh lake air bathing my face and the sounds of the seagulls grabbing their breakfast. My big sweatshirt is just enough to break the slight whining wind at my back.

The waves gently make their way to shore in a slow, melodious way, rhythmically setting the pace for our walk along the moist surface beneath our feet. With each step, the squish-squish soothes my senses and eases my mind, opening it completely—a good habit I learned while meditating.

Barney is walking one step ahead, keeping our pace as he swishes his head back and looks at me, as if to say, *Mom, I love walks.*

I decide to take this time and let him know what's been going on lately. Not knowing if he understands me or not, I try.

"Barney, I'm sorry I've been so busy and have cut down on our walk time. I'm so worried about Daddy, the baby, and the bad man who's bothering me."

I imagine his response. *I'll help get that bad man. I love you, Mom.*

I know this dog would do anything for me, and I for him. My imaginary conversation with him gives me a secure feeling, almost as if I were out walking with a friend.

Ahead, dead, smelly fish washed up on the shore interrupt our walk; I gently tug at Barney's leash, reminding him to *leave it.* He agrees, with some hesitation, and we continue northbound on our trek. Further past the foul odor, I inhale a cleansing breath through my nose, feeling the rigidity release from my upper back and neck as I exhale through my mouth, gently pressing out a resounding *ahhh*. I realize how taut and stress-filled my body has become these last few days.

After a few peaceful moments, I can no longer ignore the gnawing feeling in my stomach, so we stop to take a little treat break. I unzip the plastic bag stashed in my pocket and toss my companion a freeze-dried lamb treat while I enjoy a small piece of a mint chocolate Balance Bar. Leaning against a large, moss-covered rock, I look back across the beach and realize just how far we've walked. The path ahead is filled with jagged, slippery rocks and slimy, seaweed-covered sand. Opting to avoid bringing home a gunky, sandy mess, we turn around to head back to where we started.

Out of nowhere, Barney pulls on the leash and begins growling. Tugging gently, I tell him to *sit*. I survey the beach, looking back and forth, up and down. There are no dogs, people, or small animals anywhere that I can see. Wondering what could have spooked him, a shiver passes through me. I resume our walk, a bit slower now—calculating our next move, should I have to *run* for it. My house is about six blocks away from the beach entrance and we are about five blocks from there. There is no way I can run over a mile with a dog and baby in tow.

I hold Barney with one hand as I casually reach with my other hand to locate my left pocket—the one that contains my pepper spray. I unzip it and slide my hand inside to gently flip the toggle to the "on" position. I partially re-zip my pocket to keep my weapon accessible, if needed. With the hairs on my arm sticking straight up, I walk nonchalantly, darting my eyes from side to side. All clear. *Betsy, don't let your mind play tricks on you.*

Nothing spooks Barney for the remainder of our walk along the beach, and we make it back to the entrance leading up to the sidewalk unharmed. Letting down my guard and the recurring strain in my neck and shoulders, I kneel to scratch my pal's head and ears. It's now 6:15 a.m., according to my

Fitbit. We are on track to walk nearly four thousand steps this morning. Not bad for the start of the day.

A twinge in my chest alerts me to Barney, who is fixated on a spot down the beach. He's driving forward nonstop and won't give in to my tugs to *stay*.

I glance over to the rock where he's looking, trembling and hoping he only sees another dog or maybe even a seagull.

Not taking any chances, afraid that whoever is over there will pick up on the fact that I am aware of them, I don't look up; instead, I slowly stand then pivot on my toes. "Heel," I whisper, and we dart up the hill, stride for stride, to the main road. Looking over my right shoulder and through the thick trees, I can't spot anyone following us, but I continue to run-walk across the intersection and down my street—just four more blocks.

Breathing is difficult because my air passages are being squeezed from the pounding pulses of the racing blood through my veins. Not wanting to stop and catch my breath, I forge onward, unable to believe this can be happening again. Just like ten years ago. I'm surprised at my endurance.

"Come on, Barney, Mom has to get home. I don't want to see that bad man."

This phrase seems to get through to my dog because now he's running much faster than usual. I imagine him saying as he shoots his worried eyes up to me as he continues to run, *That bad man kills birds.*

"Yes, he does, Barney."

He's scary, Mom. Let's go.

I continue to see no sign of my stalker on the street we're on—and we're just two blocks from home.

WOOOOF! Arooof!

Ahead and to the left I finally see the man, masked and dressed in black, forging through the yard between my house and Misty's—no more than fifty feet from my entrance. I realize he must've run down the alley as we ran down the street. He really knows this neighborhood, that's for sure.

"Misty!" I scream as if my life and heart depends on it. I pull my pepper spray from my pocket, hold it up, and take a shooting stance. Barney is growling and barking furiously. The masked man stops dead in his tracks, looks left, then right. The sound of metal sliding on wood comes from our screen door as Misty opens it, spooking him. He darts back between the houses, through the yard, and disappears into the alley.

Deflated, I fall to my knees and hug my savior. My confidence is chipped away as I slide my pink weapon back into my pocket.

"Barney, you saved me."

His tail wagging, my dog gives me sloppy, wet kisses that fill my cheeks and chin. I welcome them. He knows what he did.

Misty, dressed in sweat-stained workout shorts and a thin T-shirt, wraps her sweater around her shivering arms and exposed legs. She runs over to me. I'm gasping for air.

"What happened, Betsy?" she shrieks. "Why were you screaming?"

"The stalker... the stalker was following me back from the beach. He must've noticed that Barney and I spotted him so he slid over to the alley—" I'm slowly catching my breath, "—to our house. He came between our yards and was heading straight for us. I should've let Barney loose to get him, but I didn't want my dog to get hurt. I held up my pepper spray and I think he heard the door open, so he must've gotten scared off."

Misty stands, transfixed, as red flushes her cheeks. "That *bastard*. How dare he come through our yard! He should thank his lucky stars, because next time, I will shoot his butt, you can be sure of that." She helps me up. "Let's get you inside, so you can get your kiddos ready for school while I call the police. I'll let them know that you are okay and don't want the kids to be upset with them coming over to talk to you right now, so I'll handle the report. If they still want to speak with you, I'll call you, but let me handle it. Just relax and get the boys up for school. Are you okay right now?"

"Yes, I'm okay. He didn't touch me, just scared the crap out of me." I put a hand on my stomach. "The baby's doing flips. I'll wake the boys and get them ready for school." I give her an extra-long hug and look down at my dog. "Come on, Barn, let's get in the house." To Misty, I say, "I'll see you after drop-off. And thank you."

"Sounds good. And lock your doors. Once the coward sees the cops pull up to my place, he won't be within a thousand yards of here, rest assured. That S.O.B."

———————

Barney enjoys it when I towel-dry his fur, like a massage; and after the beach incident, both of us could use some tension relief. I find such joy simply petting his rich, chocolaty fur and little white bootie paws—they're so regal. We could have named him Boots, but that would've been too ironic.

Trying to put aside the events that took place this morning, I focus on the peaceful parts of our beach walk, like the gorgeous view and feeling of serenity I had, if only for a few minutes. How dare that bully try to ruin that for us! I put him out of my mind and get down to business. "Are you ready to eat, big guy?"

Barney's wagging and smiling at me as he *chuff-chuffs, yes,* in agreement. Human words can't describe the relationship dogs have with their food.

I set down his big, blue bowl, which is now brimming with kibble and lamb patty, beside his clear water bowl, which I've topped off for an after-breakfast swig. I decide to leave the first-floor shutters closed, and double-check the locks on the patio door, front entrance, and side door, then trot upstairs to take a quick shower before the boys wake up.

———————

Kyle and Morgan love my breakfasts. I usually make a lot of food so I can give them a chance to try different things. This is a great way to form a little chef's palette, and it helps me forget that I'm missing my career in the kitchen. I start by slicing fruit, then arrange the pieces by color on a glass plate, adding a side of yogurt, topped with honey and cinnamon for dipping, to ensure they'll try to eat *some* of the fruit. Ordinarily, I make homemade pancakes, but today, with lack of time, I pop two mini bagels into the toaster oven.

Fresh-squeezed orange juice is easy to make in a jiff and is always worth the effort. My boys love the little bits of pulp that rise to the top of the glass, which they poke at gleefully with their tongues. I whip that up, then grab two precooked hard-boiled eggs from the refrigerator, crack and roll them on the counter, peel the remaining bits of shell from the firm egg white, and slice them in half to present to my diners. Kyle likes to sprinkle pepper and salt on his; Morgan likes his plain. Kyle seems to have the palate of a chef; Morgan, not so much.

After our hearty feast, I am beginning to feel balanced again. This morning was not pretty, but thankfully I've got a smart, thoughtful neighbor on my side.

"Let's go, kiddos, time for school," I announce.

"Mommy, do you like the outfit that I picked out for school?" Kyle asks.

"Yes, Kyle, you look dashing." He's dressed to impress someone today, with his khaki pants and navy polo shirt. Maybe Sasha?

I flip on the radio as we pull out of the garage. I look both ways, praying not to see the man with the black mask. "*Dream On*" by Aerosmith is playing on the radio. I've never really listened to this song until now, but as Steven Tyler's trademark high, throaty voice sings about how acknowledging that death could be only a day away, I start to pay attention. The song is like a live-for-the-moment anthem, which I find ironically inspirational right now. Wondering which angel above sent this song to me today, I trust that I'm protected, pushing aside the worries that have been rocking me to my core.

Pulling up to school is always a bittersweet moment for me; I hate to see my sons leave, but I also welcome the handful of hours to get things done. Today consists of visits to Dr. Deller, Steven, and the police department, if they need me to come by and sign the statement from today's beach incident.

"Bye, Mommy," the boys sing out.

"Love you, boys! See you soon!"

"Mommy?" Kyle hesitates, turns on his heels and asks, "When is Daddy coming home? I miss him."

I've been dreading this moment. "Soon, baby, soon. Hey, I have an idea. Why don't we make a welcome home card after school, for when Daddy returns?"

"Okay, Mommy. Have a fun day."

Pulling away from the carpool curb, I edge my car slowly along, stealing a last peek at my angel babies as I go to confront the day. The parents behind me toot their horn. Ordinarily I'd get testy with them and honk back, but today, I'm resolving to think and be positive.

Speaking of positive, I'll call Misty and let her know I'm on the way.

Making this familiar car ride with Misty, my personal Secret Service agent, is kind of nice. There are days when I roll through the motions, feeling somewhat lonely, so to have a sidekick is a much-welcomed addition. My passenger is dressed like the typical suburban mom with a rich ex-husband. Her uniform consists of J. Crew khakis, blue suede Salvatore Ferragamo loafers, an olive-green Tory Burch tunic, and a Coach handbag that I know contains her water bottle, lipstick, and gun. She's moving past her suburban persona and into the security guard role perfectly—but much better dressed.

"The police added the information to the report, but want you to stop by to finalize and sign it," she says. "They'll add it to the file. I asked them to patrol the neighborhood more this week. They agreed."

"Thank you for handling that for me. I'll swing by later. I don't know how I would've explained the police coming by again to my sons. I'm certain they must suspect something."

"As far as when we get to the appointment, do you want me to wait in the car and keep a lookout for any strange guys wearing a dark bomber jacket, boots, or even a mask?"

I nod. "Yeah, that would be great. I'll be perfectly safe with Donna and the other patients in the waiting room."

"Just keep an eye out, keep your pepper spray handy, and your phone accessible. I'll text you if I see anything fishy."

"Yes, ma'am."

When we get to the doctor's office, I exit my car from the driver's side while Misty hops out of the passenger side and runs over to enter my open door. Walking away, I look back at her, and she shoots me a thumbs-up.

Keeping my wits about me, I walk, head high, shoulders back, straight through the doors of the doctor's building. Upon entering the lobby, past the check-in desk (hospital security, at its best), I see Henry slowly pushing a broom, picking up scattered clumps of dust along his path. He casually catches my glance, nods, and moves along past the lobby couch. So far, so good—no masked man, unless Henry truly is the culprit. Right now, he looks harmless.

Just as the elevator doors are about to close, a hand slides in and pushes them open. Grabbing the railing behind me, I steady myself as Dr. Hildebrandt enters the elevator.

"Oh, hello, Mrs. Ryan," he says. "How are you doing today?"

He looks dashing as always in his dark pants and jacket, which accentuates his dark hair. I find myself blushing when he speaks to me. Thank God, I opted to register as Dr. Deller's patient instead of his; otherwise I'd be staring at my doctor in awe the entire time, and the last time I checked, that wasn't ethical. When Dr. Deller was out, delivering a baby, Dr. Hildebrandt stepped in and covered my appointment. I was so tense, staring at those dark brown eyes and that pearly white smile. There's no way I could ever have him examine me again. *I wonder if he's married? Betsy, stop it!*

"Hi, how are you?" I manage.

"I'm great. It's a wonderful day." As the elevator slides open at our floor, he says, "Looks like we're here. After you."

I can't get out of that elevator fast enough. Unfortunately, I need to follow him into the office like a lovesick puppy. I'm surprised I haven't wet my pants.

Donna is busying herself at the front desk, so I write my name on the sign-in sheet and make a beeline for a seat in the corner of the waiting area.

The usual flimsy magazines beckon my attention, but I have emails to check on my phone, so the Hollywood gossip will have to wait until next time.

But I find it hard to focus because of the events from this morning's beach visit—I'm still reeling. I search the corners of my mind, trying to figure out where the man had been hiding when I was at the beach with Barney. Better yet, why is he after *me*? It just doesn't make sense.

"Mrs. Ryan, good morning. Follow me. Here's the plastic cup, you know the drill," the nurse practitioner says.

I follow her through the hallway and back to the exam room. Donna passes by us, headed to the back room.

"I'll be back in a moment," the nurse says, letting me into one of the rooms.

As she steps out of the room, I see the janitor walk by. "That's odd. He's always working," I whisper to myself. I guess he's rotating through the building today. Henry is like a neighbor that you never talk to, but wave to every morning when you're getting the newspaper.

Dr. Deller is running behind schedule today, so I turn my attention back to my emails. I notice an email from the Village Police Department and mark it as important, planning to read it when I leave the office. I don't want to find out news about my stalker while sitting here naked from the waist down.

"Hello, Betsy. How are we feeling today?" Dr. Deller asks. Pulling the flimsy paper covering closer to my groin to avoid flashing the doctor, I hesitate, wondering whether I should share my morning incident with him. I reply, "Fine."

I remind myself that my doctor has always been very good to me. He delivered both boys and helped me through some unhappy pregnancy experiences, so why would I ever suspect him of harming me or being connected to someone who would?

He's always been very positive and proactive, in the limited conversations we've had in the past, aside from what we experienced at my house the other day. Doctors are human beings, too, even though we sometimes tend to forget that.

Why, then, do I get a sense that he's a part of my stalker situation? I can't shake this feeling. Even though I just don't see *him* injuring anyone, let alone me. On the contrary, I'd like to think he'd be the one trying to save me from peril.

The smell in the exam room is that typical antiseptic, hospital-like odor, which as of late is not a smell I'm keen on. I'm bombarded by it when I go to see Steven *and* whenever I have an appointment here. The fluorescent lights give me a headache, and their constant *bzzz-hmmm* is quite distracting. It would be nice to see a couple of end table lamps with soft bulbs; maybe even a little shag carpet to soften up the joint.

The doctor squirts the slimy gel on my belly and rubs the cold ultrasound probe to monitor the baby. He studies the screen and takes down some measurements and turns his gaze to meet mine.

"Well, my dear, you and baby are doing just fine. Growth is normal."

"That's good to hear," I say, relieved. "Do you think the most recent spotting incident was just due to the stress?"

"Yes, I'm sure it was." He nods. "Speaking of which, how *is* Steven? Any word?"

Taking a leap of faith and hoping my instincts are right, I answer honestly. "Truth be told, I've had a horrible day. I'm surprised that my blood pressure was somewhat normal and that the baby was doing okay."

"What happened?"

"Well, no additional bad news about Steven today, but I did have a scary incident at home—that I don't really want to talk about right now. It's made me shaky all day."

"I understand, Betsy. If you decide you want to discuss it, please let me know. My main concern is that you and the baby are healthy."

I release a huge breath that was stressfully caught in my lungs, as I reply, "Thank you. That means a lot to me."

———

Misty has been a rock for me the past few days; heck, she's been a rock for me ever since I met her. Picking up my pace, I spot the car with my security guard neighbor seated behind the wheel. I raise my hand to wave at her; she waves back, but within an instant, her face changes. Her eyebrows raise and her jaw drops and she furiously flags me to come to the car. Instinctually, I take off waddle-running, not sure if I'm in danger or she has a crude joke to share with me. Reaching the door handle, I open the car door and fling myself in as she puts the car in gear and takes off.

Barely able to put my seat belt on and grabbing the side door handle for stability, I scream, "What is it?"

"I saw the S.O.B. walking outside the building!"

"The stalker? Where? Are you sure it was him?"

"Coming out of the building, right behind you! I don't think he realized that I was in the car, because right when you waved to me, he took off running to the side of the building. Let's go around the block and see if we can find him!"

"What did he look like?"

"It was hard to see him. He had a dark hat and jacket on. His face was looking down. I don't know if he was our stalker, but once he saw me, he took off running."

"What? No! Misty, let's just go home."

"We have to show this jerk that you mean business and that you won't be pushed around. I personally won't stand for it."

Misty aggressively turns the steering wheel to the right, flinging me to the armrest in the center of the front seat, then she hits the gas; whiplashing me back into my headrest.

"Slow down, Misty. You are going to hurt us."

Not seeming to realize her own strength, Misty taps the brakes, looking left and right, searching for the assailant. For a minute, I think I see him crouching down between two cars. I alert Misty, and she instantly puts the car in park and leaps out of the car, gun in hand.

"Stay there, Betsy. Keep the windows up and lock the doors. I'll be right back."

I fight off the strong urge to pee my pants, so I do a quick Kegel squeeze to try and halt the urine in its tracks. Trying not to think about urine, I scan the parking lot for Misty.

I can't see much, but I think Misty is crouching down, walking in between rows of cars to find our masked man. I feel foolish for not even realizing that anyone was coming out of the building behind me. How could I not hear him? My only thought had been to motor out of there and get to the car as quickly as possible.

Could it have been Dr. Deller or someone else targeting his office waiting for me to leave my appointment? Maybe they broke into his office and figured out when I'd be there, *and* stole my personal information? That's almost ten years of facts, dates, and intelligence on my family and me. People nowadays give out their information handily to doctors, dentists, and others, not thinking they could be a victim of identity theft or abuse.

Without warning, Misty runs up to the car and flings open the door.

"Jeez-us, Misty, you scared the snot out of me! What happened? Did you find him?"

"Nope," she grumbles. "But whoever it was left this on the ground. Do you want to open it?"

The white envelope has specks of dirt on it. It has the same size, shape, and scribble as the other envelopes I've received. As I hold it up to the light, I can make out the little pink slip inside the envelope. I slowly rip it open, hesitating to look inside. I exhale and close my eyes. "Give me a minute, Misty."

She patiently sits next to me in the driver's seat with the motor running. I know Misty would rip this message open, run after the madman, and shoot him down if I let her, but I need to think straight and be realistic. I know the police have had their hands tied in helping me identify who the stalker is, but perhaps this envelope will have better fingerprints or clues?

Misty places a gentle hand on my arm. "Betsy, I know we've just tried to track him down, but I think we should drive home and look at the letter there. We'll be more secure and we can call you parents and discuss next steps. I don't want someone catching us off guard here in the car."

<hr />

At home, the dim living room has an eerie, ominous feel, so I flick on the switch and flood the room with light. Barney wakes up from a nap and steps forward to lean into his two front feet, and then he gives his back legs a good stretch. Next, he leans his rear end back and up as he lowers his outstretched front legs to do the stretch, in reverse. As a final wake-up ritual he twists and shakes his head, flopping his ears, making them slap against the top of his head and the bottom of his chin simultaneously. Now, sitting in a ready position, he stares at me. If more people did these stretches every time they woke up, we'd have fewer wars.

I ask him, "Do you want to go outside?"

He cocks his head to the right and widens his eyes, as if to say, *Huh? Me? Yeah!* This form of communication, I *can* understand.

He's been giving me that quizzical look ever since I could remember. Evidently, he's understood me for years; I'm sure he's wondering what took *me* so long to understand that *he gets* me. I continue my imagination, *A-hem. Yes, Mom, I do want to go outside. I heard squirrels chasing each other around on the roof this morning. I think I need to go and look.*

Stunned for a minute by my vivid thoughts, I catch a little chuckle in my throat. I can't believe I'm having everyday thoughts about my cocker spaniel this way. It's cool, but very peculiar.

Setting her purse on a chair at the kitchen table, Misty crosses the room to grab an apple from the fruit bowl and stands next to me at the kitchen counter. I mentally take note that Misty *does* appreciate my fruit choices, regardless of whether she enjoyed my gorgeous fruit display the other morning.

In between bites, she says, "Okay, let me see that envelope."

Her vivid green eyes practically match her tunic top, which accents her gorgeous hair. All the working out and beauty routines she's been doing have paid off. I'd love to set her up on a date with one of Steven's friends. It would be fun to double date.

As she pulls the pink slip of paper out of the filthy envelope, I say, "I've been thinking, Misty. He must've accessed my personal records somehow. Earlier, I was trying to narrow it down. My medical and dental offices have my contact information; heck, even the exercise studio has some of that stuff in their files. But they wouldn't know about my spotting or get a note to the kids' school." I shake my head and look to the ceiling—maybe for answers or just a way out of this mess. "Amazing how we are all so exposed. One crazy loon can spy on files and learn so much about people's identities."

She nods in agreement.

"Well… what does *this* threat have to say?"

Misty replies, "He says, and I quote, 'Your husband is next.'" She slaps the kitchen counter. "I am blown away by this guy's nerve. It's almost as if he's trying to see how far he can go. He knows you're going to the police, so he must also know that we've hit a dead end there. He also knows that you probably have video surveillance of him from the Village Hall. He also knows about Steven, the baby, and the boys. Jeez, what doesn't he know?" She's rambling on, which means she's trying to distract me from the weight of this threat.

My heart sinks into my chest as I respond, "This guy is sick. He doesn't have compassion or logic—he's just plain sick. The scary thing is, *I did* get an instinctive twinge that the stalker was with Steven yesterday." I shift my weight and lean on the counter as I continue, "That's why I raced over there last night. And when I pursued it with Steven, he alluded that someone strange had been in his room." My mind begins to race. What should I do? How can I stop him? "People won't believe 'mother's intuition' any more than a comatose husband talking."

My rant is interrupted by a tiny sound over by the patio door. We look over and see my dog. Barney has a way of scratching the screen door, ever so slightly, just to get my attention when he wants to go outside or just sit on the porch. He loves our fenced-in yard, but I don't always like picking up the doo-doo in the grass, so I prefer taking him for walks. But paying attention to the little things, like his gentle scratch on the door, seems to be one of the ways I'm able to cope with this menace.

While I open the door to let Barney outside, I call over to Misty, "I completely forgot, I received an email from the Village Police Department earlier today while I was at the doctor's office. I flagged it as important so I could read it when I got home. Let's see what it says."

While waiting for my computer to start up, I can't help but think how much of a distraction email is. I think back to a few years ago, when I worked in the Cranstons' kitchen and dreaded taking time away from the busy prep area to answer emails. Given that I had to be at work so early, I would wait until at least 8:00 a.m. to open and reply to purchase order disputes, vendor contracts, and any other nonsense that ended up in my mailbox.

I would plan emails precisely when I had a break from the action, once each morning and afternoon. Typically, I would prep the ingredients and dough for fresh-baked bread. While I was waiting for the yeast to activate and prove, which takes about forty-five minutes, I'd run over to my laptop and whip through a few messages. I'd remain standing so I wouldn't get too comfortable in the chair, because work would be waiting for me back in the kitchen.

Now, back in my own cozy kitchen, I scroll down the various messages in my overstuffed email box, finally pinpointing the message from the Village Police Department. I start to feel a rise in my heart rate and sweat starts to form in my underarms. My hands are shaking slightly, which is visibly noticeable as I move my mouse over the mouse pad.

"Wait, Bets, it's right there."

Click.

"'Dear Mrs. Ryan… We regret to inform you that the fingerprint sample that accompanied evidence #R35466 has an insufficient or unreadable sampling. Please resubmit additional evidence for further review."

"Wait, so it didn't work?" I shake my head and reread the email. "I don't understand… they have the originals. How can they not have prints on them?"

"I bet he used latex gloves, or they got smeared."

The mention of latex gloves makes me sit up. "I know it sounds silly, Misty, but my doctor used latex gloves today during my exam. I know you can get gloves like that from any drugstore, but when you put together the pieces, it kind of fits. Where is Jessica Fletcher when you need her?" Misty slips me a smile, probably because she knows about my TV crime and mystery obsessions. "Do you think I should go over to his office again and see if I can find any other clues?"

"I think it's worth a shot, but remember, latex gloves are not enough to prove your case. I'm sure the madman wouldn't dare follow you there again after our little chase scene."

"Let's hope. It's almost like the universe is telling me something—like the answers are out there, glaring me in the face, yet I just can't see them—even if the gloves aren't the key piece of evidence!"

Misty nods in agreement, smiling as she hands me my cell phone. "Why don't you give the hospital a call and see if there's anything new going on with Steven."

"All right. I'll text or call you later with any updates. I didn't hear anything from them throughout the night—no news is good news, I guess, but the threat about Steven from the new pink note should be taken seriously."

I watch my very best friend sashay back across the room, confident and bold, ready to take on the bad guys. As for me, I've always held my head high, regardless of the adversity that comes my way, but not as confidently as Misty. I've always believed you get in life what you're capable of handling. I guess this whole sordid mess is just a test. I need to figure out this problem and begin to shed my fears and insecurities; meanwhile, hopefully Steven will come home to us, safe and sound.

I tiptoe over to the couch to snuggle up with my dog so I can relax for a minute before calling my parents. Even though the hospital didn't have any new information on Steven, it's nice to know that he's in good hands over there.

As I rub Barney's belly, I quietly sit with him and think about what an amazing job he did today at the beach. I really want him to know that. I trust that he'll understand how grateful I am, but a new rawhide should do the trick. I go and get him one and come back to the couch.

As he hops down to the floor, then sits politely waiting for his treat, I tell him, "You know, Barney, I'm so proud of the way you reacted today when the bad man was chasing us. You protected me and kept me safe."

He lets the bone rest at his feet while sitting in silence, gazing into my eyes with the little end of his tail lifting and dropping against the floor—almost as if a puppeteer were pulling a string attached to the end of it. I love that little nubby tail.

My imagination kicks in again as I envision him saying, *I was so scared when I saw the man chase us. If you would've let me, I know I could have scared him back. I may not be as big as the German Shepherd down the street, but I can hold my own, Mom.*

I'm glad no one knows how crazy I'm acting right now, but to keep my sanity, I need to believe he's connecting with me on some level—even if I'm creating both sides of the dialogue. Knowing just how dramatic and emotional today's events were, I want to try and meet him emotionally, but where do I begin? I have no way of knowing for sure if he even understands me, but I know I'll feel better if I at least try.

"Barney, the man who chased us at the beach this morning came after me again today at my doctor's office. I wish I knew who he was so I could alert the police."

Barney shifts his weight and then stands up, alert. A thought comes into my mind. *Mom, the man who was at the beach has been outside our house before. He put the bird there. He sees you all the time.*

I close my eyes and lower my head to think. Why did I just think that? It seems as if I'm using my dog as a sounding board to think things through. Whatever the case may be, it's working so far. I should keep following this thought process. Somehow the thoughts and answers are coming to me.

When us dogs go for walks, we smell lots of things, like other animals, trash, and even an old sneaker to chew. We register who has been in the area, through our sense of smell. But, Mom—and this is very important—we communicate through our thoughts, like we are now—even with plants, trees, animals...

I sit up and regard Barney with intensity. "So, can I exchange information with the big oak tree outside, or even someone across town?"

Yes, Mom, but there must be some sort of intention. I can't just ramble around and pick people's brains. They need to connect with me in some way or be near me or our home. Barney tilts his head, as he looks deeper into my eyes, probably hoping that I get it.

"Oh, I see. So. if someone is mentally fixating on me, like the bad man, you might be able to pick up on those thoughts?" The butterflies in my belly are doing cartwheels next to Emmy Grace right now. The idea that I can have a microscope into Barney's mind just warms me to my soul. I affectionately rub under his chin.

Exactly! But it's not perfect because, as you know, I get distracted by squirrels, other dogs, and of course, food. He pulls his ears back and lifts his chin so I can get a better position to give him a good scratch.

"Thank you, Barney. This is very helpful for me to know." Looking around my tranquil living room, feeling the warmth of Barney's fur against my leg, I giggle and imagine what Mom would think if she were here; or even better, if she could read my mind. Whether I'm imagining this conversation or not, the relief that I may have some answers sits well with me.

Barney lowers his head and stares at me for several minutes, then shifts his gaze to the bone at his feet and licks his lips. A noise at the door causes his ears to pitch back. Spooked, I wonder what he hears. He jumps off the couch and runs to the side door.

"Hello? Hello, Betsy, are you here?"

Heavens to Pete! It's only Dad. I *must* remember that he has a house key.

Hopping up, I make my way over to meet him at the door. "Dad, you startled me right out of my skin!" I giggle. "I was hanging and relaxing with Barney for a few minutes. I was going to call you. Come sit down, I have to fill you in."

"Okay. Your mother is at home… she said to say hi and to ask if we can go visit Steven."

I gesture to join me in the family room. "I spoke with the hospital a little while ago, but we can visit any time during ICU visiting hours." I shift on the couch to get more comfortable and continue. "Here's where we're at with everything." Dad is fixated on me, more serious than I've seen in a long time as I share the morning's events at the beach *and* the doctor's office. He props his elbow on his knee and rests his chin on the palm of his hand. Intently, he formulates his thoughts.

"I think we need to drive over to that doctor's office again," he says. I nod in agreement. "Can you call them and say you're having pain and you need to get back in? That way, maybe we can figure out these coincidences surrounding the doctor's office. And we can pop in and see Steven. Let's go get your mom."

He gets up from the sofa and navigates his way into the kitchen pantry, calling out to my dog, "Barney, who's a good boy?" Barney hops up and hightails it into the kitchen. "Do you want a treat from Grandpa?" Dad loves spoiling my first *baby*. Barney chomps down the freeze-dried lamb nugget in one chomp.

"Stay here, Barn, we'll be back soon. Now that you've had two treats in one sitting, you should be content for a little while longer." I've often wondered if I'm the only one who tells their dog that they'll be back soon. I always feel like he might be upset when I leave him alone. Now my dog seems to understand me and perhaps realizes that I *will* be back soon. My mother-guilt lessens a bit.

Barney grabs his half-eaten rawhide and walks over to his doggy bed. There he sits, looks back at me, and appears to nod his head.

"Did you see that, Dad?"

"Huh? No, what?"

"Never mind."

———————

I don't think my father has ever been to my OB-GYN office. After all, why would he? I guess there's always a first time for everything. And this time is important; we're on a mission. Mom has been here with me before, but she's my *mom;* women do things like that. I'm glad she's staying in the car to be on lookout from the parking lot. She may spot the stalker outside the building, like Misty did the last time I was here.

The elevator seems to be moving slowly, and is ever so slightly wiggling from side-to-side as we await the *ding* announcing our arrival on the floor where we'll get off. The elevator is empty so we have a minute to talk.

"I'll go right up to the desk," I say, my voice barely above a whisper. "I'll tell them I need to see the doctor again today, while you go and sit in a chair near the corner. I'll let Donna, the receptionist, know that you are with me so she doesn't approach you and make a big deal."

"Perfect. I'll wait for you there and see if I can snoop around and find clues."

I snicker at his comment as I imagine the big orange letters on the side of the *Scooby-Doo Mystery Machine*, carrying five of the best cartoon mystery sleuths of all time: Shaggy, Scooby,

Velma, Fred, and Daphne. I loved the voice of Shaggy, played by the actor and radio personality, Casey Kasem, who was also the voice of the syndicated radio show *America's Top 40*. Even back, then they had creepy stalkers, but Shag and Scoob would always foil them. I wonder if my boys will ever watch *Murder She Wrote* or *Scooby-Doo*? Every kid I knew in grade school watched those shows religiously. They're innocent and timeless. I guess I've always had a thing for mysteries. How ironic.

Donna's warm smile is very welcoming to my father, which eases any apprehension.

"Mr. Anderson, it's very nice to meet you. Make yourself at home while Betsy meets with her doctor. Would you like some coffee?"

"No, Donna, I'm good."

The nurse calls my name and brings me down the hall to the exam room, placing my file in the plastic holding container attached to the wall.

"Let's get your weight. We won't be needing a urine sample right now since you were just here this morning." This nurse is quick and efficient, unlike Donna. She's medium height, with brown curly hair and perfectly manicured nails. "The doctor will be with you shortly."

I wonder what Dad is doing in the waiting room. Hopefully he can unearth something, anything, to shed some light on this case.

From down the hall and through the exam room's slightly opened door, I hear my father's familiar voice. "Excuse me Donna, where's the closest men's room?"

"Oh, you can use ours. It's down the hall on the left, next to the supply room."

Dad has always had a way of working through obstacles with ease because he looks so sweet and innocent. People trust him and he's brilliant, which would explain why he was the head of ABC-TV here in Chicago for years. After his heart surgery last year, he decided to retire; now he travels the world with Mom and works with Scooby-Doo and the gang, protecting and saving me from danger.

———————————

While Dr. Deller does a manual exam to make sure the baby is doing okay, I move my gaze to the sink on my right—anywhere but in the direction of the doctor, whose hands are currently in a compromising position, a situation I've been in a lot over the past few years.

"All set, Betsy." My doctor says as he wipes off the ultrasound goo covering my belly. "Things are moving along nicely. I'm surprised to hear that you are having sharp pains. I trust you know what labor pains feel like, so I'm assuming the pain you were feeling was different. Perhaps you were having gas or indigestion?"

I search my mind to falsely answer his question, then reply, "You know, you're right. Maybe it *was* just gas pains."

"Well, there's no sign of distress with the baby, but let's take another look with the ultrasound again on Monday to make extra sure. Stay off your feet when you get home, but first, to ease your stress, why don't you go and see Steven?" He pauses. "I'm sure you're tired of always having to come over here several times a week, but I want to monitor this baby all the way to delivery. Never hesitate to call and come back in."

I agree with my doctor, but as he is speaking, my fleeting thoughts raise suspicions about his involvement with the menacing envelopes. In my heart, I know that he's not guilty, but an unrelenting pull is directing me back here.

"Thank you so much. I agree it will be nice to have a day or two off from getting poked and prodded." I let out a desperate laugh and hesitate for what seems like an eternity. Finally, I turn to face him head-on. "Just wondering, doctor, do you go over to the hospital much? Reason why I ask is because the ICU nurse told me that a man came to see Steven the other day, claiming to be his brother, and I thought maybe you might have seen something that appeared out of the ordinary."

He shoots me a surprised look and instantly replies, "Why on Earth wouldn't I tell you if I knew something like that, Betsy? I am just as worried about him as you are. As a doctor, we take an oath for the health and the wellbeing of all people." He tilts his head and looks at me. "What aren't you telling me? What's wrong?"

I can't help but wonder if he's being truthful with me, or throwing me a line that he prepared ahead of time if he were ever to be confronted. I'm not sure why I feel this way, but I do. Something is just not right—about this doctor, this office, and this building.

"Oh, I know, Dr. Deller. I'm distraught about so much right now, so I am shaking the bush on every front, trying to figure things out. Just disregard my question." I decide to avoid telling him more details until I find out how he or his office fits into this puzzle.

As I gather my belongings, I deduce that my question was an odd one, and I should have realized it the moment it formulated in my mind and then spilled from my mouth. I'm certain that he won't take offense.

But if he is guilty, this will certainly motivate his timeline for attack.

As I exit the exam room and make my way to the reception area, I catch a glimpse of my father's furrowed brow and intent glare. I can tell something is not right. Hopping up, he raises his left eyebrow, then purses his lips, nudging his head towards the exit. Our steps are in unison as we quickly leave the office.

"Betsy, keep walking; don't say a word, just keep walking, and go directly to the car." I always know when my father quickly talks this way he means business.

My heart races as I pick up the pace to match my dad's. Wow, those walks he and Mom take every morning on the beach and around town are really keeping them in fabulous shape. He's putting me to shame. After several silent seconds, he sighs cautiously, darting his eyes around the perimeter of the parking lot all the way to the car.

Safely inside, with Mom in the back seat and me in the front passenger seat, we are free to talk. He locks the door and puts the car in reverse to pull out of our spot. Driving slowly, he circles the large U-shaped parking lot, looking in between cars, searching.

"Can you tell us what's going on, Dad?" I push. "Everything went okay inside the examination room; the baby is fine. I felt horrible making up this fake pain, but in reality, I did just have spotting, so I guess it's warranted."

Dad looks in the rearview mirror, acknowledging what I just said, before speaking. "You have to listen to me and don't interrupt. I think that your doctor, or at the very least, someone in his office, is involved with the stalker. I highly doubt it's your doctor, but there is some link that we have to figure out."

"What evidence do you have, Scooby?" I'm trying to keep things a little light to offset my shaking body—make lemonade out of lemons, if you will. I visualize me as Daphne and Mom as Velma.

Somehow my dad manages a smile and Mom follows suit. "That's funny, dear, but we have a real problem on our hands and it's not getting any better. When you left for the exam room, I went ahead and asked to use their bathroom." Dad is talking very quickly, as if he's trying to get it all out before someone rushes the car, or worse. "When I walked by the supply room. I peeked in and saw an open box of pink sheets of paper. Next to that was a box of white business envelopes and a sheet of paper that looked like it came from your medical file! I read it quickly because I didn't want anyone seeing me, but your name was on it."

I'm trying to stay calm as I reply, "A copy of my file was in the storage room?"

My dad nods in agreement, then continues. "I know it sounds like no big deal, but then, when I was at the front desk, I also noticed your medical record was up on the computer screen. I'm not sure why it would still be up on the screen after you left the waiting room to go into the exam room." He waits for our collective gasps before finishing his thought.

"Call it coincidence or whatever you'd like—maybe a sloppy stalker—but when I got out of the restroom and back in the waiting area, I overheard Donna talking to herself asking, 'Why was that sheet with Betsy's medical information in the supply room?' That made me very anxious, so I strolled over to her desk and made light conversation about how they have a very comfortable, laid-back office.

"I then asked what computer system they used for clients because I was thinking about getting a system set up for my work clients."

"Dad, you don't have work clients."

He nods his head and says, "I know, but she doesn't know that. And by the way, who in God's name doesn't close out of patient files in this day, and age of patient privacy?" Before we can answer he continues talking, "I'll tell you who. A stalker who's opening up your files when the receptionist is away, that's who."

The idea that a stalker may have been reading my medical files sends numbing panic throughout my entire body. I push my feet against the floorboards and squeeze the door handle to stabilize myself. Trying to believe everything will be okay, I breathe in deep, peaceful breaths aiming for tranquility. "Whoever wrote those notes wore latex gloves or something like that, because the police couldn't pick up any prints on the on paper. But it's way too coincidental that a page from my file was in that storage closet next to the paper."

I fight back a sob as the violation blends with the rage boiling within me. I need to find out who this is and confront him directly. The thought sends terror down to my bones. How could I defend myself against a man who's six feet tall, if confronted face to face?

"Betsy, your mother and I will go over to the hospital with you to see Steven, then we can head over to pick up the boys at school. We can figure out dinner later. Why don't you call or text Misty and fill her in? If we get delayed at the hospital, she can always go get the boys."

The reflection in the mirrored elevator doors at the hospital reveal dark circles under my eyes and hair out of place—a woman at her wit's end. Yep, that's about right.

My father keeps his hands lightly on both of our backs as the doors open onto the ICU floor. He gently escorts us down the hall to see my husband. No wonder my mom loves him so much; his consideration is boundless.

We enter Steven's room, and find that he's nowhere to be seen. A swell of panic instantly fills my body. Worry powers my steps as I run over to the nurse's station, Mom and Dad falling in behind me. Their support gives me the burst of confidence I need to form my question.

"Excuse me... excuse me!" The words come out of me like a popped cork. "I'm Betsy Ryan, and—"

"Mrs. Ryan. We were just going to call you," replies a nurse I've never seen before. She looks alarmed. "Unfortunately, there's been an incident, and the police are on their way up right now. But I can assure you we're doing everything in our power to keep your husband safe."

"Keep him safe from *what*? What are you talking about?" I wail helplessly.

Dad tightens his grip on my shoulder. "Ma'am, please, just tell us what's going on. Is Steven okay?"

"I'm really sorry," she says, "but that's all I can say right now. I promise to update you as soon as I can. Please sit tight and we'll check in again, okay?"

I nod weakly. Nurses and doctors are running this way and that, and a couple are on their phones demanding extra security. I realize that the mass confusion going on behind her is probably about my husband, wherever he is.

I back up several steps, feeling my legs give out from under me as I fall into my father's arms. My heart is knocking against my chest, pain searing my solar plexus. Mom is standing right next to me, ready to catch me if I fall again.

With soothing tones, they steer me over to two metal chairs that are situated no more than fifteen feet away, near the ICU desk. There's no way I'm leaving this seat without information.

Waiting, Mom sits beside me, tenderly rubbing my forearm in a protective sort of way. I notice movement in Steven's room and realize Dr. Abbott has gone inside. I summon the energy to get up and wobbly-march over to him, my parents close behind.

"Excuse me, Dr. Abbott," I ask, peeking through the space, between the security guard's hip and the door. "Can I please speak with you?"

He motions us into the room, as he tells the security guard to let us pass by. Steven's room feels lonely, impersonal, and smells of death without him in it. I sit down in that chair I hate so much, immediately searching my mind, trying to select the right questions to ask Steven while I picture him in my mind— not the husband who's lying unresponsive in some hospital bed, in some other wing of this place—but the husband who lifts our sons over his head to his shoulders, who helped me plant the bushes in my front yard, who proposed to me wearing a Northwestern sweatshirt on a crisp fall day.

"Thanks for letting us in, doctor," Dad says as he gently pushes past me. "Now please, for the love of God, tell us what's happened here. Why is there a security guard at the door? We have a right to know!"

"Folks, trust me, I understand you're worried; so are we," Dr. Abbott offers gravely. "Here's what we know. About twenty minutes before you arrived, the ventilator alarm in this room went off. Our head nurse raced over here and discovered an unauthorized needle protruding from Steven's IV line. She removed it immediately, and we've sent it to the lab."

"How long will it be before you know what was in the needle?" my father asks. "My daughter is very distraught about this."

"I'm not sure how long, but I'll let you know when we know. We moved him to another room after they flushed his system because the police needed to search this room."

"Is he stable?" I ask, searching for answers in his eyes.

"I want to reassure you," he says, looking directly at me, "I've just come back from checking your husband's vitals, and yes, he's currently stable."

Numbly, I fish around my purse for a tissue and catch the drip coming out of my right nostril. I fold the tissue in half and dab the corners of my eyes to drain the tears that have pooled there. Mom scoots her chair closer to mine and squeezes my knee.

"Still," he continues, "we can't be too careful. We've drawn blood and rushed that to the lab. We've also introduced a new fluid combination to further flush his system of any potential toxins. And the lab is currently in the process of analyzing the needle and its contents, so we'll have a better sense of exactly what we're dealing with." He puts Steven's chart down. "Meanwhile, the police have arrived, and as you can see, we've stepped up our own security throughout the ward as well."

Dad clears his throat. "Well, I'll be. With all due respect, sir, I cannot begin to imagine how some unsavory character could have gotten into this restricted-access room in the first place, let alone poisoned my son-in-law in broad daylight! I mean, he might as well have been in a—"

Mom cuts in with her most calming yet authoritative voice. "My husband's right, sir. We're angry and concerned. But right now, we just want to know a few of things: How can we help our daughter? Can we stay here past visitor hours, for example? How can we trust that your newly increased security will be enough to protect my son-in-law? And when, for goodness' sake, can my daughter get in to see her husband again?"

The doctor's expression is one of apology and regret as he replies, and he sounds sincere when he does. "I personally assure you we are doing everything in our power to keep Steven stable and safe. We will keep a security guard on duty at his door twenty-four hours a day until he's released from the hospital. Unfortunately, we do need to wait for the police before we can grant visitation rights to anyone, including family. I'm so sorry about this."

My parents look at each other, stunned. Mentally racing through my list of questions, I realize one of the elephants in the room has not been addressed. "Doctor, may I ask, do you have any idea who might have done this?"

"Honestly, Mrs. Ryan, we do not. No unknown visitors or new staff members have been in the hospital today to our knowledge. The police are combing through the guest and staff entrance manifest as we speak to see if they can come up with any leads."

"Okay… but I have a favor to ask. If you discover that anyone from Dr. Kevin Deller's office was here today, can you please let us know?" I ask, hopeful.

"I will do what I can," he says, gently, "but the police are handling it from here, so they'll know more than we do. I'd suggest you go to them with any concerns and questions you have about this. In the meantime, we, your doctors and nurses, will do what we do best: give Steven the best care we can."

The cafeteria is just about as typical as you can get for a hospital, with its stainless-steel countertops, stark wooden tables, and deeply unflattering lighting. The smell of meatloaf and mashed potatoes triggers an unwelcome memory of the institutional food we were fed in grade school. Being in the food industry, I know all about the variety of chemicals, fillers, and general crap that often goes into food prepared in large quantities.

With Mom, off to pick up the boys, Dad indulges in vending machine cuisine, a bad splurge habit he never gave up after heart surgery. The Snickers bar, packed with peanuts, he claims, is a wonderful bridge to dinner later tonight. My stomach is in knots, unable to even think of food. I opt for Sprite and Ritz crackers.

"Let's look at the information we've gathered so far," Dad begins as he starts counting on his fingers. "We have someone looking at your personal file from your doctor's office, who's also grabbing pink paper and envelopes from their storage room. A crazy person is tracking you from his office building on this hospital campus, which is not far from where we are currently sitting."

As my father speaks these truths, I start to shake in my chair, pressing the heels of my shoes into the floor beneath the table, trying to stay calm. *Yoga, don't fail me now.* I visualize three of the most positive and loving things I know—my baby, Morgan, and Kyle.

"What if we're in danger right now?" I whisper furtively. "We don't know who would do this, so we have to keep our eyes open."

"You saw the security detail and police all over the hospital. We should be safe here. What *is* important is the activity that's been going on the past few days and right now, here in this hospital. You told me that the stalker said he wanted your husband next, and now he's trying to make good on that promise."

"If he's doing exactly what he says he would, based on the letters, then my whole family hangs in the balance. Steven, the kids, Barney, me…" I take a deep breath and reposition myself in the cramped cafeteria chair. The light chatter from diners in the background masks our conversation. "We need to be the aggressive ones here. No more standing around waiting for him to come to us. I can't sit by and let this happen any longer." I feel a sense of exhilaration as the bolder version of myself takes a proverbial step forward.

"I agree with you one thousand percent, honey. Why don't we go up and see if Steven is back in his room yet? It's been over thirty minutes."

"Remember, Dad, I have the ability to tap into Steven's subconscious mind. I'd like to take a few minutes and get quiet here, before we go up."

He raises his left eyebrow and smirks, indicating he's still on the fence about my ability to communicate with Steven, as he says, "Okay… I'll go grab a cup of coffee and be right back."

───────

I've gotten good at honing-in on my husband's consciousness over the last few days. I've discovered that if I quiet my mind of unwanted thoughts, breathe deeply, and visualize the person I'm communicating with, it works; the waves start floating between us.

I believe the stressful emotions over the past few days must have exploded my transmission superhighway wide open, because otherwise, how would I be able to understand him? Thinking back, though, Barney has also been trying to get my attention for years, but I was too preoccupied to notice. Now he's pitchforked his way through, and he has a better understanding of my emotions and words. I think I'm imagining his thoughts, but maybe a pet psychic could confirm whether they really are his thoughts or not.

Steven's conscious mind, meanwhile, is somewhat blank and relaxed due to his inactivity right now, making him a near-perfect receiver for my communication.

Steven, I love you. I am so worried about you and want you to come back to us. Please.

Silence.

Honey, someone tried to hurt you. We're trying to find out who this person is so we can have him arrested.

Silence again.

Finally: *Betsy… it's hard to breathe… my mind is a blur… but I will try to remember…*

It's okay, honey, I can help you! The doctors say you're stable now, but we need to get to the bottom of this. Do you think maybe you saw someone in the room that didn't belong here, or gave you a bad feeling?

Silence.

Betsy… the man… who put the needle in… was here in the hospital when you were here.

What man? Dr. Deller? Was the man you're talking about here when Dr. Deller and I were here, or was there another time?

Same time.

Silence.

The quiet is somewhat deafening, but I'm glad I can feel the love passing between us like a river flowing in both directions. More love than has passed between us in months.

Who could it be? A deranged nurse or security guard gone rogue? Henry was there at the same time, of course, but it's hard to know. Dr. Deller said he was here meeting with Dr. Hildebrandt, but I barely know him. I must look outside the box and consider, who has a motive? I discreetly punch the armrest of the chair, hoping to relieve some of the pent-up frustration. I know that my obvious negativity won't help the communication between Steven and me, but it probably doesn't matter because it looks like Steven has checked out for now.

"Hey, Betsy." My father returns. "I brought you hot tea to help calm your nerves."

My father sets the tea down on the table in front of me and takes a seat directly across. Chamomile, with honey and lemon to add to it. Dad's sweet gesture helps relieve some of my immediate stress. The gentle heat from the beverage rises and fills my senses as the calming takes effect. He watches as I slowly squeeze the thick, golden syrup into my steaming cup of tea, add the lemon, and stir it all up. Holding the cup in both hands warms me. The chill within my bones begins to exit with an uncontrollable shiver. The small hairs on my neck start to lay flat again.

"Thanks. I need this right now," I murmur, wondering if a bite of that Snickers bar would hit the spot, too. Maybe I can go grab one for myself on the way out, or better yet, a piece of pizza—my go-to cheat food.

"Steven had a lot to share just now. He says the man who put the poison in the IV had been here before, and in fact, was here when Dr. Deller and I came to visit."

Watching my father accept this explanation from Steven gives me a reassured sense of stability. Knowing that he's on my side and believes me is all the fuel I need to motor on.

"Of course, there were several hospital staff members milling around that night with Dr. Deller, what with all the interns, nurses, and custodial staff who are in and out all the time. Remember that we also saw Henry, the guy who cleans Dr. Deller's office; and, Dr. Deller also mentioned that he was at the hospital meeting with his office partner, Dr. Hildebrandt, before he bumped into us?"

"Betsy, wait," my dad pleads. "If you do the calculations, Dr. Hildebrandt *or* Henry could actually make sense. I don't know them, but either would jive with what I found at Dr. Deller's office earlier today."

"What if it is one of them? I see Henry around here all the time. It's absolutely crazy, thinking he's so close to me in this medical setting and yet, he could be a stalker; and Dr.

Hildebrandt is a respected doctor." *Not to mention extremely handsome.* "That, too, is insane."

"I agree, the whole thing is crazy." Clearly Dad is determined to follow this line of reasoning, he raises one bushy eyebrow and gives me that "listen to me" look.

I sigh, in agreement. He's got a good point. "All right, maybe we should follow them around and see where they go. One of them may slip up. But I don't know much about Henry, and Dr. Hildebrandt has only met with me once, when my doctor was delivering a baby—he hardly knows me and would have no motive."

"Maybe you can find out where Dr. Hildebrandt lives the next time you go into their office," my dad suggests.

"Dad, all I do know is, it's *not* Dr. Deller. I'm scratching him off our suspect list. When I'm with him, I can tell he's safe, trustworthy, and totally on my side. He'd take a bullet for me, if he had to. I know for sure."

The "listen to me look" is still zeroing in on me. "You know, Betsy, sometimes people don't show their true selves to others. Sometimes even the nicest-seeming people have odd obsessions and fixations. I'd watch both of those doctors *and* the janitor."

While Dad is talking, I look over his shoulder and notice Dr. Deller coming into the cafeteria, headed straight for our table. Feeling sweat form on my upper lip, I wipe it off with my index finger inconspicuously just as he approaches our table.

"Hello, Dr. Deller! Wow, lucky me, I get to see you more than once in one day! How are you?" I say, feigning surprise.

"Me? How are *you*? I heard that there was some incident with Steven here today, so I called over to the ICU and they told me you were here in the cafeteria. Do you know what happened?"

Shrugging my shoulders, I vaguely admit, "It's all a mystery to us." I shoot Dad a look, trying to signal him that I will handle this. "Have you heard anything from the doctor-types?"

"Not yet. I was going to press them for answers after talking with you."

Well, if talk is what he wants, then he came to the right place. It's time to get to the bottom of this mess and break my silence about what we know. I check my intuition for certainty and get a good feeling that it will help us clear the decks. "Dr. Deller, please sit down with us. We need to talk." He sits across from my father, who gives him a hard look, then turns to me as I spill the beans.

Dr. Deller's expression deepens into a serious frown after we explain the whole sordid mess to him. He's obviously as shaken as we are, but I am glad I'm finally sharing the story with him.

"We have reason to believe that someone who has access to your office is responsible for what happened to Steven. We don't know who it is, but we also have reason to believe that this same person is the stalker that has been terrorizing me." I don't openly admit that I think the culprit could be Henry or even Dr. Hildebrandt, because we haven't confirmed facts yet.

My father is sitting, nodding his head in agreement while keeping a watchful eye on Dr. Deller. What I have said leaves my doctor speechless. Leaning against the wobbly cafeteria table, Dr. Deller combs his fingers through his thick, gray-streaked hair, then looks down at his shoes. After holding that pose for a few minutes, he exhales and looks up at us. My thoughts race, from guilt to accusations and back to innocence. My heart is hoping he's honest.

His eyes are clear and direct. "Betsy, I *swear* to you, I don't know anything about this, at all. However, some hospital staff have access to my office, which could answer the questions you have."

Dad also outlines what he discovered at Dr. Deller's office today while I fill in other details about what else has been happening, recapping every point I can think of. Hoping he'll be our ally in this fight, I plead that he keeps this information from everyone. Dad and Dr. Deller agree that we should keep our eyes open and try to catch the assailant red-handed. Then we would have legal proof—that would assure police assistance and action.

"I know you have nothing to do with this, Doctor, but from my perspective, I hope you understand what I've been going through," I say.

"I do, and I'm sorry for all of this." He shakes his head, then leans his elbows on the table to hold his chin in his hands.

As I look back on the many years I've been Dr. Deller's patient, I realize I've always been satisfied. I'll never forget the traumatic day I had to get the dilation and curettage procedure, known as a D&C, to remove the tissue from inside my uterus due to the blighted ovum. Go figure—I ended up having an empty amniotic sac with no fetus inside. Dr. Deller told me then that the fetus had been destroyed by my own system. The next pregnancy was a success thanks to his smart medical approach; he administered weekly immunoglobulin IV treatments, which literally saved my son Kyle.

Morgan was born without a hitch, thanks to the hormone treatments, but the miscarriage a year after he was born threw me back into a tailspin. I couldn't understand why my body continued to fight some of my pregnancies. Dr. Deller explained that sometimes the immune or endocrine systems take over and supersede medical understanding. Lucky for me, my doctor is on the cutting edge of this treatment approach, giving us the opportunity to build and raise our wonderful family. My family means everything to me, and I know that if—*when*—Steven makes it through this whole mess, I am going to dedicate whatever it takes to build upon our marriage and make *it* strong again, too.

Getting up from the table, Dad and I agree that we will keep Dr. Deller up-to-date on anything we find out, and he offers to do the same.

The three of us walk together to the elevator to go see Steven. As we approach the elevator, we are startled by a loud crashing sound. Looking over, we see an overturned trash can, with a janitor picking it up. Fear surges in my veins as I see what I hoped would not be true: Henry. He kneels to scoop up trash strewn on the floor. Dad shoots me an urgent look while we join Dr. Deller, who is approaching Henry to offer him a hand.

Hanging a few steps behind, I whisper to Dad, "Don't say anything to Henry just yet. Let's see how he reacts. We aren't one hundred percent sure he's our man."

"Henry, let me help you with this," Dr. Deller is saying.

I've never spent any time with Henry, but as my father and I approach, I pick up a very strong negative energy from him—rage-filled and bold—the way he acted when I approached the van the other day. Something has set him off, but I don't know what. He's acting very erratic.

He tilts his head on an angle to look up at Dr. Deller. "No, leave it! I'm fine." He looks down and ignores us, going back to his work.

We pivot and turn around, heading back to the elevator. Looking over my shoulder, I realize just how big and menacing Henry is. Could *this* be my stalker—the crude, letter-writing jerk, trying to terrorize me?

I'm seething under my breath as I tell Dad, "I have half a mind to go over there and confront that—that—that horrible man."

Dad pulls me close to him and whispers, "Just be calm, honey. This doesn't prove anything."

Dr. Deller, obviously taken aback by the response from Henry, slowly walks away, stunned that a hospital staffer would take that tone with a doctor. As he steps through the open elevator door, he signals for us to get in. Inside, he slams a closed fist into his free hand and shakes his head. "Are you kidding me? That man was so incredibly rude," he says. "I was only trying to help! I didn't want to get into an altercation with him, so I just walked away."

Dad and I nod in agreement. I say, "Henry is our best bet right now. We think he could be the one who has been writing the pink notes and doing all these horrible things."

"If you look at the big picture," Dad adds, "he could have easily followed Betsy to the beach and still made it to work on time."

"But what would be his motivation?" Dr. Deller looks baffled. "He's been working for us for years. It doesn't add up."

I shrug and offer up my best guess. "His motivation could simply be a sick crush. A vendetta. Anything. He's passively seen me go through hell and high water over the years, coming to your office dozens of times. He could easily have access to your files and know where I live *and* what I've experienced. Those notes were very specific about my life. Only a select few people would have that information. It could even be a reaction to drug use?"

"That's right, Betsy," Dad says. "We don't know that much about him, any one of those reasons could be true. However, we don't have enough evidence to pin it on him, so the police won't get involved yet. But we could keep a sharp eye on him for the next day or so. What do you think, Dr. Deller?"

"I agree. I could text you when I see him at work. And I know which car he drives, so I can keep track of his comings and goings. I can also find out where he lives and figure out when he'd be in transit," Dr. Deller says.

We agree on this makeshift plan and exit the elevator to Steven's floor.

Steven is back in his room, and the security guard on duty lets us enter the dimly lit room. Dad and Dr. Deller give him gentle touches on the arm, and I lean over and give him a sweet kiss on the cheek.

"Hello, Mrs. Ryan and Mr. Anderson," Dr. Abbott says as he walks into Steven's room.

"Hello, doctor," I say, then introduce Dr. Deller. "This is my OB-GYN, Dr. Deller."

They shake hands. "How's the patient doing?" Dr. Deller asks, nodding towards Steven. "I know his wife is on pins and needles, hoping for good news."

"He was exposed to arsenic through his IV, but we caught it in time and flushed his system, so no damage was done. For now, we need to focus on his healing. He needs to rest for the rest of the day and tonight," Dr. Abbott says, "but please stay as long as you want."

"Oh, my God. Who would do that?"

"At this point, we don't know," Dr. Abbott replies, as he looks down shaking his head.

Dr. Deller seems to sense the tension as he chimes in, "Thank you for that update. I know it's important for Betsy and her family to know what's going on."

"I know the police are investigating the case, as we speak," he quickly replies.

Dr. Deller turns to us. "Betsy and Cary, now that you've gotten some answers and are settled here, I'm going to make my way home. I trust we'll connect sometime tomorrow, yes?"

"Yes, doctor, thank you for everything." I watch him leave, carrying the secret we've shared with him this evening. I wipe away tears as I look over to Dad standing at Steven's bedside.

Quietly I whisper to Steven, "Get better, please, so you can protect me from Henry in the future."

Dad is silent as we drive down the winding road that leads to my house. I'm looking out the window at the array of gorgeous homes whizzing by as we travel.

I break the silence. "Dad, what do you think we should do first?"

"I've been thinking about that," he says. "Since we almost bumped into Henry at the hospital and then observed his little dustup with Dr. Deller, I believe he's going to keep a low profile for the rest of today." He's staring out the front windshield but is razor-focused on me. "I think you go about your business, lock up, and make sure you set the security alarm when you to go bed tonight. We are just a few minutes away, plus I know Misty is *armed* and ready whenever you need her. We'll meet again in the morning and go see Steven and circle the wagons. Sounds good?"

"I don't know what I would do without you guys," I reply, quickly and gently squeezing his left knee. "I feel so safe and protected, even during this terrifying experience. I think we have enough evidence for the police to get more aggressive with my case now. Maybe even question Henry?"

Nodding my dad agrees. "That's a great idea, honey. Now get some rest tonight."

"Sounds good. I think I'm going to invite Misty over so the kids can hang out and us moms can talk. I'll feel safer with her here with me."

The driveway leading to my garage is short, so we pull right in after Dad clicks the door remote. As I hop out of the car, I run into the garage, and before the door shuts, I slowly watch his car back up and disappear. I throw one last wave goodbye before exiting the interior garage door—quickly making my way up the walkway to the house.

The pavers leading to the house are lined with a gorgeous array of fall flowers that partially spill over the walkway of speckled rocks. A sweet *Quan Yin* statue that Steven gave me for my birthday years ago watches over them. He knows I've taken a liking to the female version of Buddha ever since I started my meditation class. The patio, situated closer to the house, is made up of a sturdy bluestone, housing my teak patio dining table with a navy umbrella and two teal-, white-, and navy-striped lounge chairs. It matches my house colors perfectly. It's the ideal yard for family entertaining.

While walking toward the house, I take in the tumbling sound of the fountain in the corner of the yard and fixate on the beauty and functionality that we worked so hard to create in our backyard retreat. I don't notice the landscaper, Antonio, who's also looking down and walking straight toward me. Startled, and trying to avoid a collision, I lurch back and give my him an alarmed look. I'm frozen as I size up the man before me. He's about six feet tall, wearing a dark cotton bomber jacket, and sturdy black work boots—like what my attacker in the city wore and the stalker was wearing when I identified him after my walk at the beach with Barney. *Why am I pointing fingers at all these people?* Everyone has become a suspect. *Snap out of it, Betsy.*

"Hello, Mrs. Ryan," he says, smiling at me. "Beautiful day."

"Oh, Antonio, hello, you startled me," I cautiously reply, not sure if he understands why on earth I'd be startled.

Antonio smiles and goes about his work as I quickly scurry to the side entrance, unlock the door, and slip inside. What am I thinking? This landscaper has worked for some of my friends for years and came to work for us with excellent recommendations. I truly believe he would never think of harming me.

Thankfully, I gave a copy of the new side gate key, after I changed the locks, to

the landscaping office, so he could enter the gate without me having to be home. That reminds me, I should add *Give a new key to dog groomer,* to my to-do list when I get inside.

I decide that before I get suspicious of Antonio, I need look at the solid evidence. I've not encountered him during one of the incidents.

The quiet rumble of thunder off in the distance grabs my full attention as I stride over to the window and peek out. I watch Antonio complete his excellent, detailed work in my yard. Pausing, I scan the property as I form a brief grin on my lips and nod, feeling very appreciative that he keeps my yard the sanctuary that it is.

213

Without notice, Misty unlocks and slides open my patio door, causing me to jump back from the window. I slide the shutter back to its closed position. Barney greets her with an affectionate lick as she enters the room. He's grown to love her as much as I have.

I smile and meet her at the kitchen island. She's smartly dressed in a pair of dark Levis and a leopard skin belt, a crisp white button-down shirt, and brown Coach loafers—looking like my perfect Secret Service agent. I fill her in on the latest developments with our case. She nods in amazement as I share the next steps of the plan.

"For now, though, we should just have an ordinary evening with the kids, like any other Friday night. We can order in some Chinese from *PF Chang's* and splurge on kiddie cocktails, direct from my secret stash of Cokes in the wine fridge." Steven has never understood why I filled it with soda, given that I don't drink the stuff, but I think tonight's a good night to let loose and sip on pops intended only for company. Soda twice in one week… I'm living large. I'm determined to focus on my kids, our friendship, and Steven's recovery—not that psychopath.

"That sounds great to me," Misty responds. "By the way, I wanted to tell you a secret."

"Oh, sounds juicy! I could use something else to think about right now. Do tell."

"I met someone… on a dating website. Before you start lecturing me, just hear me out."

"Okay, I'm all ears."

"To avoid hitting the bar scene again, I decided to go online to a dating website and create a profile. Within a couple of days, I've gotten three responses."

"Wow, you go, girl!"

"I agreed to meet one of the guys today for lunch, and boy, was he a cutie. Tall, dark, and handsome… and would you believe it? He's a doctor."

"Just what I've always dreamed for you! After a few dates, if things go well, we should go on a double date—of course, after Steven recovers."

"Geez, you've already got a double date planned and I've just met him. Slow down, buckaroo. Oh, I hear the door opening, your mom must be home with the boys."

"Don't think you're getting out of this conversation that easy, Misty. We *will* discuss that lunch date of yours, after dinner while the kids are watching the flick."

"Sounds like a deal. I'll grab the backpacks and get the kids geared up for a fun movie night."

"Any requests?"

"I was thinking maybe we could watch *Mulan*. I know it's an oldie, but given your heroism lately, it's fitting. I can be the sidekick, *Mushu*, to your *Ping*. I do look good in red-orange dragon garb."

Laughing at my always-positive and energetic friend as she heads out the door, I visualize a cartoon version of Misty taking on *Shan Yu* and the rest of *General Li's* army, kicking, punching, and taking them down. I know I picked the right person to be my *protector*. Barney looks up as if to say, *Mom, I'd like to be Mushu, if it's okay with you? I seem like a better sidekick.*

"You're right, Barney, old boy. I'll talk to Misty about that later. *You* are my number-one protector."

I'm starting to enjoy my one-sided conversations with Barney—they're rather interesting.

The slow, rhythmic sound of the falling rain on the rooftop and the intermittent cracks of lightning piercing the early evening's sky set the backdrop for our family movie night with Misty and the girls. The storm has set in for the long haul, offering low rumbles of thunder to keep us aware that a bigger storm is brewing in the distance. The kids probably don't hear the rumble over in the living room where they're talking and giggling.

"At least I don't have to water the yard tomorrow," I say to Misty as I lower my voice. "The sprinkler system is on the fritz, so the landscaper told me to water everything a few times a week. Those plants and bushes are worth a fortune, so I want to make sure I keep up with it. I almost walked right into Antonio in the yard today. Nearly jumped out of my skin. Everyone is making me on edge." As Misty replies, I throw back the final bite of my eggroll.

"Aw man, Betsy, even Antonio is on the suspect list? What motive does he have? On another note, that's why I said you should've created a rock garden, instead—no watering required."

"Ha. Why don't you grab the kids' plates and rinse them in the sink? I'll go take Barney for a quick walk to get the job done. I could use some fresh air before the rain starts to pour. I'll stay close. Then later this evening we won't have to go for a walk, he can just piddle in the yard." It seems that Barney likes to go number two when we're on leashed walks, and not in the yard. I completely agree with him. Who wants to poop in their own yard?

"Sounds good. We'll start the movie now and then later we can eat that awesome chocolate cake you baked."

"Correction, the gourmet grocery store baked that cake. There's not enough time to bake these days, given that I have a stalker to keep track of." My humorous defenses can't overshadow the constant pump of adrenaline in my veins.

"Very true. Either way, I'm going to indulge. I've been working out all week and I'm ready for a sweet."

Misty starts the movie as the four kiddies snuggle on the couch under a fluffy blanket. Misty hops in my tan chair and nestles in, just the way it's intended to be sat in. I can wrestle her for that spot when I get back. I hesitate before I attach Barney's leash to his collar and watch the kids jockey for position, giggling and smiling. Life is good. I smile along with them.

"You can catch me up on the movie when I get back from our walk," I call, as I step out the side door with Barney, realizing the rain has beat me to the punch. We'll make this walk quick. With a burst of confidence and strength, I step out the door.

With an umbrella in one hand, I wrap Barney's leash around my other wrist and latch my thumb inside the loop at the top. I learned this trick from an animal trainer back when we first adopted him. She taught us so many useful dog training tips, most of which I use to this day. Ironically, if I'd known back then that Barney could understand me, I could have just told him what to do. Then again, what toddler, or even teenager, listens to their parents? It's probably best that I discovered our special bond at his midlife stage. This way we can bond as adults, without the immature stunts that most kids go through. Barney *is* like my grown-up kid, after all.

A startling flash of lightning brightens up the sky and the follow-up roll of thunder comes seconds afterward. The full moon hangs hidden behind thick clouds in a pitch-dark sky. We forge ahead several feet on our soggy walk, determined to get a number one and maybe even a number two in so we can skip our late-night bathroom stroll—every dog owner's dream.

Barney has always been a true champion when it comes to peeing on demand. All I need to say is, "Let's go potty, hurry up," and he gets the cue. And now that he understands me, I can just reason with him and explain that it's cold, or hot, or raining, or whatever and, ideally, he should get the job done.

I encourage him so we can get back inside. "Barney, let's try to get all of our business done on this walk so we don't have to go out late tonight. Does that sound good?"

While he sniffs around fervently, I giggle as I imagine his reply. *Uh, yeah, okay, Mom. Just give me a couple of minutes. I'm picking up a few scents from some German Shepherd and poodle friends who were near this tree earlier. I'd like to pee here to make my own personal statement, if it's okay with you.*

I smile, thinking how funny I must look and sound. "Oh, by all means, Barney. Take your time. I'm sure the rain won't melt me. I'm in no rush. Thanks for sharing."

Sniffing and walking in a circle near another tree, distracted, Barney continues his doo-doo quest.

Causing myself to laugh even harder I get carried away. *Um, yeah, Mom. Thanks for not tugging on my leash and pulling me away from this juicy gossip, like you usually do. It appears that the cute little schnauzer from across the street and the crazy Doberman from the block over were both here a little while ago, too. I'd like to leave my own scent, just so they know I was here, too.*

Now that I realize just how social this behavior is for my dog, I come to recognize why he always wants to go on walks and why he wants to go in different directions. He must get bored with the same old gossip and scents. From now on I must remember to give him more variety and social stimulation.

My mind wanders further past my make-believe conversation with my pet as we walk along the sidewalk, lit only by the streetlights and glow of the moon behind the rainclouds.

Then my mind shifts to my current stressor: the stalker. What makes someone want to hurt or stalk someone else? There must be a need or longing that has not been met. Maybe they've been abused or bullied or tortured. These thoughts pepper my mind as Barney has success with number two. I poke around in my soaked raincoat pocket to find a doo-doo bag to gather up our mess as Barney kicks his back feet into the wood chips, attempting to cover his deposit; I toss it in a trash can along our route.

Making our way back around my property, I hear a couple of teenagers scrambling from the storm to reach their cars. I silently send a little prayer of protection their way so they drive safely. You never know how slippery the roads might be. I throw in a prayer of protection for us on the walk, too.

Everything has gone still and calm except for the cadence of the rain. "Barney, do you hear or smell anything or anyone?"

Sniffing into the air, my dog stops, then continues his pursuit of animal scents along our path.

A chill works its way up my spine and settles in on the small hairs on the back of my neck. An odd sensation has taken over me. I decide to walk in a measured pace to clear my mind and get back to the house, keenly paying attention to my surroundings.

Barney's ears pinch back, and he stops walking, causing me to stop, too. The rain is beating down harder now, making it difficult to see.

"Let's get in the house, boy. I'm getting drenched. Plus, I'm not in the mood to bump into some crazed stalker this evening. That's why our walk was a quickie tonight."

We enter the gate, and hear a crashing sound near the garage that causes me to jump. The garage light isn't on, so I am unable to make out who or what is over there. Looking back at the house, I see and hear Misty and the kids sitting on the couch talking, thanks to my view of the patio door. The shutters prevent me from seeing the television screen, but I can tell they are watching intently. I make a mental note for my to-do list to install some sort of window covering on those patio doors. From outside we are very exposed on a dark night; anyone could see in from the back of the yard or even the alley behind our garage.

Barney starts to pull me in the direction of the garage, causing me to slip and stumble on the wet sidewalk. The grass is spewing mud and bits of plant material on the walkway from the flowing stream of water heading to the sewer drain at the back of the yard.

I gently tug on Barney's leash and ask him to *heel*. He yanks his head forward and instead starts to growl. He's pulling me harder.

I can't resist his strength, so I let the leash go. He runs over to the garage and starts barking and growling and scratching at the door.

Shoot. I forgot my phone. In the barking confusion, I hesitate, wondering if I should go run to the house and get Misty—and freak out the kids for possibly no good reason—or should I just quickly check the area by the garage? Maybe there's a skunk or a raccoon?

I catch up with him, as he growls and scratches at the door. I turn the handle as we enter the dark, damp garage, and flick on the light. It doesn't work. I wish I had brought my flashlight on the walk. The drain in the yard has partially overflowed and seeped under the trim of the door's threshold, causing water to empty into the garage like flowing rapids.

"Shoot. Look at all of this darn water, Barney!" I let him enter to run in the containment of the garage.

I hear Barney barking, and from the corner of my eye, I see him running in circles where Steven's car is usually parked. I attempt to use the wooden broom to swish the water back toward the doorframe to prevent a flooded garage. It's a futile effort at fixing the water situation, but I try anyway.

As I hold the broom in my hands, I glance over at Barney again in the dark, trying to see him over the hood of my car. His barks echo in the closed garage, and then they become violent growling, as if he's trying to bite something.

Bark, bark, bark!

Out of nowhere, someone comes from behind me and places a white rag, filled with a pungent liquid, over my mouth.

I struggle, but can feel myself passing out. The last thing I hear him say, as he's slamming the door, is "Get out of the garage, mutt." Barney whimpers, as if he might've been shoved or kicked. I black out.

In a foggy, dazed state, I feel my hands bound in front of me with duct tape. I'm sitting on an old milk crate in the dark garage. I keep my head down in the unconscious position as I try to access the situation. The baby is kicking and rolling around furiously as I try to focus on a way to escape.

"Wake up, Betsy. I know you see me." My attacker walks toward me. His sweaty stench fills the air around me. The smell brings me back ten years ago to my city attack, causing my heart to hammer with fear.

My cover is blown. I slowly raise my head, fighting off the dizziness and the taste of vomit in the back of my throat. I inhale through my nose and exhale silently, trying to maintain focus and clarity in the haze of the garage, which is only dimly lit from the light peering in through the door and window located in the middle of the wall.

"Before you speak, I would be very careful." With a shock, I recognize that voice. It's Dr. Hildebrandt. "Do not attempt to call out to anyone, because if you do, I will kill you. Understood? I should have killed you at the beach when I had the chance."

I nod, trying to focus on a spot by the wall, remaining silent. The realization that I am, once again, being attacked by a man while I'm pregnant turns my body numb. *Not again.* I won't let him or anyone harm my baby. I'm wishing inside my heart with all my might to fixate on my dog, Barney, who is somewhere outside. *If there is a God, please get him to bark loud enough to alert Misty.* I know it's crazy, but it's all I have right now. Within seconds, I hear a muffled sound outside the garage in the pouring rain. It's my dog, Barney, barking ferociously.

Dr. Hildebrandt is walking around me in a circle, eyeing my every move, however he doesn't seem to register that my dog is frantically trying to alert Misty.

God, please, this is important. Get Barney to go to the patio door and scratch very hard and bark. Otherwise this man will kill me and my baby. Begging and pleading with all my soul, I hope my prayers are answered. *If there are angels or something watching over me, please. Help me.*

In my foggy state, I hear, *Mom, I hear you. I am already here, but Misty can't hear me. I will run to the side door and try.*

Dr. Hildebrandt comes closer to me and bends down, resting his weight on his bent ankles, eye level to me. He asks, "Do you wonder why I am here and why I have been trying to communicate with you through the pink notes?"

I nod, trying not to look at him. His good looks are deceiving and fading away.

"Well, I will tell you, Betsy." His gruff voice continues, "I've wanted you, ever since you came to our practice ten years ago, after your miscarriage. But you've never given me the time of day or acknowledged me the way you should... Oh, I've tried." He's circling me, spewing saliva with each filthy word he utters. "When you lost your second baby, you came in to see Dr. Deller, not me! During your crying and blubbering in the waiting room, I was there in the office. I sympathized with you, but you paid no attention to me. Instead, you went to him." He grimaces as his face gets red with anger.

I look up with a blank expression on my face. I don't want him to see the hurt, anger, and confusion in my eyes. "I took his pink sheets of paper and placed the first note," he continues. "No one suspects accomplished, good-looking people like me. We get professional courtesy in most situations, unlike what you gave me. I knew where you lived and everything about you, including your medical check-up schedule—written in your medical file. Dr. Deller keeps very meticulous notes. Lucky for me, it was child's play finding out your details." He points to me, and then over to my house and back again—encompassing everything about me, my family, and where I live. "Seeing you pregnant again gave me the urge to make my move—after so many years of wanting you."

Tears roll down my face as I remember that horrific day when I had my first pregnancy loss. *Never again, Betsy; fight for this baby.* I nod *yes*, as if to acknowledge his words. Inside my heart, I'm frantically begging, pleading: *hurry, please, someone help me. I hear Barney frantically barking. Hurry, Barney.*

"Then, when you had to have the D&C procedure, I was in the hospital, hoping you would be okay." He squats down again, resting on his knees, inches from my face. "I came into the registration area, and still again, you did not acknowledge me the way I expected and craved. You could have come to me for support, but no!

"When you gave birth to both of your sons, you stayed in the hospital to recover. I was there, but did you even notice me? No!" He gets up and screams down at me, "You were more concerned with your baby and your doctor, not me!" His voice is cloaked behind the pouring rain, but ringing in my ears—his face inches from mine. His breath is sour, filthy. Nothing like the image of the man I've casually seen over the years.

He exposes a large hunting knife and taps the point on the tip of my chin, pricking it to expose several droplets of blood, then a quarter-inch slash. The cut stings.

I struggle to choke back sobs that are caught in my throat—lungs protesting to take in any additional air. Feeling dizzy, I drop my head and look down at my feet, where drops of blood are accumulating. My baby, Emmy Grace, is sitting motionless, evidently sensing my gripping fear. Am I going to die here? *Please, God, protect me. Touch my dog's heart and soul and guide him to protect me or go get help.*

"I watched your children go to school, your dog walks, fights with your husband in the backyard, trying to shield it from your children. I knew you needed me to rescue you, but you refused me. He was in the arms of another woman and you never knew!" His diabolical laugh echoes as he nods his head.

I lift my head, rage surging through my entire body, and scream, "How dare you? How dare you, Hildebrandt! I'll be damned if I'm going to let you hurt me, or anyone I love." I don't even know his first name, and yet he feels a need, after ten years, to get even—for what?

He's caught off guard by my scream, which I hope caught someone's attention. I wish Misty could hear me over this pounding thunderstorm and the movie. "I never did *anything* to you to deserve this treatment. I love my family. My husband loves me! I don't believe you."

He takes a step forward and swings the back of his opened hand, knuckles toward my face, and smacks me across the cheek, knocking me to the floor. Unable to use my bound hands to soften the fall, my hip hits the floor first, then my cheek. Tears are streaming, mixing with the blood, creating a puddle on the floor right next to my cheek. I hope the baby is okay. She's still. I breathe slowly, taking in air at a measured pace, hoping she can feel my love.

Feeling my baby's love in return, I muster up the courage to fight. Behind my closed lips, I grit my teeth, fueled by love and faith, and hang on.

He grabs my hair and pulls me back onto the crate. "Get up! I almost killed your husband in the hospital, but those damn doctors had to butt in, just like Dr. Deller coming in between us. He's always interfered with my life, with *you*. That made me angrier than you'll ever know." He starts to pace the room again, obviously thinking about what to do next. His eyes are dark with fury; he's huffing and puffing heavily as he scans the garage. Any physical beauty that he once had is gone. With each exhale, the stench of hateful, dirty breath fills the air.

I zero in on my baby and become very still, helping me focus and go inside to ignore my physical pain. I focus on Barney. I close my eyes and picture my dog running in circles in the yard, trying to get Misty's attention so he can bring her to the garage. Somehow, I can visualize her whispering on her cell phone in my yard. I wish my imagination were true, but I'm afraid this may be my last thought before I die. I hear the pounding rain, I hear my dog, I think I hear Misty.

The many thoughts of my life start to flash in front of my face, like quick flickers of film. My thoughts stop and focus on a flashback of a *Lassie* television show rerun that I once watched as a young girl. I can see the collie leading Ruth and

Paul Martin to find their adoptive son, Timmy, who'd fallen in the well. Barney is my Lassie, but will he bring me help?

Hildebrandt's raging voice jolts me from my thoughts as he surges back over to where I am sitting, knife above his head. I hear him speak, almost as if we're under water in slow motion. "If I can't have you, no one will, Betsy. I will kill you. And then I'll kill myself."

In that instant, I'm thrown back into reality, where I clearly hear Misty scream, "Hold it right there, asshole! Don't make one more move or I'll blow your head off!" Misty's gun stance is impressively threatening as she squints and then suddenly lowers her weapon and stares at Dr. Hildebrandt.

"Gary! What are you doing?"

He swerves his head and sees Misty with Barney standing by her side, growling. Both are frozen for what feels like minutes, then he charges straight for her and throws her to the ground. Her gun flings over, near where I'm being held captive.

Little did he realize Misty has serious black belt capabilities. They grapple on the muddy pavement for several minutes as Barney runs to my side, licking my leg. I struggle to a stand and scramble to seize the gun. I see the cold steel end of the weapon as I point it at my stalker, screaming for Misty to duck as I shoot three times—hoping Misty heard me and isn't in the bullet's path.

Bang-Bang-Bang!

Everything is happening so fast as I drop the gun and run over and tend to Misty, whose arm is cut. Dr. Gary Hildebrandt is unconscious on the ground; I don't know if he's dead or not, but blood is soaking his chest wounds. The searing pain on my cheek and hip increase by the second as I struggle to help Misty to her feet.

I hear sirens in the distance.

Being inside an ambulance can be rather telling, as it gives you a better appreciation for the dedicated paramedics who work in an even-tempered fashion to fix you. To observe their skill and ability—tending to victims in a moving vehicle—is awe-inspiring.

The paramedic wraps the cuff around my bicep to check my blood pressure, then shines a light over my eyes to check my pupils. Next, he gently presses his fingers on my vein to check my pulse, then uses the stethoscope to listen to the baby. Another person applies a butterfly bandage to the blood-crusted knife cut on my chin, while I hold an ice pack against my cheek where Dr. Hildebrandt hit me.

The driver whizzes through a red light, only slightly slowing down to confirm there is no oncoming traffic, then proceeds through the intersection at full speed. I can hear the person sitting in the front passenger seat talking my parents, letting them know I'm okay and am headed to Good Faith Hospital. I'm certain I won't be taken to the ICU, but interestingly Steven and I will spend the night in the same building tonight.

The paramedic turns to me. "Mrs. Ryan, when we arrive at the hospital, we're going to take you in on a stretcher, so please remain in this position when the driver parks the ambulance, okay?" His slender build and thick head of blond hair, cut in a surfer-dude style, perfectly match his laid-back demeanor—ironic for an EMT.

"Sure, no problem," I say. "Can I give you this ice pack or should I keep it on my cheek? It's cold and making my hand numb."

"Aw, I'd keep it on until the doctor sees you, if I were you. You don't want that shiner to take hold."

The familiar hospital sights, sounds, and smells permeate my senses while the paramedics check in at the ER reception desk and I wait to be seen by a doctor. They transfer me to a wheelchair sitting next to a wall, where I close my eyes to have a few minutes of privacy.

My quiet reprieve is interrupted when a young and energetic orderly pushes my wheelchair into an exam room housed behind a flimsy curtain. The patient next door is complaining about her broken leg and something about pain pills.

A police officer comes in. It's Officer Flaggler.

I nod and wait for him to continue.

"I'd like to get a statement from you while you wait for the doctor to arrive. I've been filled in on the details of your attack," he said. "I am so sorry that we could not have been more helpful in arresting this person. We just did not have enough descriptive evidence and manpower to stake out your home. I truly apologize."

"Yes, of course, I remember you, and yes, that is correct." Trying to focus, exhaustion pulls at my eyelids. I just want to get this over with so I can get some sleep.

"Your neighbor, a Miss Misty Nicks, called the station earlier this evening when your dog showed up at your house without you. She sensed foul play. She said she was the person who called the station the other day when the assailant was outside your home. We immediately dispatched the ambulance and a squad car to your residence." He's reading from a notepad, to make sure he gets the facts straight.

PINK
SLIPS

"I thought I heard the ambulance in the distance when I was in the garage. Thank you for coming so quickly."

"From what I understand, you and Misty Nicks were in inherent danger, and you would've been stabbed to death if you hadn't gotten ahold of her weapon to stop the attack. Is that what you remember?"

"Yes, that's exactly what happened. It was self-defense," I reply, trying to rack my brain to remember. It all happened so fast. All I can remember is hearing Barney bark nonstop and the sound of the gun going off. I hope Misty recalls the story with more clarity... I just can't remember. "Is Dr. Hild... the suspect... dead?"

"Yes, ma'am. He died at the scene. Ms. Nicks arrived in the other ambulance and is with the doctors in another exam room having her laceration stitched up. She'll be able to leave after we get her statement. Your neighbors, the Swansons, are at your house with the children." Given what we've been through the past few days, I must admit, Misty has been ready to jump in and help me, without question. Ironically, I ended up being the hero of my own attack. Whatever the outcome, though, Misty and Barney saved my life.

Now that I have signed my police statement and it's on the books, I can meet with my ER doctor. Hopefully, it'll be quick so I can get to my room for the night, because my eyelids are winning the battle for sleep.

———

This hospital room is much cozier than where Steve is in the ICU. I will have a beautiful view of the lake in the morning. The dim lighting in the hallway, and in my room, is soft compared to the stark fluorescent glow of the lights and machines Steven is subject to. I realize he is not conscious right now, but it must be hard on the folks who need to work there, day in and day out—not to mention the visiting family members. I'm thankful they're keeping me overnight to monitor the baby after that horrific attack. We really took a beating.

Since I forgot my cell phone when I went on the walk with Barney, I need to use the wall-connected phone in the room, located on the movable bedside table. I want to give Misty a quick call to check in with her. She must be eager to talk with me.

The door opens. "Oh, Betsy," my parents cry as they enter my room. "We were so worried about you." Arm in arm, they approach my bed and swoop in for a hug.

"Well, thanks to Misty, I'm okay," I say. "The baby's okay, too."

Mom holds back sobs as she runs her fingers through my curls. "Misty is on her way back home to be with the boys and get them to bed, until we get there. Luckily Mrs. Swanson was able to come over and stay with them after the ambulance took Misty."

"Did Mrs. Swanson know what was going on?"

"Your father told her there was a bit of an accident and we had to meet you at the hospital. As far as she knows, it wasn't a big deal. Surprisingly, I don't think she heard the gunshots."

"How did you know what was going on?"

"Misty called us when she saw Barney barking at the back door, without you. She asked if we had heard from you, then told us to call the police while she searched the garage and areas around your house. Misty called and told us everything. I can't believe how brave you are, sweetie. Between you, Barney, and Misty, you fought off that horrible man!"

"It's all surreal. I just hope the police know it was self-defense."

"Honey, they do. Misty is your witness. We'll be here to help with any legal issues. Do you know why did he do this to you? A doctor, of all people?" Dad asks as he sits on the edge of my bed, gently rubbing my ankle. Mom stands next to him, relief fills her face.

"He said he's been watching me for several years, ever since I started going to their medical practice—right after the city attack. Never in my right mind would I have imagined that someone who gave me medical attention at one time would target me. He snooped through the files, just like Dad said, and found out everything personal about me. As a doctor of the practice, he had free reign. It's truly scary to think how patients can be victims this easily."

Right on cue, Dr. Deller enters the room in a rush and joins my parents at my bedside. "Oh, Betsy! Are you okay? I am so sorry this happened to you. I can't believe it was Dr. Hildebrandt! You think you know someone..."

"I know it's hard to fathom that a loyal employee of the hospital and your business partner would do such a thing, but it's true." Feeling more energized, I wiggle myself to an upright position in the bed. "He told me how he was able to find out everything about me through your files."

"Dr. Deller, we were just talking about this. It must have been very easy for your medical partner to get to Betsy's personal information," Dad points out.

"Well, from what I've figured out, he must have snooped through Betsy's file. And, you're right, being a doctor in my practice, there's no way I could've prevented that." He gestures with his hands, as if he's trying to make his point. "And since he was a registered doctor of our office and cleared for passage throughout the hospital campus, he had access to many doors."

Nodding, I chime in. "It looks like if a doctor goes rogue, I agree, there's really no stopping him."

"Oftentimes, after I see a patient, I take their file into my office and recite audio dictation for Donna to transcribe into your file later that day or even the next morning, depending on when she gets to it." While he's speaking, Dr. Deller looks at my parents and then over to me. "Typically, I also add handwritten personal notes about my patients in their file folders, then I place them in the outbox on the top of my desk for Donna to refile. Gary may have come into my office after hours to peek at the personal information and then put the files back. By doing this, no one would ever know. If he snooped hard enough, he would find the key to the master files up at the front reception desk, hidden in Donna's top desk drawer. Not very secure, I must admit." He shakes his head and quirks up the left side of his mouth in discontent.

A flash of aggravation fills my voice. "I agree, since he had access to all of my personal information. Let's say, for example, if Donna was in cahoots with him, it could've happened anyway. There's really no stopping the personal information intrusion."

Dr. Deller sighs, shifting uncomfortably. "I know, Betsy. We do follow the HIPPA guidelines in our office, and in this case, it wouldn't have mattered because he's a doctor and he has access to files—whether it's legal or not, he was able to gain access. Monday when I get back to work, I will work on a more secure file system with Donna."

Interjecting, my mom inquires, "Doctor, how did you know our daughter was here in the hospital? My husband received a call from Betsy's neighbor and the paramedic in the ambulance, but I don't think she has your phone number."

Dr. Deller catches my sudden glance and crooks his bushy eyebrows as he winks at me. "Call it intuition or *a little voice* in my head. I just had a feeling about the Ryan family and called over here. The ER nurse's station told me Betsy was here after I informed them that I was her doctor."

I knew exactly what that bushy-browed wink meant; Dr. Deller must've had a hunch. I remember how he'd shared the gifted experience he had with his wife when she was on her deathbed. I imagine he's been aware of it ever since. He must be better at this communication method than he lets on.

While Mom and Dad continue to talk with my doctor, I close my eyes and breathe deeply. I visualize the hazy amniotic fluid within my belly, which houses my beautiful Emmy Grace. I see her sucking her thumb, floating. She does a roll inside my belly, which is visible to Mom and Dad.

"Hey, Karen, did you see that? The baby just did the wave to her grandma."

My mom blushes and softly rubs the moving mound on my belly as if to high-five her granddaughter.

Dr. Deller shoots me another wink. "Well, folks, if you'll give me a few minutes alone with Betsy, I'd like to give a quick exam and check on our rolling, high-fiving baby, here."

"No problem, doc. Betsy, it looks like you are going to be okay," my mother says. "Your father and I will stop over at the ICU and peek in on Steven on our way back to the house. Your father will come by in the morning to bring you home."

———

The stress is ironed out of Dr. Deller's face after he examines my baby. The deep, furrowed brow is less creased, and his smile is softer. I adore this man, in a patient kind of way. He has been here for me for years, and has always made the right decisions related to my health and that of my babies. How could I have ever doubted his sincerity or loyalty to me? He would never hurt me. I truly believe he was unaware of Dr. Hildebrandt's plan or obsession.

"Betsy, you two will be just fine. You believe that, don't you?"

"For sure, doctor." I meet his hand with a high-five.

"I can't even begin to tell you how my awareness of your attack came about."

It seems like he's going to try anyway.

"I was blown away by the power of it all. I was relaxing and reading a book in my living room when I heard a sound. I put my book down and looked around the house. I couldn't find the source of the sound, so I decided to go back to my book. I was seriously engaged in the next chapter when out of the blue, I heard the sound again. I stopped and listened, intently… like a bolt of lightning, I realized the sound was coming from my subconscious. I didn't realize it at the time, but I had been focusing on you, deep down. I was so worried when I left the hospital that I must have planted a deep-rooted seed in the recesses of my mind that I would keep my senses open for you. I know it sounds crazy," he says, but I shake my head and he continues.

"Anyway, I heard someone screaming and then crying, from deep inside my consciousness. When I realized, it was you, I panicked and called the hospital. They told me you were here." The glimmer in his eye told me what his words didn't. He must have been proud and honored to show up and help me in this special way.

Not surprised by his fantastic story, I share a warm smile with my doctor. I will only ever be able to tell a short list of people who are close to me about this connection that I share with him; a gift that has brought my family together. We have been given a light into a world that is not known to many on Earth, and with that gift, we will do good things.

"I am so glad that you came to the hospital to check on us and even more happy that my baby is going to be okay," I say.

"Thank you so much, Betsy," Dr. Deller replies, a tear rolling down his cheek. "Thank you for trusting in me and for letting me help you. It's been hard since my wife died, but I feel a stronger sense of purpose once again. You have given that to me. Now let's get this baby to term and bring your family a little girl."

The shimmery light of day peeks through my window at the crack of dawn. The sounds of happily chirping birds chattering outside my window as they enjoy their breakfast gives me a chance to wake up slowly before the hospital floor starts buzzing with morning traffic. I stretch and move the monitor that's connected to my arm so that I can slide my hospital gown up and look at my watch. I can't locate it, and then remember that after I called Misty last night I left it on the rolling bedside table, next to the hospital phone.

My door is ajar and the light from the hallway exposes the dry erase board on the wall by the entrance to my room. On it I read, *Betsy Ryan, age thirty-eight, pregnant. Administer fluids upon waking, obtain urine sample, and take vitals.* Now that I know what's in store, I might as well wait to get up and pee.

A nurse comes in. "Good morning, Mrs. Ryan. How are you feeling this morning?" she asks as she turns off the signal on my monitor. I smile instead of responding. "I'm here to get a urine sample from you. Your doctor has instructed that we do a few labs and, if your vitals are okay, you are free to go this morning. Sound good?"

"That's perfect, because I really have to pee!" Maneuvering off the bed and into my plastic slippers, I add, "I'll be right back."

From outside the bathroom, the nurse calls in to me. "Once you're done here, I'd be happy to take you up to the ICU to see your husband. He is now conscious and is asking to see you. We haven't told him about your condition, but I suggest you avoid talking about that for now."

She waits while I'm in the bathroom. A few minutes later, I emerge. "Here you go. One cup of pee for your morning enjoyment," I sarcastically offer.

"We've got a funny one here, huh? Now hop up on the bed, Ellen DeGeneres, and let's check your vitals." She shoots me a sly smile.

It's great to have a nurse with a great sense of humor this early in the morning, especially since she thinks *I'm* funny. I wonder if she'll be here when I have the baby? I could use some cheer after going through labor again. I can't believe how much time I've spent in this hospital; I've joked before that I should just get my own private room, but this isn't what I meant. Just a few more weeks, and I'll be here giving birth to our daughter.

Out of curiosity I look up at my nurse and ask, "I'm just wondering, did anyone on this floor know much about the man who tried to kill me? Dr. Hildebrandt?"

The nurse stops what she is doing and intently watches me as I speak. She replies, somewhat hesitantly, "Yes, we all knew him. On the outside, he seemed like an ordinary doctor, but deep down, I hear he was troubled. He has had an OB-GYN practice through this hospital for years, but no one really talked about his past. We're learning a lot of details now."

"What do you mean, *troubled*?" I sit up with more interest.

"Evidently, his pregnant wife was killed late one night by a woman who was driving home from work. It was an accident, and the woman was never charged in the murder. He was never the same, from what people are saying, but at work he seemed to cover it up rather well. Once, he told one of the nurses about his wife, Betty, and showed her a picture. Evidently, she had blonde, curly hair…" In that moment, my nurse sees my expression and stops talking.

She starts to fidget with her stethoscope, then mutters as she leaves the room, "Would you excuse me?"

The weight of what I just heard bears down on me like a ton of bricks as I search my heart for answers—I feel burdensome and sorrowful. How could I have known? This man was reaching out to me in a very abnormal, broken kind of way, a way in which I would never have known. How could I know? I was never unkind to him, yet I never acknowledged him as my doctor, either. Was I wrong in the way I disregarded him unknowingly? I shake the self-blame from my thoughts, but the bitter chill inside, remains.

The nurse returns to my room, her eyes moist and pink in the corners. I meet her gaze and share a compassionate smile; we silently agree to never discuss Dr. Hildebrandt again.

"All set, Mrs. Ryan. You are good to go once your labs come back normal. Your belongings are in the plastic bag on the chair in the corner. You can probably grab a bite to eat at the hospital cafeteria. It opens at seven."

"Thanks so much—for everything." I smile brightly, sending her warmth and appreciation from my heart. My gratitude begins to melt the guilt-laden frost that had started to form deep inside. By her sharing this information with me, I have gained a better understanding and closure for my stalker's actions.

My heart is pounding a little faster with the anticipation of seeing Steven. What will I say to him? Will he remember anything from the past few days? I grab my clothes to get dressed as fast as I can so I can get going, and call Misty from the bedside table phone. I get her voicemail.

"Hey, Misty, it's me. I know you're probably in the shower right now. I'm calling you from the primeval, wall-connected phone in my hospital room. I wanted to let you know that I'm leaving the hospital this morning. I'm all right—just looking rather bruised and battered—but am going to see Steven shortly, then I'm coming home to shower. I smell."

Hopefully, Misty will check her messages, because I've got some interesting news for her.

By now, the nurses in the ICU probably know me by name. Let's hope this little relationship that we've developed will soon come to an end so I can get my husband home to heal in his own bed. The security guard lifts his chin slightly to acknowledge that he knows who I am, and as I slide by, says, "Glad to hear you're okay, Mrs. Ryan." He's a strong and sturdy man, perfect for his chosen profession. His mustache floats above his top lip like a brown, fluffy caterpillar, matching his set of eyebrows.

I meet his gaze, smile, and mouth the words, "Thank you."

I take slow, quiet steps into the room to meet Steven's bedside. His eyes are closed, but his breathing tubes are out of his mouth, which is a good sign. I sit back on the ugly upholstered chair and wait for him to awaken. The hallway outside his room is starting to fill with muffled sounds of the new day in the ICU, but he doesn't seem to hear it. I sit and gaze at my husband, imagining what I will say to him when he wakes up. I've run our last real conversations in my head a hundred times and am trying to figure out where we go from there. I know we were arguing about moving to California, but given all the confusion with the accident, his hospitalization, and our communications, I'm not sure that will be an issue now.

The words Dr. Hildebrandt uttered before his death keep playing over and over in my mind, like a broken record: "*He was in the arms of another woman and you never knew.*" Who was this other woman, and when was she in my husband's arms that the stalker could see them? Perhaps Dr. Hildebrandt had simply made it up or jumped to conclusions, based on the arguments he witnessed; but how in God's name had he even seen us fighting? It's creepy to think he was nearby, listening and watching us. But I decide that today is not the day to bring up that subject. What I want is a peaceful and pleasant reunion with my husband.

Sitting for over thirty minutes in this room, waiting for him to wake up is making me go stir-crazy, so I decide to head home and let him rest. I can come back later after I've cleaned up and regrouped.

———

Dad is parked in the loading zone outside the hospital, waiting for me. I'm thankful that he's on time so I can get home and shower; I spent more time in Steven's room than I thought I would, but I'm glad he didn't wake up and see me this way. It's for the best that he fell back asleep before I got there.

I hop in the front passenger seat of Dad's car and click in the seat belt across my pregnant belly. As we drive off, I glance back at the hospital, thankful that the stalker threat is out of my life. Now I need to confront the threat that is my crumbling marriage… or maybe not.

"How ya doin', kid?" Dad looks freshly shaven, his partially dried hair combed back, exposing his distinguished high cheekbones and perfectly placed wrinkles around his dark eyes.

"I'm doing okay, just a little freaked out about last night. Are the boys doing okay? I'm sure they're so confused about what's going on."

"Not really. Misty diverted their attention beautifully when she ran out to find you. Luckily, she gave them dessert right before she stepped out, so they were happily eating. In fact, they had just finished up when we arrived later."

"I really thought that I was a goner for a minute there. I can't get the image of his bloody dark hair out of my head, or the stench of the blood." I shake my head. "I found out some of the reasons why Gary Hildebrandt was stalking me for so long."

"Really?" My dad throws me a quick glance, then focuses back on the road.

Nodding slowly, I look out the window and watch the trees zip by the window as we drive. "Yeah, I guess I looked like his pregnant wife, Betty, who was killed in a car accident years ago." Looking down at my hands, I reflect on the comparison he must have made between his wife and myself. "He must have fixated on me, and over the years, it grew and grew every time I came in to see Dr. Deller. He was extremely jealous of my connection with my doctor and the mere fact that I was his patient."

"That's a shame. Sad really, when you think about it. Betty and Betsy sure sound alike. The scarier part is that he was able to get all of your personal information from the files in his own office." Dad's tone goes from compassion to angst and then anger. "There needs to be an overhaul on their security policies. I may just make some calls on Monday to see if I can shake the bush. I know they followed HIPPA laws, but how do you protect against someone who works in a particular practice from exposing your personal information, law or not?"

"That's a good idea, Dad. I'm not sure what we can do, but it's worth researching. On a happier note, I'm excited to see the boys and give them hugs! I also hope Misty's injury is okay. I'm glad her daughters were with their father last night. I know she left the hospital after they stitched her up and took her statement. Did you see her after she came back home?"

"Yes, she popped in quick to say hello, but the boys had already gone to bed. I told her we'd stop by and see her after I picked you up this morning."

Being back home and in my own kitchen gives me a silent moment of joy. I love the aromas of the food, working on my gorgeous countertops, and being surrounded by the soothing colors that meld perfectly with the muted living room décor.

As I watch the kids play on the other side of the room while Barney sits at my feet, I only half hear Misty asking me a question. "Were you able to talk with Steven?"

"Actually, no. After I was released from my room, I went down there to see him. He was still sleeping, but thankfully the tube was out of his mouth. The IV was still in, though. I think he'll have to stay there for a couple more days to let the heart surgery stiches heal, but his blood was flushed of the toxin, so that part is in the clear," I say. "I can't even imagine what would happen to him if I were to tell him about the crazy incident with Gary's murder. He would probably have another heart attack!"

"Yeah," she says. "Gary, my dream date."

"What!? Was he the doctor you were telling me about? Oh, My God!"

"Unfortunately, yes. I sure have a way of picking them, don't I?"

"There is no way you could have known this, Misty. Plus, you only just met him. I'm sure he targeted you because you were my neighbor and he could get close to me, to us. Don't give up, your prince will come." I get up and hug her tight.

Quickly changing the subject before giving me one last pulse in her return hug, she says, "We don't want the kids to get wind of last night's attack. Right after I gave them the chocolate cake, I heard Barney barking at the door—and you were nowhere in sight. I told them I was running outside for a minute because you had run over to your parents' house—and luckily, the frosting kept them busy." She shoots me a quick grin, then continues. "I'm glad they didn't see me running around following Barney as I tried to find you. I called your parents when I realized you weren't in the yard." Misty gives me a confident look and nod. She really handles everything with ease.

We casually glance over to the kids to see them wearing capes and masks, running around the furniture. Even my big boy, Kyle, is taking part in the adventure. My smile stretches from ear to ear. I realize it's been quite some time since I've smiled like this. "Oh, the joys of being young and naïve. I hope there will never be a day when I'll share this story with them. It's bad enough that I've got to process it."

"Three cheers for therapy!" Misty laughs. "It helped me through a hell of a lot of divorce pain. So, do you think you'll tell Steven about what Gary said?"

I know she's referring to his comment about Steven being in the arms of another woman. "I have no choice. It will come out somehow. After he gets home from the hospital, I'll pick a day to sit down with him and share what happened. He's going to flip. But more importantly, I want to watch his reaction."

Misty dries the last breakfast pan and places it into the drawer. It's funny how she knows my kitchen so well. I hang the dash dishtowels over the oven door and join my friend at the kitchen table. I sit to her left so I can keep my view of the kids playing. I realize that I stink. I hope to cut my time at the table short so I can run upstairs and freshen up.

"Your face looks a little rough, Betsy. What are you going to say to the kids?"

I shrug and gingerly rub my cheek. "I hadn't even thought of that, to be honest. How's your cut feel? It looks like it hurts."

"Nah, I'm okay. They didn't seem to notice it when you came in, but they were distracted. Maybe you can put some makeup on the bruise and a regular bandage on your chin. The white tape and gauze looks too medical," Misty says as she points to my chin. "You could tell them you slipped in your parents' kitchen last night, or something. When I mentioned that you ran over to their house, they seemed to believe it."

"I guess that'll have to do! What's that old joke? 'Does your face hurt you, because it's killing me'?" Getting up from the table, I tell Misty, "I think, if it's okay with you, I'll run upstairs and go take a shower and put some makeup on. I'll hurry up because I'm sure you have plenty to do today." Barney follows me as I start to leave the room. He hasn't left my side since I returned from the hospital.

"Honestly, not really. I'm yours all day, if you need to go to your parents or something, please feel free to call me." Flashing me a smile, Misty continues, "I know you would do the same for me. Life has a way of balancing out. It's a give and take, my friend. "

The hot stream of water pulsing on my back feels so relaxing. I hadn't realized until just now that my arm and lower back also have bruises. I thought I had only whacked my hip. I must look like a spotted leopard. My scalp hurts, too, from Gary's yank on my hair when he picked me up to place me back onto the crate. Water is so therapeutic, unless it's forcefully piercing stitches on one's face. *Ouch.*

Toweling off is a slow process with a pregnant belly and injuries, but I carefully pat each part of my body, taking my time and making sure not to press too hard on a bruise or stitch. I throw my towel over the chrome towel rack next to my bathtub and tell myself to take a hot bath later today. The bubbles will be healing.

My elastic-waist maternity jeans work well with my purple V-neck T-shirt, which accentuates my eyes. I grab my silver Tory Burch necklace and silver pearl earrings to show off my expert makeup cover job. A glide of pink lipstick and push of my toes into my black suede ballet flats, and I'm as good as new.

Heading down the stairs, I hear Kyle talking to Misty. I stop where I am, waiting on a step, so I can listen. "Aunt Misty, is Mommy okay? I saw she cut her face. I know she's been sad lately, and I don't know why. Is she mad at us for something we did? I try not to fight with Morgan, but he gets me angry sometimes."

"Oh, heavens no, Kyle! She has been so happy with you. She is upset because the baby is tossing and turning in her sleep and wakes her up, so maybe she's just cranky."

"Really?" Peeking through the banister, I see Kyle's face. It looks as though Misty's story worked.

"I know she's not mad at you, because I'm her best friend and your aunt, and she would definitely tell me. You would be the first to know, because you are my secret buddy, right?"

That answer seems to have satisfied Kyle, because he retreats to the living room, appearing fine. Thank goodness Misty is great at thinking on her feet. My heart sinks in my chest, and I choke back the tears welling up in my eyes. This woman is a saint—a sailor-mouthed saint, but a saint nevertheless.

It makes me wonder when and how I'll tell my family the truth. How am I going to handle this Gary situation with Steven, let alone my sons?

Two Months Later

Sleeping among a mound of pillows and a tangle of blankets is one of my favorite things to do. Whenever I wake up throughout the night, I just happily hop back in bed and fluff and puff them around my body and snuggle up again to continue my slumber.

Barney sits at attention at the side of my bed crooking his head to the side and yelps as if to say, *Wake up, Mom. I need to go outside.*

I momentarily protest. Eventually, I roll over and think about how difficult it would be if I were told to "wait" to pee, so I muster up the energy to rise at 5:30 a.m. and take him out. The baby was up at 4:00 a.m. for her feeding, which Steven had covered, so I can't really argue with Barney's pleas.

Life with a new baby has offered us a few schedule changes, but we welcome them with open arms after what we went through two months ago. Now, we give thanks for every single day.

Coming back upstairs from doggy detail, I catch Steven's wanting glances as I approach him in the master bathroom. We stand together for a thankful moment staring into one another's eyes. We embrace, gently swaying to imaginary music as we giggle like teenagers. After a loving shower together, we quickly get dressed and wake the boys for school.

The baby is gurgling and cooing in her crib as we walk in and scoop her up for morning hugs and kisses. Steven agrees to get her changed and ready for the day as I head downstairs.

"Boys," I call. "We are heading down with your sister to get breakfast ready. Brush your teeth and get dressed!"

"Okay, Mommy!" I hear them reply.

The copper teakettle on the stove whistles like a harmonica as the steam swirls from the spout. I gently pour the boiling water over the teabags that Steven has chosen for us this morning, and sprinkle Stevia and a dollop of whole milk into each cup. I dish out healthy scoops of freshly cut fruit, scrambled eggs, and two slices of turkey bacon on the boys' SpongeBob character plates. Breakfast is one of my favorite meals to make for our family because it's easy to prepare, tastes great, and looks impressive. Steven adds butter to the mini bagels and pours two small cups of orange juice for our sons. It's so nice to have a kitchen assistant this morning. He's rather good-looking, too, if I do say so myself.

"Hello?" Dad hollers as he and Mom enter the side door and cross the room to our busy kitchen.

Mom and Dad are right on time for breakfast, so I grab two extra plates and place them on the kitchen table.

"How is everyone this morning? And who's driving with us to school today?" I love it when Dad offers to drive the boys for me. It can be tricky to get the baby bundled up for the cold and into the car on these busy mornings.

The boys shout together, "We are!"

I quietly lean against the kitchen counter, sipping my herbal tea, observing the mechanics of my family unit—I'm happy watching them interact together. Steven glides over to stand hip-to-hip with me as we watch our boys smile and laugh with their grandparents.

Steven turns to me. "I'm glad Morgan got that smelly cast removed last week."

I nod, smiling.

"Say, I wanted to ask you," he says quietly, "did you ever go with Misty to get your gun permit?"

That's kind of an odd question for my husband to ask me, right now, with my entire family sitting here watching. "Um, no, not yet. Why do you ask?"

"Well, I was thinking, it can't hurt to have you familiar with how to properly handle a weapon. I understand you're an expert shot, but a few lessons might come in handy. Let's face it, your pink pepper spray isn't going to do much if you're ever in trouble again."

"Agreed. I'll talk to Misty about it later this morning when we're out on our baby walk. Which reminds me, I need to find Emmy Grace's fleece blanket to tuck over her coat. It's chilly out there."

"I saw it in the mudroom last night," Steven says.

I follow him in there, out of earshot of the family. "What did your boss say about accepting the Chicago area regional sales position? I know he was hoping you'd take it."

I realize this is a sore subject with my husband. He loves the West Coast and this was such a bone of contention between us in the past. But he agreed to take it for the good of our family.

"I called him yesterday and accepted," he says, beaming. "The position doesn't start for another four weeks. He wanted to give me more time to rest and heal from my surgery and the whole ordeal. Plus, with the new baby, he tacked on some extra time off."

I'm relieved. Thankfully, now that this subject is settled, I need to find a clever way to find out if Gary's "other woman" comment has any validity. I still don't want to believe it to be true.

Back in the kitchen, I look over at the boys and my parents and say, "Hey, guys, you'd better go grab your coats so you can get going to school." Dad lowers his chin and raises one eyebrow and sends a thumbs-up.

As the boys go to the mudroom to get their bags, I turn to my husband and continue, "Steven, before I forget, I have a call scheduled with Candy Cranston today. She emailed me and asked if I would consider coming back to work, part-time. After she saw my parents at the fundraiser a couple of months ago, she decided to make me an offer to come back. I told her we had to discuss it, but honestly, I don't think I want to schlep into the city for work anymore. I just love it here in Westin Heights and I was thinking … it might be nice to open a shop here. Maybe a quaint little breakfast spot."

Steven purses his lips, glances down, and then raises his face, smiling from ear to ear. "I am so glad you're asking me this. I have wanted to talk to you about this for a week. I really want you to get back into doing what you love, but was hoping you could find a business opportunity around here, maybe with a partner, so you could just work half-time. I know you would miss the boys and the baby if you were working long hours in a kitchen in the city." He looks at me. "Am I right?"

"When did you start reading minds? That's what I was thinking!" I twirl on my heels and purse my lips into a kiss that I throw over my left shoulder as I cross through the kitchen to grab the boys' backpacks on the hooks by the side door.

Shuffling the boys out the door, kissing their heads, and hugging my parents, I softly push the door closed behind them with a *click*. I peek out the window, holding my palms on the glass, as I watch them hop into the back seat of their Lexus.

"Steven," I call as I come back into the kitchen, "I have a quick question for you."

"Uh-oh, what did I do?" My husband smiles with his eyes as he joins me at the table.

"I want to be serious for a minute. Before I shot Dr. Hildebrandt, he told me something about you."

"Oh?"

"He told me he saw you in another woman's arms." I pause, watching his eyebrows furrow as he shakes his head.

"Oh, my God, Betsy. I would never in a million-years cheat on you. I already told you that kiss with my secretary was a one-time thing. You know I wouldn't do that to you. What sick kind of stunt..." He takes my hands.

"I know he tried to kill you in the hospital and I think he was delusional enough about his sick crush on me that he was willing to kill you for hurting me. I know that sounds crazy, but I had to ask you. Otherwise, it would bother me forever."

I can see the genuine love in his eyes, but I let him squirm a little just to be double sure. "I believe that doctor was a sick man, and he said and did some horrible things to you. The way he manhandled you and hurt you... I am still broken up about the fact I was in that hospital bed, unable to help you."

He pulls his chair closer and slides his legs next to mine, gripping my hands in his, then pulls them up to kiss my knuckles. I search his soul, reading his thoughts. Seeing and feeling nothing but genuine sincerity, I inhale with my nose and exhale as I ask him, "Steven, do you remember anything from when you were in the coma? Anything at all, like visitors, people talking to you, or whatever?"

"No, not really. Why?"

Barney makes a little groaning sound in response to Steven's comment, as I imagine him saying, *Mom, how can he not remember"*

"Well, there were times when I came to see you and would talk to you, but obviously, you couldn't respond. Then one day, I meditated and tried to tap into your subconscious mind. And... I did."

Barney wags his tail.

A look of surprise flashes across Steven's face. "What? Really? What did I say?"

"We talked about a lot of things, but you definitely were able to tap into me. It made me feel more at ease, knowing that you knew I was there and that I loved you," I say. "One day, when I'm not on my way out the door to go walking with Misty and Emmy, I will sit with you and show you how I have mastered it, if that's what you call it."

"Hmm…"

"Oh, and by the way, Barney completely understands what I'm saying, all of the time. Remember I told you he did that Lassie thing with Misty when Gary had me captive?"

"Oh yeah. That's the same thing? I thought you were just saying it was a coincidence or something. Betsy, this is cool! I can't wait to experience it in action!"

Barney stands up on all fours and looks at Steven, then over at me, hoping to be included in the conversation. "Good boy, Barney. Do you want to join Mom for a walk with Misty and your sister?"

Chuff-bark. I'll take that as a yes!

I pick up our teacups and squeeze by Steven as I walk over to the sink to rinse out the cups. I glance back at the table where he is still sitting. He's looking at me with a huge smile on his face.

"Steven, I'm going to run over with Emmy and meet Misty for our walk. Are you off to physical therapy this morning?"

"Yes. But will I'll see you later for lunch?"

"You've got a date." My face feels warm and tingly as I flirt with my own husband.

———

Misty always has a way of making me feel important. The week after the baby was born, she came over to help with the kids, making sure they would get breakfast and get off to school with Mom and Dad on time. She even helped my dad install a remote window shade on the patio door so no one can peek in at night. I've returned many favors for her lately, too. She's started to date a new guy (not a stalking doctor) and needs nighttime and weekend sitters while she goes out with him. I love having Samantha and Abby here, and they love seeing the boys and playing with the baby. They call Emmy their new baby cousin. Misty and her girls have become an important part of our family.

"Hey, girl," I call to Misty, who is standing on the sidewalk in front of her house. She skips a step and jogs over to us, zipping up her fleece jacket. Her matching leggings and pink sneakers are quite the ensemble. I'm wearing baggy yoga pants and a Cubs sweatshirt under my jacket.

"Hello, little Emmy. Are you ready for a winter walk?" Her obvious baby talk gets Barney very excited because he knows that he's included in that equation. Sensing his attention on her, Misty turns to him and says, "Hello, Mr. Barney. How are you today?"

Not expecting an answer, Misty looks startled when Barney replies, *Garoof!*

The light frost on the grass and the tied-back perennials are a sure sign that winter is on its way. Soon, neighbors will start hanging holiday lights and greens. We comment on the gorgeous landscapes and architectural details along the way. This is an area that takes pride in the look and feel of their neighborhood; I am proud to live here, and walking with Misty always gives me a great reason to get out and see more of it, winter, spring, summer, or fall.

"Misty, remember how I started to tell you about my idea for a local business, right here in Westin Heights?"

"Uh-huh."

"Well, I found a little space that is available, right in town. In fact, we'll walk by it on our walk today."

"Tell me more!" Misty cheers.

"It's perfect! I was wondering if you'd be interested in talking with me about a possible business *together*. I've been working on the business plan all week and have crunched the numbers, and I think I can make it work. I have a friend who worked with me in the city, years ago, who also lives up here, and she's open to working the days I would take off. You can be a silent partner, or active in the day-to-day run of things, depending on what you decide."

"Interesting, Betsy." Misty glances over to me and grins.

"Well, that's what I wanted to talk to you about. Now that your bathroom rehab project is complete, I know you're looking for something else in your life in addition to your new boyfriend, and I think this would be perfect. Our friendship fits like a glove and we've learned how to give and take, giving us a strong foundation for working together. What do you say? Will you at least consider it?"

Misty picks up the pace to make sure I keep my heart rate in my target zone. I unzip my jacket to let in some cool air. I grab an extra gulp of air and double step to get back on stride with her. Pushing this stroller is quite the workout.

She turns her head to the left and grins at me again. "Of course! I'm sure we can figure something out! I know you want to open your own little café here in town, and honestly, we could use another tasty food spot for the locals. I think it could be really great!"

Barney woofs in agreement.

"Really?! Really?!" I stop walking. There I stand, in the middle of the sidewalk, jumping up and down while hugging my best friend and new business partner.

acknowledgments

Thank you to the wonderful people who assisted and supported my writing throughout this book, including Daisy Simmons and Sarah Dinetz for your first round of edits, which truly launched this project into reality and gave it wings. Katie McCoach, Jennifer Zaczek, Rebecca Mahoney, Jessica Hatch, and Jovana Shirley, your eagle eyes and candid professionalism helped give this book the final touches it needed to soar. Wini Nimrod, thank you for letting me read countless passages, bouncing ideas back and forth, giving me more clarity. Sarah Hansen, your cover design is impeccable, embodying the true essence of the story and genre. Dina Silver, your friendship and guidance pushed me over the finish line into a whole new world of publishing. I will pay my gratitude forward, tenfold. Lisa Beacom, thank you for lending your perfect voice to my audio book. It's like listening to Betsy Ryan—in real life. I appreciate the love and patience from my entire family and many friends while I spent hours, days, weeks, and months confined to my office—only coming out for food, water, and dog walks. Bonsai, Karma, and my mom's dog, Bailey, thank you for being the inspiration for Barney, and always giving me a reason to stop and smell the roses. Thank you to my readers, for taking time to read my debut suspense thriller novel. I invite you to visit my website and register for my newsletter so you can keep in touch and stay in the loop on my writing news. My next novel is a heart-warming holiday story about an unlikely chap who becomes an angel to save a grieving mother's life. Happy Reading! BethAldrich.com

about the author

Photo credit: Melissa Song Photography

Beth Aldrich is an award-winning and Amazon bestselling author for the book, *Real Moms Love to Eat* (Penguin/NAL, 2012), and former publisher and host of the magazine and PBS-TV series, *For Her Information (FHI)*. The series aired in 60 cities, nationwide, as well as in Turkey and Israel. Beth lives in Chicago's Northshore with her husband, three sons, and two loyal Tibetan Terriers. She believes life is more delightful when filled with laughter.

Reviews for Pink Slips

"Atmospheric and chilling with a feisty and relatable EveryMom heroine, Pink Slips will keep you in suspense until the gripping climax."

~Eve Adamson, nine-time New York Times bestselling collaborator

"Not since Rosemary's Baby has a book revealed how vulnerable women are when pregnant... Aldrich has Raymond Chandler's (The Lady in the Lake), gift for portraying violent scenes, but has a woman's insight into the especially serious consequences it could have for pregnant women."

~5-Star, Indie Reader Review

"In her delicious first novel, Beth Aldrich has written a spine-tingling thriller about the power of motherhood, friendship, communication, and love. Interwoven with humor and suspense, Pink Slips takes us on a fast-moving ride with unexpected twists and turns along the way. I couldn't stop reading or caring about the characters, and, upon reaching the end, I found myself longing for a sequel!"

~Dr. Sheila Flaherty, Award-winning and a bestselling author of East of Mecca

As an avid suspense/thriller reader, Beth Aldrich kept me hooked until the very end! The ending of each chapter will keep you wanting more, it's a true page turner! Get in your comfy reading chair, you may not get up until it's over!"

~Deanna A. Amazon Reviewer

Made in the USA
Lexington, KY
14 June 2017